TWICE IN A LIFETIME

R.M. NEILL

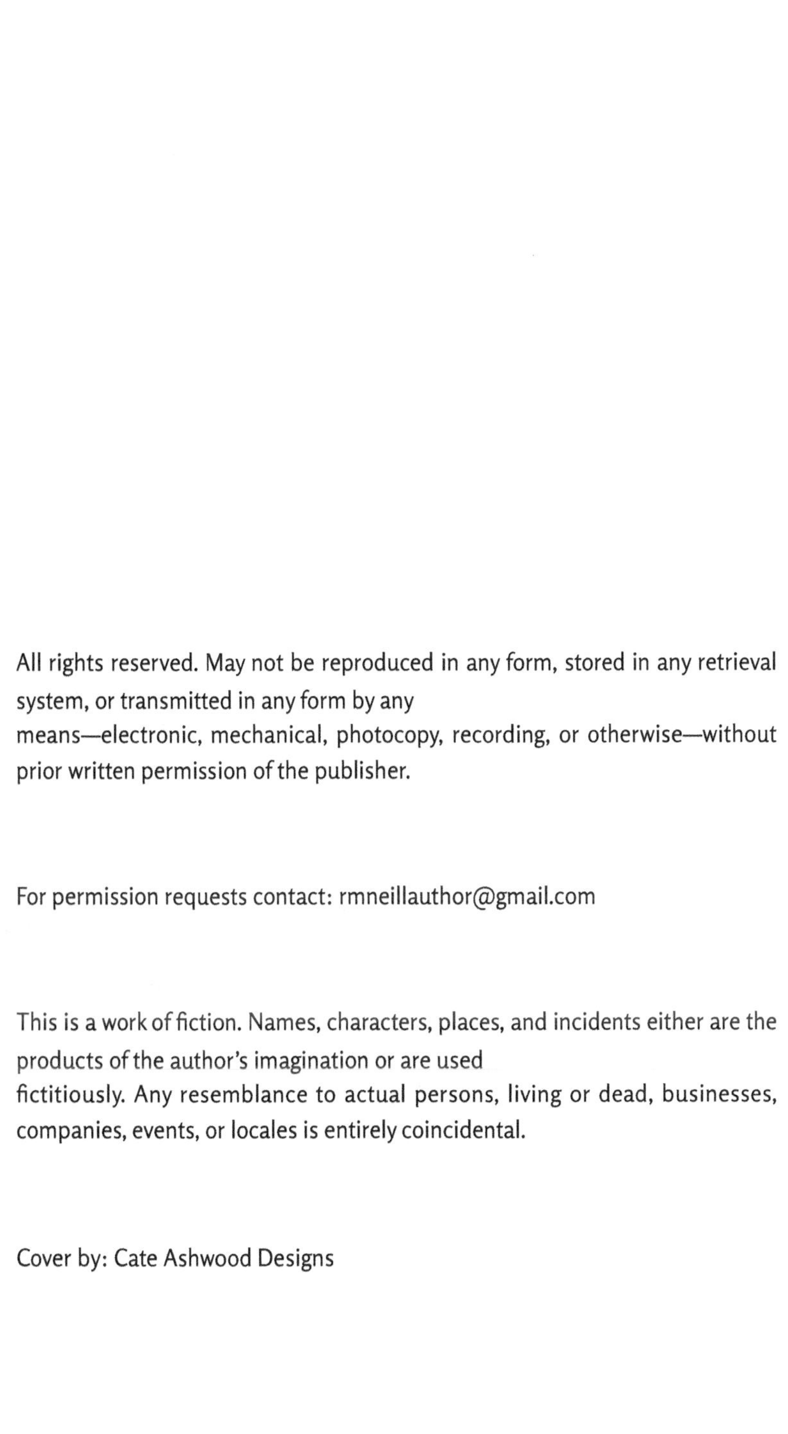

Introduction

Twice in a Lifetime is the first book in the Sheltered Connections Series.

Events in my book The Perfect Pass inspired this series. You don't need to read it first, but you will get a background on several of the characters that appear in this series, as well as the history of how the shelters in this book came to be. Animals and their unconditional love are truly inspiring. If you would like to help a charity that pairs animals with members of the LGBTQ+ community, consider looking into the Don't You Want Me Project.

From their website:

The Don't You Want Me project examines the lives of queer people and their rescue dogs, and creates a visual global platform for them to tell their stories. Finding strength *and purpose in the unconditional love, compassion and non-judgemental nature that is embodied in dogs, we watch the participants heal and transform. This bond - and the stories and personal growth that spring from it - forms the backbone of Don't You Want Me.*

Coupling compelling images and personal narratives, Don't You Want Me shows that individuals of all stripes have the ability to transform their lives when they are given love. The question of 'who rescued who' IS universal, no matter how you identify.

ONE

Dominic

THE DOORBELL BONGS AS I enter the Screaming Bean, my best friend's coffee shop and bakery. Owen looks up from his task behind the register to greet his newest customer, just like he always does. A giant grin splits his face when he sees it's me.

"Dominic! Have a seat buddy and I'll bring our lunch out shortly."

I wave in acknowledgement as he hands over the duties to his staff and I pull out a chair at our usual table. The Screaming Bean has evolved so much in the five years since Owen opened it. He grew The Bean from a quick stop for your morning coffee to a bakery and now offers light lunch. He even hired a pastry chef recently and has taken on custom orders.

I cock my head and smile at how far Owen's come. Since we met in first grade, we've been inseparable. Our history runs through my mind, like an old jerky film you'd watch in public school history class. Our first dates, prom, winning the championship football in senior year, graduating college. They all stutter through my mind, jumping from one scene to the next. When the sad memories start, I turn the movie off. I don't like to keep replaying those.

"I can tell by your frowny face you didn't have a good date."

Owen slides our lunch tray onto the table and pulls out the chair opposite me, plopping into it like he's a teenager and not the successful entrepreneur who owns the place.

I run my hand down my face with a sigh. "I guess she was nice enough."

"I feel there's a but coming on here." He slides me half of the clubhouse we always share, and I take a bite while I consider my next words.

"We didn't connect. We had a conversation over dinner and that's where it ended. I didn't want to ask her out again. I didn't want to bring her home. There was nothing beyond a friendly conversation." I look him in the eye. "There was no spark."

Stirring the tomato macaroni soup he placed in front of me earlier, I wonder if I can find an answer to my loneliness at the bottom. Maybe today's macaroni can magically spell out an answer for me. I feel Owen's heavy stare and I finally raise my eyes back to his. He's my best friend, he cares for me, and I know he's concerned. But it's the pained glance and half smile I don't want. I'm done with the pity. I don't want it anymore.

"Nobody will ever be like Jenny, Dom. She's never going to be replaced." He sighs. "She would hate to see you struggle like this."

We eat our lunch with the weighted grief of remembering someone we lost. I know he's right; Jenny would hate this version of me. I'm angry with myself for being like this. That familiar thickness builds in my throat, and I sigh.

"I just don't want to take the first person I might like even a little, ya know? I need to find someone that I connect with on all the levels. Someone I can talk to about everything and burns a fire in my soul, too. I need passion. I don't want lukewarm love."

I lean back in my chair and stare at the ceiling. It's very white today.

"I'm not asking you to accept anything you aren't one hundred percent happy about Dom. I'm just asking that you make sure you're not pushing these women away simply because they aren't Jenny."

He has a point. When I first started dating again a year ago, I compared every date to her. Her smile, her laugh, how she could hold a conversation about how to clean a wild turkey. Even how she dressed. I wanted to replace my Jenny with a replica. After several failed dates and a long talk with Owen, I knew that was no way to live. I had to find someone who brought me joy and connection like Jenny did, but be a completely different person. It was a difficult task.

"It wasn't that. She was nice enough. I just didn't feel it. I think if there isn't even a teeny, tiny spark at the first meeting, I won't try to force it. Maybe I'm being too hard, but I honestly feel like if I meet you the first time and nothing draws me to you, why continue?"

"Sorry boss, can I get you in the back for a moment?" Owen's pastry chef interrupts and I notice a flicker of annoyance cross his face.

"Sure, Parker, give me a sec."

He watches Parker sashay his way back to the kitchen before turning back to me. "This guy really gets under my skin some days. I'll be right back. He probably wants me to count the chocolate chips or something ridiculous."

Owen leaves me at the table while I finish my lunch. I watch couples come and go while I eat. Some of them hold hands and turn a lovesick gaze on their partner, and my heart pangs with yearning. I'm not afraid to admit I'm lonely. I have been since Jenny died. It's been two years since her death, and I want to feel whole and happy again so badly my entire body aches for it.

My phone rattles on the table, and I glance at the display. It's Tara, Jenny's best friend. With a fortifying breath, I take the call.

"Hey Tara."

"Hey Dom! How are you? I've been trying to reach you to hear how your date was."

"Uh, it was okay."

She tsks loudly in my ear, causing me to pull the phone away. "Nobody can be as good as Jenny. We knew her best. I think it's a good thing the date didn't go well."

My back stiffens. "Pardon?"

"She's not good enough for you. Who is though, really?" She honks an annoying donkey laugh and I grip the phone tighter. "I thought we could have dinner tonight. I'll come by for 6 P.M."

The last thing I want to do is have her over for dinner again. "I made Jenny's favourite. You know how she loved my lasagna."

She knows I won't turn her down when she brings up Jenny. With a resigned sigh, I accept my defeat. "Fine. I'll be home."

I end the call and pinch the bridge of my nose. I don't understand why Tara still feels the need to keep checking on me and bringing me food. She was Jenny's friend. I accepted her because of that and no other reason. Other than Jenny herself, we have nothing in common. I wish she would fade away and leave me alone, but I know she misses Jenny, too. It would be cruel to shut her out.

Owen has been my rock through this entire ordeal. From diagnosis to the day she took her last breath, to today; where he still has lunch with me twice a week and texts or calls every day. He's never stopped holding me up. He worries so much about taking care of me; I wonder if he bothers taking care of himself.

"Sorry Dom." He plunks back into his chair and his cheeks are flaming. "I was right. He needed me for something he could have handled on his own." He rolls his eyes and resumes eating his now cold soup.

"Is he really that unsure of himself?"

"Honestly, I think he just enjoys trying to make me lose my shit, you know?" He rips a bite from his sandwich.

"You think he's doing things on purpose to make you angry?"

"I think he's just testing limits. But he mentioned something to me the other day, and I thought about you."

"Um... that seems strange, but I'll bite. What did he say?"

"I don't know if I told you this before, but he had a rough childhood and spent some time at the youth shelter by the lake. You know the one for the LGBTQ kids? Auslo's Loft I think it's called. Anyway, he said when he stayed there, part of his therapy was helping at the animal shelter next door, Austin's Animal House. He said caring for the animals really helped him get over his loneliness of losing his family. He even adopted a cat when he left."

I hate hearing stories like Parker's. It makes my heart hurt. I donate to their fundraiser every year and help if I can, because I'm beyond grateful to have a supportive family. If there was more I could do, I would.

"So, what's that got to do with me?"

"I think you should adopt a pet. Maybe a dog. It'd be something for you to love on and take care of. You'd have a fishing buddy too, maybe."

I consider this. It's actually not a bad idea. It would be nice to have someone to greet me when I get home every day. A purpose to go home to the empty house at night.

"I don't hate the idea. I might do that. I'm not sure what I should get. A dog I could always have bones and scraps for, that would be cool."

"See! It even has another purpose. You have a creature that will adore you bringing home soup bones."

When Owen opened The Screaming Bean, I opened my butcher and specialty meat shop next door, Wild Baloney. With all the butchering I do, I often have scrap meat, bones and fat left over. The odd person will ask if I can save bones or fat for something, but I end up throwing more out than I give away.

"I might swing by there tomorrow. I'll get some info and go from there. I've never owned an animal before, though. Do they help you with all that stuff?"

Owen brushes off his hands and starts gathering things to clear our table.

"I bet they do. From what Parker told me, it's part of their duties to stay at the shelter. They assist in everything the animal shelter does. Animal care, education, adoption drives, fundraising. The whole nine yards."

I help Owen carry our dishes to the bussing area and wait for my coffee to go. Now that this seed has been planted, I'm excited to pursue this. A cute fuzzy face to greet me and bring some joy to my home. To give me a purpose every day. I want that. Actually, I need it. I know I do.

I wave a goodbye to the staff and Owen and walk the short distance back to Wild Baloney. My employee, Jade, greets me with a smile as she assembles gift baskets of gourmet treats.

"Hey boss man, did you have a good lunch? You're smiling, I like it." She beams a high voltage smile my way.

"Thanks. I had a great lunch, and I have an idea in my head now. I'm going to adopt a pet."

"Oh, my god! What a wonderful idea! What do you want? Dog, cat, short hair, long hair, hypoallergenic, working... as you can see, there's a lot to think about."

My eyes widen. "Wow, that is a lot. I think I'm going to look for a dog. Then I can bring him soup bones and maybe take it fishing."

"Can dogs have bones like that?"

I pause. "I don't know. You mean some bones are bad? I guess I'll add it to my research then. I'd hate to give them something that doesn't agree with them." That would make me feel horrible. I couldn't do that.

Jade and I finish our day with her making gift baskets and arranging the store front to look amazing, and I do what butchers do. I slice and cut the best cuts of meat to fill our showcase. Everything from the finest T-bones to chicken breasts and stew beef. Even the best salami and capicola for charcuterie boards.

When I leave work, I drive by the animal shelter and check the hours for tomorrow. They open at 10 A.M., I'll be there with all my questions and maybe I'll find a fuzzy butt to take home too.

TWO

Micha

"**F**UUUCKK."

I roll over and slam the blaring alarm clock for I think the seventh time. I'm not a morning person. At. All. I can hear my landlady, Roberta, walking around upstairs. Bless her, she probably hates hearing my alarm every day, but she never complains. She greets me with a grandmotherly smile and has coffee waiting for me every morning. If it really bothered her, I think she would have said something by now.

Meow.

I peer over the side of my bed to find my sweet little kitty, Tuxedo, staring at me with his big green eyes. I scoop him up and scratch him behind the ears. A little rough just how he likes it.

"How's my beautiful man this morning? Big plans to lie around in a sun patch today, buddy?" He rubs his head against my face and taps my lips with his tiny paw, like it's a polite cat way to tell me to shut up. "Okay buddy, let's get you fed, and I need to get ready so I can get to work on time." I glance at the clock; it's going to be close.

I rent a room in Roberta's basement, but I also have a private bathroom and a small kitchenette that has a tiny sitting area. It's not much, but it's enough to work for me. I'm barely here as it is, and I don't have a tonne of friends to entertain. I certainly don't have to worry about bringing anyone home for mad nights of sex. I snort out loud at the absurdity of it.

I scoop Tux his wet food in a tiny dish and set his kibble for the rest of the day next to it. I wash out his water bowl and refill it too. Leaving him to his breakfast, I hit the shower. There won't be much time for me to look fabulous today. I pull my long, blonde wet hair into a ponytail and dab some concealer around my eyes to hide the dark shadows that never seem to go away. A bit of black eyeliner and pink tinted lip gloss, then I'm pulling on my jeans and a T-shirt in record time.

"Be a good boy today, Tux. I'll see you tonight." I squish him in a big hug, and he purrs with his full belly. He follows me up the stairs as he does every day, and I find Roberta in her kitchen with a takeout mug waiting by the coffee machine for me.

"You're too good to me, Roberta." I peck her on the cheek as I fill my mug and glug a generous dose of milk into it.

"I'm only giving you a hand getting yourself out the door, Micha. It's not a hard thing. I make the coffee anyway. Maybe one morning you'll actually have time to share one with me." She reaches down and gives Tux a scratch as he rubs all over her legs.

"When mornings start later than 8 A.M. I just might do that." I smile as she settles into her sitting area, and Tux finds the sunbeam to splay in. This happens five days a week. Tuxedo follows me upstairs, Roberta hands me coffee and the two of them don't do much as I go to work. I'm not jealous. I'm grateful.

She's a widow and retired. She's lonely, and she saved my life. She offered me a low-cost living option to get me out of the youth shelter after I consoled her when her cat passed away. She was all alone, and I was very intimate with the beast of loneliness myself. But I wouldn't accept charity. We came to an agreement and for the last year it's worked out really well. For both of us.

When I qualified for the funding to help me open up my pet grooming business, she was the one popping champagne and celebrating with me. Well, her and my best friend Travis.

"Try not to get into trouble while I'm gone, you two."

"We're going to solve a mystery today, Micha. It's a Murder She Wrote marathon. Tux and I are going to spoil ourselves, aren't we?" Tux swishes his tail in agreement and stretches out longer into the sun. Spoiled cat.

I slide my feet into my most comfortable pair of runners and start my walk to work. On cold days it feels far, but on a beautiful late summer morning like today, it feels like it's too short. The cool morning air and the bright warm sun bring me happiness. When I take a break at lunch, I'll walk around the lake nearby and hopefully drag Travis with me. If not, I'll just enjoy the beauty of it on my own.

I sip my coffee as I enter the business district and watch some businesses in various states of their opening process. Hard to believe I'm one of them, a business owner that is.

Two years ago, I was homeless, jobless, and wondering if life was even worth living. Now I have a place to call home, I own a business and I'm back to being my usual confident self. Mostly. Fuck you very much, to the people that were supposed to love me unconditionally and didn't think I'd amount to anything. Look at me now, bitches.

My shoes crunch over the gravel in the parking lot as I come to the door of my grooming shop, Fuzzy's. Every day when I arrive and turn the key, my chin is high with the knowledge I came out on top. I flick the open sign on and hang my coat in the tiny room I call an office. It has a single chair and tiny table crammed inside, and it's where I take care of my paperwork if I have time to, during the day. I slide my laptop bag onto the table and close the door behind before booting up my front computer to pull up today's appointments.

Looks like I'll have a busy morning. Two Shih Tzus and a Lab before I break and tackle a German Shepard and a Pug in the afternoon. I can handle that. A knock comes on the door connecting Fuzzy's to the Bloomburg Veterinary Hospital. Not just any knock, the special knock of my best friend Travis.

I slide the deadbolt open and peek through a crack. "What is the airspeed velocity of an unladen swallow?" I cackle in my best bridge troll voice.

"African or European?"

We both snort laugh at one of our favourite parts of Monty Python's Holy Grail. I step aside and let Travis in.

"What's your day looking like? We going to have lunch today?"

"As long as we aim for a one o'clock lunch. The Shih Tzus can be nippy, so they take me longer, but today's animals are all well behaved. What about you?"

"I'm on lab duty today so I can leave for lunch when I want to. I'll put up the notice now that's for 1 P.M. and I'll come back to meet you."

"Sweet! Can you pick up one of those awesome lunch time charcuterie boards at Wild Baloney and we can eat by the lake?"

"Oh! Great idea! I'll give Jade a call and order ahead. I'll grab it before I come meet you then."

"Thanks Trav. I'm looking forward to it."

"Oh, and we should talk about the fundraiser thing the animal shelter has coming up. They need volunteers and ideas so let's talk about that too."

Travis goes back to his post as I nod in agreement that we need to talk about that, and I lock the door behind me as my first client of the day arrives.

I check in on little Gizmo, the Shih Tzu, make sure I have his owner's cell phone number and take the little dude to the back to get him spit shined.

"So, Mr. Gizmo, do you have any requests for the day? Are we changing your look?"

He snuffles and snorts and gives a short woof while cocking his head at me.

I mimic his look. "I'm taking that as no and it's the standard wash, brush, dry and bow?"

Bark.

"That's what I thought. I agree. Why change when you're already so fabulous?" I laugh and his tongue lolls out and his doggie lips stretch into a comical grin. It's a grin that says he knows I get his doggie thoughts. Truth be told, I just might. Seems like I'm way better at communicating with animals than I am with people. Not like Dr. Doolittle level or anything, but that would be cool. More like a Disney princess, all the animals love. That's more my style.

I secure him in the tub and don my waterproof apron. He really is a fabulous dog. The cutest thing ever with his smooshy face and his fancy bows. One thing that's always bothered me was how we're so quick to accept male animals wearing feminine bows, but when a human does it, it's somehow wrong. It should never be wrong. People should always just wear whatever the hell they want to. Individuality sets you apart. Who wants to be boring and follow the sheeple?

Wear a star, be fucking fabulous people!

As I brush Gizmo out and set him in front of the dryer, I decide Gizmo is a damn star. I find my sparkliest bow in the bin, and once he's dry, I gather the hair on his head and fasten it.

"Gizmo, you're a man after my own heart."

Woof!

"You're welcome. I think I'm pretty fab, too."

THREE

Dominic

I FORCED TARA OUT the door after she'd been here long enough to grate on my last nerve. From giving me unsolicited opinions on how to change the décor in my house, to trying to invite herself back tomorrow, I was done with her company. I need my space without her in it. When she insisted on hugging me after I walked her to her car, I allowed it, but I didn't like it.

I've spent the rest of the evening researching dog and cat breeds until my eyes burn from staring at the computer screen. I had no idea there were so many choices and things to consider. Sporting and working breeds. Miniature and giant breeds. Long hair and short hair. That's just for dogs. Cats have just as many categories it seems, but one thing I know for sure is they are more self sufficient.

I learned there are pure bred animals and cross-bred animals. Some dogs only like to have one owner and some dogs like to make everyone happy. Surprisingly, some cats even like water.

I made a list of a few dog breeds I think would fit my lifestyle. While I love any kind of Labrador, I think I need to dial back the activity level. I'm at the shop too much for that. As much as I'd love a dog to take exploring, I think I'll need to look for something smaller and less active. If that's even possible. All dogs need activity. I'd prefer one that doesn't need to jog 5 kilometers every day, though. I hope the shelter can help me decide.

I even researched bones, and it dismayed me to learn that it's bad to give a dog bones. While a raw bone is better than a cooked one, it still posed some nasty risks if something went wrong. I already lost Jenny through no fault of my own. I wouldn't be able to live with myself if I made my furbaby sick and I could have prevented it. If I can't give it bones, I found several homemade dog treat recipes I could make from scrap meats. I'll take it as a win.

Tucking my list of wants and preferences under my wallet by the door, so I wouldn't forget in the morning, I mix myself a rye and ginger. I take my drink with me to the living room and do what I do every night for the last two years. I sip my drink and stare at the rose bush I planted in Jenny's memory two years ago. In the beginning of this ritual, I tried to imagine her there, smiling, laughing and whole. I would hear her voice telling me how much she loved me, and the same movie reel would play in my head on repeat. Our prom, our wedding, her beautiful face, and her broken body as she took her last breath on this earth, still holding my hand.

Every night I did this ritual, I would cry. Until the last six months. The crying has eased and I'm smiling more. I'm happy I had the time with her, even though it ended too soon. When the rose bush flowered after its first winter, a beautiful shade of yellow, I knew it would be just what Jenny wanted. It made me feel like a part of her would never leave.

Now I've graduated from sitting in the dark crying, to sitting here with a small, sad smile. The ache inside me has waned and I can breathe again. It's a small step to move on, I suppose.

I leave my half-finished glass in the sink and head to bed. Tomorrow feels like Christmas, and I hope to find a furry friend. It's the first big step for me to continue travelling the road of finding my way back to life again.

M Y PULSE RACES AS I jam my truck keys in my pocket and bound up the steps to Austin's Animal House at 10:15 A.M. My list is in my pocket, ready to impress the shelter workers. I throw the door open and bounce inside, but my steps falter because it's nothing like I pictured. At. All.

The lobby has a few chairs scattered around, a welcome desk and one lonely fake tree in the corner. While it may be empty of furniture, the walls are covered with pictures of people and the pets they've adopted. I'm immediately drawn in and I scan each one.

Everything from grandmothers smiling with new kittens to a toothless child with a new puppy. There have to be hundreds of adoption photos gracing the wall. What an honour it must be to have your photo on the adoption wall. The front wall behind the welcome desk has a photomural of the history of the shelter. There's a photo of a young couple hamming it up with shovels at the ground-breaking ceremony. Next comes a series of photos in the stages of building of the shelter.

On the largest wall at the back of the room, there's a beautiful engraved plaque. It's heart shaped with small paw prints walking across the bottom. As I read the engraving, tears prick my eyes when I realize it's not just a dedication plaque, it's a declaration of love from one founder to the other. Logan has laid his heart out for everyone to see. This shelter is for his husband Austin because Austin only ever found true, all accepting love with pets as he grew up. Animals were his safe harbor as a child, giving him the affection he lacked at home and the unconditional acceptance he wanted. This is Logan's reminder to Austin that his love for him has no conditions, and every animal to come through these doors will find the same support with their forever homes.

Our town is very fortunate to have the Larkman family and their generosity. Logan's charity, Logan's Wish, built the youth shelter next door and the animal shelter. While Logan is a famous model, his husband is an NHL hockey player and together they are the nicest couple you'll ever meet. They come here every summer during Austin's off season and sporadically when there are events they need to attend for the shelters. Very hands on and very down to earth. If they needed a photo to place next to relationship goals in the dictionary, these two are it.

A throat clears behind me, and I whirl around. A young man waves with a loopy grin on his face and something about him seems familiar.

"Beautiful plaque, isn't it?" He nods at the wall I was admiring.

"It is. I was just thinking they're a wonderful couple and their love shines through like nothing I've ever seen."

The young man's smile grows bigger. "Nobody loves like those two. That I will agree with." He puts his hand forward for me to shake. "I'm Jacob Maloney, Austin's little brother. I manage both shelters. What can I help you with today?"

That explains why he looks familiar. I glance back at the photo of Austin, and they have the same strong jawline and kind eyes. I firmly squeeze his hand and feel how sweaty they've become. "Nice to meet you. I'm Dominic and I'm here to adopt a dog. I even made a list." Wiping my hands on my pants, I hope he didn't notice.

"It's wonderful you've done research, Dominic. Not everyone does. Tell me what you're looking for."

He motions for me to sit in the chair nearby and pulls another one over. We settle in like old friends, about to catch up with a long overdue chat. I review what I've learned about dog breeds, pull out my notes and explain in far too much detail what I'm looking for. He smiles and nods, adding to my comments along the way.

When I'm finally done, he aims his charming boyish grin my way, but it's tinged with a hint of sadness.

"Dominic, I wish everyone that wanted to adopt was as thorough as you. Our shelter has an abundance of cats. Simply because there are so many wandering that aren't fixed, we're constantly exploding with kittens. We very rarely have puppies and occasionally we have older dogs that got lost or were left behind by owners who we can't locate."

My shoulders slump. "Oh, I hadn't put much thought into the cats. I had my heart set on a dog."

"We have one dog in the shelter right now. She's a black lab mix. We think she's around six years old. Would you like to meet her?"

I had a lab on my list of dogs to avoid because of activity level. If this one is older, maybe it's not so bad?

"What's the process if I want to adopt her?"

"Well, you can meet her first. Even take her for a test walk and see if you like her. If you think she might be the one for you, we can talk about the paperwork and fees."

I suck in a breath and wipe my damp hands on my pants again. Am I ready for this commitment? I know I want company, but this suddenly seems overwhelming. I feel his hand gently on my thigh.

"Are you okay Dominic?"

My eyes find Jacob's and his non-judgemental aura sets me at ease again. He's been a fantastic help and host so far. I shouldn't lay out all my nervous anxiety about adopting a dog in his lap.

"It's a big step is all. I feel ready, but I'm still nervous. Does that make sense?"

"Of course it does. You know, we have a program where we match volunteers with new pet owners, and they guide you through pet ownership for a few days or weeks. Whatever you need to get comfortable. We always take a pet back if it doesn't work out too."

I consider this piece of info. I could have someone who knows what they're doing alongside me while I adjust. Like, when a new mother has her mom or grandma to call for baby advice. I don't hate it.

"I think that would make me feel better." Laughter bubbles out. "I own a business. I can handle firearms and I buried my wife. But the thought of bringing home a cute fuzzy animal is sending mild terror through me. I'm quite the piece of work, aren't I?"

"I'm sorry for your loss Dominic." He squeezes my hand. "And there's nothing odd at all about what you're feeling. Don't feel bad about it. Let me check the schedule to see who's up next on my list for the home help match."

Jacob walks over to his desk and consults a laptop and grins.

"I have the perfect match volunteer for you in line. I'll message them and arrange for a meeting with the three of you. If they're available tomorrow evening, will that work?"

I puff out a sigh of relief. "Yes, I can be here as early at 5:15 P.M. if that works?"

"I'll get your contact info and we'll make it happen."

Jacob hands me a card with a name and time on it.

Micha 5:30 P.M.

"Micha has a key so the door will be open. Just come on in and you'll get walked through it all."

"Thanks Jacob. You're really good at this. I feel much better about getting a pet now if someone can help me with the ropes."

Even though I'm leaving the shelter empty handed, I'm oddly buoyed with knowing I won't be going into this on my own. A complete stranger to help me, but that's okay. It's short term. It's like training wheels for pet ownership.

I don't see a single bad thing about this plan. Tomorrow can't come fast enough.

FOUR

Micha

TODAY MY ALARM ONLY blares six times instead of seven. I'll take it. Any improvement is huge. Celebrate all the small stuff, right?

Meow.

"Come here gorgeous. How's my main man?" I'm rewarded with head butting from Tux and a lick on my ear. "We need to hang out this weekend some, don't we buddy? I feel like I'm just never home anymore."

Tuxedo kneads his paws on my shoulder and snuggles under my chin. He's the snuggliest cat I've ever met, and I love him more than the air I breathe. I hate leaving him all day, but I know Roberta enjoys his company, too. That eases my guilt to a degree.

"I have to get ready for work, buddy. But you and me, we're gonna hang on Sunday."

He's totally fine with that plan as he bounces down to head to his dish. We do the same old morning routine, with me rushing to feed Tux and get out the door at a decent time to make it into work without calling a cab.

Same ponytail. Same dab of lip gloss and eyeliner.

Taking the stairs two at a time, Roberta already has my coffee poured and the cream waiting.

"Roberta, have I told you how much I love you lately?"

She laughs and blushes, shooing me away. "Micha, you're always so sweet. You know I love you darling, you don't have to butter me up."

I place my travel mug on the counter and allow myself a moment of seriousness. Taking her hands, I pull her close to me and envelope her in a big hug. I rest my head on top of hers so she can't see my face. "Roberta, you saved me. I love you for that and I can never repay you. You're the only family I have, even if we aren't blood related. I love you for everything. I'm not buttering you up, it's true."

When I release her, her eyes are shiny, and she swats my arm. "Don't make me so sad first thing in the morning."

I peck a kiss on her cheek. "Never sadness. Always love and sparkle from this guy."

I gather my things and give Tux a quick smoosh goodbye and begin my walk to work. It's another beautiful day and I have much to be happy about. It's going to be a great day.

M Y PHONE PINGS AS I finish my brief break in between brushing out a Golden Retriever and trimming the nails of a squawky Chihuahua. I find a message waiting from Jacob at the shelter and a grin splits my face at its content.

Jacob is asking if I can assist a man with a pet match for the shelter's only canine occupant. I call him back right away.

"Hey Micha, thanks for calling back." I feel his warm smile through the phone. I adore Jacob and would do almost anything he asks of me. He's too kind not to help.

"No problem, Boo. Now tell me who needs help with a pet match. What do I need to prepare myself for?"

Jacob's soft laugh travels over the phone. "He's a widower, young... super cute. He's looking for a pet, so he's not so lonely."

"Jacob, are you setting me up?" I tease.

"Pretty sure he's straight, Micha, he mentioned burying his wife. I just think you might bring some of your sparkle to his life and help him out with Maggie. If he's not a match for her, then maybe you've made a friend, anyway."

"I adore Maggie, so I will vet him properly at the same time. She just doesn't go to anybody, Jake. You know that."

He chuckles again. "I do know that, and I know you love her, so you're the perfect person to make sure she finds her perfect person."

"Thanks for the heads up, Jake. You know I'll be there. Anything for you."

I make some kissy noises in the phone and tap in a reminder, so I don't forget I have an errand tonight and go back to brushing out Briggs, the Golden Retriever.

The blower has him dry enough and there's enough fuzz swirling around in here that I'll be vacuuming for an eternity after he leaves. Good thing he's cute.

"So, Briggs, hot date tonight? It's a Wednesday and you usually come on Fridays. What's shaking my man?"

He thumps his tail against the wall, sending more fuzz flying and shoves his giant wet nose into my ear, snuffling like he's telling me a wild dog secret.

It tickles, making me laugh at his goofiness. "Briggs! Say it ain't so! You're planning on hooking up with the neighbour's Shepherd tomorrow? The scandal!"

His giant tongue lolls out and he barks.

"You know you're a real ladies' man, Briggs. Or a man's man too. I'm definitely not pigeonholing you there. You do you, buddy."

He thumps his tail in response and grins like a maniac. Maybe he goes both ways, who knows, but he's happy with our conversation, so I'm happy he's happy.

My day passes quickly and before I know it, I need to freshen up and get over to the shelter to meet the possible owner match for Maggie.

I finish cleaning up the shop and step into my uber tiny office to fish out a fur free shirt. The aprons help, but when you groom fuzzy animals for a living, you find fur in all kinds of places. I change my shirt and lint roll my jeans, lock up, and walk around the front of the building to get to the animal shelter next door.

The animal shelter was built immediately after the LGBTQ youth shelter. One large parking lot separates the buildings. When I was lost and alone, it was Roberta, my now landlord, that brought me to the shelter, Auslo's Loft. With Jacob and the help of other staff members, I changed my life for the better.

Austin's Animal House, the animal shelter, was being finished as I arrived, and it gave me something to focus on. They tossed me into the ragtag crew led by Jacob and I found a true place of belonging. Being with the animals and helping people find the right match for them never made me feel so alive. We came up with the idea to help match people and pets, and it's taken off. Most first-time pet owners appreciate the extra help and guidance.

I'm early for the meeting so I let myself in and wait for the man named Dominic, who wants to adopt Maggie, our black Lab cross. Usually, any dog that resembles a purebred is adopted quickly, but Maggie is older, and everyone wants puppies or younger dogs. So, she's been here for six months already, which is a really long time for a dog to be homeless. I'd love to have her, but I just can't have a dog. It's not fair. I barely have time for Tux. Instead, I'll have to settle for helping find Maggie the best darn owner out there.

There are photos on the wall of previous adoptions. Stepping closer, I remember helping with every single one, and how great it felt to be a part of something so monumental in someone's life. I'm so caught up in my memories, I don't hear the door and a person enter, until a rough voice saying my name makes me jump.

I spin around to find one of the most delectable morsels of man I've ever laid eyes on. Tall, dark and shoulders broad as a house. While his shoulders are wide, the rest of him is anything but. Strong muscled arms appear to threaten the armholes of his T-shirt and his lean body fills his jeans to perfection. His tousled brown hair throws a boyish vibe, but his dark brown eyes tell me he's anything but carefree these days. His strong jawline is peppered with stubble, my Achilles heel. God, I love a sexy five o'clock shadow.

This must be Dominic. Straight Dominic. Dammit, the gods are cruel today.

FIVE

Dominic

'M AS NERVOUS AS a teenager about to go on my first date. After coming home early, I showered, changed my clothes twice and now I'm clutching my keys, trying to calm my guts before I climb out of my truck and enter the animal shelter.

I'm meeting a dog for crying out loud.

My phone rings as I reach for the door handle, and I delay further by answering it.

"Hey."

"How long are you going to sit in your truck before going in?"

I chuckle and look up the street to see Owen standing on the sidewalk, and he waves my way.

"I'm just trying to settle the nerves."

"Dom, it's okay. You've got this. If this dog doesn't work out, you keep looking. You'll be okay."

I swallow the lump building in my throat. "Thanks O, I know it's just a dog, and I was so excited earlier, but now that I'm here it feels...final? Does that even make sense?"

Owen is quiet for a moment. The connection hangs silent. "It does, buddy. Just remember, you have a lot of life to live still. You owe it to yourself to live it. It's scary, but I'm here for you. Lots of people are here for you. You can do this."

I draw in a deep breath. "You're right. If I can wrangle a moose carcass by myself, I can meet a dog and give it a loving home. I've got this."

"There you go. If you can handle that, you can manage a pet. Now go fall in love with a pair of puppy dog eyes. And I promise I won't be bad Uncle Owen. I'll be good."

I throw my head back, laughing. "When did you ever become a good influence?"

"Ouch, Dom. I can be good."

"Uh huh. Listen, I need to get inside before I lose my nerve. I'll let you know how it goes."

We hang up and I see him wave before going back into The Screaming Bean. I climb the front steps to the shelter, and with another deep breath, I finally enter.

It's quiet when I enter the lobby and I expected to see someone waiting at the front desk for me. I'm about to call out to announce I'm here when I notice someone at the end of the room, lost in thought while gazing at the adoption photos.

I stand frozen and watch as she caresses some photos with her fingertips, lost in memory perhaps. It seems rude to interrupt what feels like a private moment. So, I use the time to appreciate the person in front of me. A ponytail of shining blonde hair sits low at the nape of her neck. My eyes track down her body and I appreciate the tight, firm ass in her jeans. For the first time in two years, my dick jumps in interest. So, I continue to look. The tapered waist, the strong muscled shoulders, and the toned arms, tell me she takes care of herself and works out.

I wonder if this is Micha and if she looks as good from the front as she does from behind. It's obvious she still doesn't know I'm here. I steal a final perusal and call her name. "Micha?" My voice is rough and sounds weird to my ears.

She spins around, her hand comes to her chest, and I see her face. Beautiful brown eyes peer out under the longest eyelashes I've ever seen. Her face is make-up free except for a small amount of eyeliner. Her lips are red and full and very... inviting.

She takes two steps towards me and holds her hand out to shake.

"You must be Dominic. I'm Micha. It's so wonderful to meet you."

I mange to take the offered hand and do something that resembles a handshake, but my mind is in overload. That's not a female voice. As I scan the front of her body, there's a definite bulge in the tight jeans. Yep, not a woman. But my body hasn't got that memo yet since I'm still holding Micha's hand and staring at him.

I snatch my hand back. His eyes widen in surprise. "Yes, I'm Dominic. Sorry to interrupt."

He smiles, and it punches me right in the gut. It's a gorgeous smile. What the fuck is wrong with me?

"You didn't interrupt. I was waiting for you and just taking a walk down memory lane." He sweeps his hand back towards the photos on the wall. "I've been involved in almost every adoption here since we opened. I remember them all."

"Wow. Every adoption? That's pretty incredible. How did you do that?"

He chews his bottom lip, as he chooses how to answer the question. My heart thuds. "I found something I was good at, and it just came to me. This is where I belong, and I do some of my best work here. I don't want to bore you with the long, sad story of my life, but that's the short version."

Micha claps his hands together and aims another smile my way. His smile is forced, but it sparkles. He sparkles. Everything about him sparkles. Why can't I focus on another word to describe him?

"Do you want to meet Maggie now?"

"Yes!" He chuckles at my enthusiastic response and my cheeks heat with embarrassment. "I'm nervous, sorry. But yes, I want to meet Maggie."

He leads me to the door leading into the area where the pets are contained. "Would you like a quick tour while you're here?"

"That would be great. Lead the way. Show me everything." I cringe. That sounds creepy. Thankfully, Micha doesn't comment and sends another one of his smiles my way.

He walks ahead of me down the hall and I notice his hips sway as he walks. I'm fucking noticing his hips. Maybe I should have said no to the tour because clearly, someone else is inhabiting my body right now. I'm checking this man out and I can honestly say I've never done that before. Maybe I'm just disappointed Micha isn't the woman I first thought he was.

He pauses outside a large plexiglass window into a room with enough cat toys and climbing towers to make any cat feel like they're in heaven.

"This is where the cats get to spend some time every day for exercise and socializing. Sometimes potential adopters spend time in here playing with the cat, before they decide to adopt too. It's very important for a person to feel they can play with the animal and bond before they take it home."

I nod and continue to follow him. He opens a door, and we enter what he calls the cat holding room. Row upon row of kennel banks line the two walls. At one end of the room is a small room with a fridge, kitchen sink and a large laundry wash basin. On its back wall there are shelves stuffed with towels and blankets. There are piles of litter boxes next to the washbasin and piles of food dishes on a rack on the counter.

My eyes bug out of my head at the sheer number of cats in the room. Micha notices my surprise.

"I know it's rather sad to see so many here without homes. But we do our best to make them happy until they find one."

I stick my finger into a kennel at a little kitten poking his foot out. He bites playfully and jumps around, pulling another smile from me. Man, I haven't smiled so easily in a very long time. I've been here ten minutes and I already feel my cheeks hurting from the effort. I'm going to have to admit Owen was right about the animal thing.

"I don't know how you leave here every day without one hidden in your pocket."

"The temptation is strong, believe me. Come in, we still have more to see, and you need to meet Maggie yet."

We continue down the hall to the back of the building. There's a massive laundry and storage room where more blankets and towels are stacked, bags and buckets of cat litter, and cat food are piled everywhere. Leashes hang on a wall with matching collars.

Micha opens the last door at the very end of the hallway, and we step into the dog room. Eight dog runs line the back, each one has its own plexiglass door, and the runs are all concrete. Micha walks over to the one immediately to our right and smiles.

"Hey pretty girl, do you want to meet someone new today?"

I hear the crazy thumping of a tail on the floor and a small whine followed by the stomping of dog feet. "I'm going to take that as a yes."

"Since she's the only dog right now and nobody else is here, I'm going to let her out off leash if you're okay with that? If you meet her and like her, we can take her for a short walk together and I can answer any questions you have."

His smile still sparkles, and my heart does that dang beat too fast thing in my chest. I'm not sure if it's because of him or the excitement to meet the dog. Should it matter if it's because I really like his smile? I smile back. "Yes, let me meet this beautiful girl."

I wipe my sweating palms on my pants and shift my feet. Okay, this is the big moment. Micha unlatches the kennel door and a hyper ball of black energy bolts out towards him. He immediately drops to greet the exuberant dog, wrapping his arms around her neck as she slobber-kisses all over him. Her tail swings so fast it becomes a blur, and she obviously loves Micha. She hasn't even noticed me yet.

"I missed you too, girl. I brought a friend today. Go say hi."

Micha points in my direction and Maggie, without pause, bolts in my direction and stomps her feet for my attention. Her giant tongue flaps out and she has the happiest dog grin. It's impossible not to smile back. So, I do.

I bend over and pet her head, but she wants more than a gentle pet and butts her head harder into my hand.

"She likes rough attention." Micha laughs. "I should have warned you. The harder the scratch, the more she likes it. She's a bit of a masochist that way."

Maggie is definitely a unique dog. I love her personality already, but I'm worried I'm not enough for her. She's so spunky and full of life. How would she be in my home? It can't be much different than the kennels here all day, but I'm away for nine hours or more at a time. Doubt is now filling me, but I can't deny I love how I feel in her presence.

I puff out a breath and find Micha observing our interaction with a watchful eye. Damn, he has really pretty eyes. Why am I still noticing things about him?

"Can we still take that walk? I have a lot of questions."

SIX

Micha

I TAKE THE COLLAR and leash hanging on Maggie's kennel door. As soon as she hears the clacking of metal and the snap of her collar, she's bouncing like a two-year-old high on pixie stix.

"She loves walks, so we can absolutely take that walk. She also knows the word walk, so now that we've said it, we have to take her. Pro tip though, she can't spell it yet, so that's still safe."

Dominic laughs, and it's a deep no cares in the world laugh. It lights up his entire being. His eyes sparkle and the lines around his eyes smile too. Dominic's giant brown eyes are happy in what feels like the first time in a very long time. I only know what Jacob told me about him being a widower, but it seems like I have the privilege of seeing him in a state no one else has witnessed for a long time.

I secure the collar around Maggie's neck, and she waits patiently, smacking her tail against our legs.

I hand Dominic the leash and he pales.

"I'm holding her leash?"

"Well, that's what happens when you walk an animal. A person holds the leash. Are you nervous?"

His smile falters. "Is it stupid if I say yes?"

"Oh my gosh no. It's important you're comfortable, Dominic. The animals know if you aren't. I can start if you want and then hand her over once we walk a bit."

He runs his hand behind his neck. "Is that okay?"

"More than okay." I rub my hand along his arm to reassure him, but he steps away.

"Thanks. I'll follow your lead."

I make sure I have my keys to the building, and we exit out the back door, which has a path directly down to the lake and walking trails. It's a beautiful area and I know it well. So does Maggie. We take a lot of walks out here when I need to clear my mind.

Our feet crunch on the gravel and Maggie stops to sniff and pee everywhere. She loves being outside and walks well on a leash. She's either really smart or someone spent a lot of time training her.

As our small path links up to the main one to start the lake loop, I turn to hand the leash to Dominic, and he gulps in air.

"Do you want to try now?"

A wordless nod and he holds out his hand. I slip the leash over his hand and hold it there. "If you slide it over your wrist like this, you can then grab the top of the leash. This will give you leverage if you need it, and if she pulls, it's less likely to fly out of your hands that way, too." As I speak, I've run my hand from his wrist and covered his hand with my own to show how to hold the nylon leash. His eyes are wide and bright as he watches me, and I feel my own cheeks heat. I do this kind of stuff all the time. Why am I feeling self-conscious around this guy suddenly? And why does it feel so good to touch him?

I step away and smile. "Do you think you've got it?"

He nods. Eyebrows furrowed in concentration. "Let's do this."

I chuckle at his determination at something so trivial as walking a dog. But I suppose those things that come easy to some can feel like insurmountable challenges to others. I know that feeling too well.

The gravel ends and we walk along the boardwalk that partially surrounds the lake on this side of the shore. Dominic is hyper focused on Maggie and I'm sensing a nervousness he didn't have before. His jaw has tensed and some of the joy has faded from his face.

"What would you like to know about Maggie? Or owning a dog in general, Dominic?" His eyes never leave Maggie. "You're doing great, by the way."

He glances my way and runs his free hand through his hair. "I need to chill out. I'm so worked up over owning a dog. Could you imagine me being a father?" He chuckles, but it's hollow and sad.

"I think you'd be a great dad. You're very concerned you're doing even the simplest thing right. That's a caring quality. You want Maggie to be safe and do right by her."

"Jenny wanted kids." He says it so softly I almost don't hear him. I don't know how I should respond either. We're supposed to be talking about all things canine and I don't know what's happening now, but I think he needs to get it off his chest.

We come to a bench along the path and without a word, Dominic takes a seat and Maggie automatically lies at his feet. My smile grows. She's comfortable with him already. She's not the only one.

"My wife died two years ago. We were going to start a family, but she found a breast lump when she went for a routine exam. It was cancer. We thought at first she'd be able to beat it, but it spread so fast." He gulps and blinks back tears. My hands itch to provide some kind of physical comfort for him, but I'm not sure he'd want it. "I lost her fourteen months after her diagnosis. I've been lost ever since. My friend Owen thought I should try to get a pet to share some of my love with, to help me move on. I thought it was a great idea until two minutes ago."

He turns to me, and I see his struggle. His pain. He doesn't even have to say the words. I know what he's thinking. I also know I can never turn away another person who's hurting.

I place my hand over his and squeeze. "Pets are a great way to help ease grief. It's okay to feel conflicted over it. I know Jenny loved you very much. She'd want you to share that love with anyone or any thing that could use it." He tips half his lips in a smile. "You're not replacing her; no other person or pet could fill that void for you. But I promise, this dog, she's one in a million and she'd be there for you."

He squeezes my hand back. "Thank you, Micha. That means a lot. I'm sorry for unloading that on you. I don't normally spill that to total strangers."

He hasn't let my hand go and I like it. I know it's just a friendly gesture of comfort, but it feels nice to be needed by someone.

He puffs out a breath. "Okay, what do I need to learn to be a dog dad?" He drops my hand and stands, and I miss the feeling. Maggie is quick to follow him. She's an explorer and will walk until her paws fall off.

"First step with the shelter is to fill in the application. It's pretty straight forward but we like to know you're able to provide the animal the basic care it needs. For example, Maggie would prefer a yard over apartment living and while she's not overly accepting with other dogs, she loves cats."

Dominic laughs. "Isn't that weird? Aren't dogs supposed to chase cats?"

"Generally, yes, it's common because most dogs like to chase. Maggie is truly a Zen dog. She's unlike any dog I've ever met." Truth be told, she reminds me of me. Go with the flow when your world goes to shit.

"How come she's been here so long? Is there something I should know about her?"

It's a valid question and I press my lips together. Something about Dominic makes me feel like I can come clean with him, and he wouldn't rat me out. I also don't feel comfortable lying to him. Truth it is. "There's nothing wrong with her. I've been keeping her here for myself. I've always wanted a dog, but I can't have one. I don't want her to go. So, I've never let her get adopted."

Dominic is silent and I'm worrying I made a mistake telling him that. I wring my hands and watch Maggie stop at her favourite sniffing spot.

"Would you let me adopt her if you could keep visiting her?" His warm brown eyes find mine and I'm shocked to see he's serious.

"You'd let me visit her? I'm a complete stranger to you, just someone who loves animals and one crazy black dog." I shuffle my feet.

"Strangers are just two people who haven't become friends yet."

I look up to find his eyes roaming all over me, but I can't read them. He holds his hand out to me.

"I'm Dominic Morenzo."

I smile and accept the offered hand. "Micha Jones. It's a pleasure to meet you." I drop his hand and we stare at each other with goofy smiles. Damn, he has a great smile.

"I'm pretty sure we shook hands back at the shelter, but now it's official. We're no longer strangers. So, if I want to be a dog dad, are you going to help?"

"Are you going to tell Jacob I've been keeping her for myself?"

"No, but I have a feeling he probably already knows." He waits expectantly.

"Okay then, let's walk back and I'll fill you in on what you need to know and do to get your house ready for a dog."

His fist pumps the air. "Woohoo! I'm gonna be a dog dad!"

As we finish the walk and return to the shelter, Dominic's previous sadness and nervousness has disappeared. I go over a few things as we walk about what kind of stuff he'll need immediately and how she's good with travelling. When we secure Maggie back in her kennel, he sits with her for a few minutes and it's a sight to make my heart burst. She'll be loved, and that's all I could ever ask for.

He hugs her and tells her she's going to be his girl real soon. As soon as he has his dog space set up, he's going to bring her home. I wouldn't be lying to say I feel a pang of jealously over Maggie being hugged and not me.

Dominic is going to be a great dog dad and I'm going to miss seeing Maggie as often as I wanted. A part of me regrets letting him do this, but I know it's the right thing and I think I made a new friend.

I lock up the shelter and walk over to his truck with him. "Do you need a ride anywhere, Micha?"

"Thank you, but I'm going to use the time to walk home. It's a beautiful night."

"Okay, be safe. Meet you tomorrow at the Screaming Bean? 6 P.M. okay?"

"I'll be there."

He waves and drives off and I start my walk home with a weight in my chest I can't describe.

SEVEN

Dominic

M Y MEETING YESTERDAY WITH Micha and Maggie has left me in a tailspin. I have so many questions swirling in my brain. I need to talk to Owen before I explode. Micha is meeting me at The Screaming Bean tonight at 6 P.M. to do my paperwork for the adoption. He also agreed to help me shop for some dog items. I have no idea what I'm doing with a dog or what they need. Which is why I'm grateful for Micha's offer of help and guidance.

That's my next issue. Micha himself has me in knots. Which is why I need to talk to Owen. I need to sort so many things out before 6 P.M. I wanted Owen to take a drive with me instead of meeting me at The Bean, but he said he needed to help Parker with something later and wanted to stick around. It's not like Owen to keep a staff member around for so long if they can't do the job on their own, but I'm not about to question him on that just yet.

I don't even know where to start with our conversation. I've never felt so off course before, and I need someone to point me in the right direction. Owen can usually help me with that, and I hope today is no different.

I wave at Owen and take a seat at our usual table. I watch as the customers flow in and out, always happy to get their caffeine fix here. From the corner of my eye, I see Parker leave the kitchen with a scowl and Owen arrives with my favourite lunch again. I suspect he only has tomato macaroni soup and clubhouse sandwiches on the menu just for me. In fact, I don't even know if they're officially on the menu.

He settles across from me and while he looks tired, he still shows up when I ask.

"Hey O, you sleeping okay? You look tired today."

He separates the sandwich and passes my half over. "It's been a long night with the upgrades to the kitchen. Electrician and contractor opted to work overnight to finish the job." He yawns and barely covers his mouth. "I came and did some paperwork while they were here."

"Is everything okay? Is the new oven set up already?"

He swallows his mouthful and nods. "Yep. Gonna give it a test run tonight. That's why Parker left in a pissy mood."

"Because he has to do his job?"

"No, because I'm going to stay here with him and watch. He got the lessons from the company about all the features of the oven. I want him to show me. He's not a fan of the idea." He barks a laugh. "So, tell me about yesterday. Am I a dog uncle yet?"

"Not quite." I run my hand down my face. "Fuck, Owen, I don't even know where to start to tell you what happened." Which part do I start with? Which part is bothering me the most?

He stops eating, placing his sandwich down. "This sounds deep, Dom. Is this why you wanted to take a drive? Are you comfortable here?"

I wave it off. "I'm comfortable here for now, yes." I lean back in my chair. "Last night I didn't have a drink and stare outside. First time in almost two years I didn't spend the night thinking of her. I feel like I've betrayed Jenny." My eyes lower. That's exactly how I feel. In my mind, if I'm not thinking of her every night, her memory is forgotten. It's a guilt I can't shake.

Owen nudges my shoe under the table, and I raise my eyes to meet his gaze. "Dom, I know you feel guilty, but this is a big step for you. You're moving your life forward. Nobody expects you to sit and grieve forever. You're thirty-two years old. There's a lot of life ahead of you. It's not wrong to move on."

I know this. I see it in everyone's face when they know I'm still grieving for my dead wife. Counsellors have told me this, my family has told me this and Jenny's family has even echoed the same. But knowing it's okay to move on and accepting it's okay has been a rough road.

"God, I know Owen. But there's more." A flash of Micha's bright smile plays in my mind. "Last night was all kinds of... weird."

He leans back. Both of us have now stopped eating. "What else happened then?"

I swallow hard. "I met the person from the shelter last night that's going to help me with all the new dog stuff."

"Right, you said her name was Micha? Is that what has you feeling off? You met another woman and you're interested?" His smile returns. "If so, that's fantastic! Tell me about her."

I chew on my lip. This is what makes all this weird. I've never been in this kind of spot before. Owen will be cool with it, but it's no less strange uttering the words. "Not a her. Micha is a man. A very pretty man, with a gorgeous smile and beautiful eyes. I went to bed last night thinking of him."

Owen sits up straighter and arches an eyebrow. "Dude, how pretty are we talking here?"

That earns him a chuckle. "I thought he was a woman from behind. When he turned around, I still thought he was beautiful. He has the prettiest eyes. Then I noticed he most definitely had a dick, and he was a he." I clear my throat. "I also couldn't stop watching his hips."

He whistles low. "Damn bro. So, what happened?"

I lean forward and Owen matches my movement. "That's the thing, O. I watched his ass; I loved his smile. I couldn't stop thinking about his fucking lips and when he touched my hand, I felt like I stuck my finger on an electric fence. I was so into thinking about him, I went to bed, and I didn't even have my nightly drink." I sigh. "Or think about Jenny."

"Wow."

I nod. "Yep, wow is right. But the really crazy thing." I lower my voice. "I dreamt about him and woke up with the biggest hard-on I've ever had."

Owen's lips tilt in a smirk. He leans back and picks up his sandwich again. "So, what are you going to do about it?"

I stir my soup. "About what? The fact I might be attracted to Micha or the fact he's knocked me off my routine so much I dreamt about him and stopped thinking about Jenny?"

He snorts. "The fact you wasted a hard-on. You know how I feel about wasted hard-ons."

I throw my head back and laugh. "Something along the lines of why waste wood when there's always a fire somewhere you can throw it in?"

He grins. "Well, that's the general idea, yeah. So, you're not freaked out about being attracted to a dude?"

I thought about that a lot this morning. While I'd never been with a man, I had many friends in college that had. I had never waded into that scene because Jenny was my high school sweetheart, and I was in love. I knew Owen had been with men, though, and while he also had girlfriends, he never gave himself a label. Sexual orientation in our crowd was never a big deal. We viewed a partner as someone who had qualities we liked, as well as being attracted to on a physical level. It was never anything more than that to us. We were a liberal crowd and found no reason to make a big deal out of it.

"I'm not freaked out, no. I think a better word is shocked. I mean, I've never had this happen before. Not even in college."

"Well, you were in love with Jenny, and she was all you focused on. If you would have been single, Addison would totally have hit on you. Remember him? Blonde guy in engineering that was totally obsessed with The Stone Temple Pilots?"

I smile. "I remember Addison. Well, sort of. It's been years and memories are hazy, but I remember The STP fascination."

"He had a huge crush on you. Settled for me instead."

I raise an eyebrow. "You banged STP guy? Did I know that?"

"I don't know if you knew about it. It was a one-night thing, but he was good with his mouth. Really good."

Owen laughs while I shake my head at him. Owen was a playboy and still is. Since he opened the business, he doesn't go out much and since he started babysitting me; he goes out even less. Which makes me feel bad. I take up so much of his time. I really need to stop leaning on him so much.

My phone lights up with a call and it's Tara. I roll my eyes and send it to voicemail. I don't need to hear anything out of her mouth today. Not when I'm excited about adopting a dog and having met someone I like. I can guarantee she won't be thrilled to know it's a man I'm interested in. She always turned her nose up at our friends in college who were bisexual, including Owen.

I tuck my phone into my pocket and turn my attention back to Owen and our conversation.

"There's also a dog adoption on the table. Her name is Maggie, and she's the sweetest thing."

"So, I *do* get to be an uncle! What kind of dog and when do you take her home?"

"She's a black Lab mix. Micha is meeting me here tonight to fill in the adoption papers. Then he's going to come shopping with me."

"Whoa, whoa. Back up here, Dom. Micha is going shopping with you and doing paperwork tonight? This isn't a date, is it?"

"What? No! The shelter has a program to help first-time pet owners. Since I have no damn clue about what to do with a dog, Micha is going to get me set up. Help me learn the ropes, sort of thing."

"And you're going to be okay being around him? In your house and space when you admitted you're attracted to him?"

"Of course, I will. We're friends and he loves Maggie. I promised he could visit, since he's going to miss her."

Owen shakes his head, laughing. "If only I could make a bet on how this will play out."

I cross my arms. "What kind of bet?"

"I give you a week. $50 says you can't last a week before you make a move."

I hold out my hand to shake on that bet. "You're on."

"Anybody that has you thinking about the future instead of the past has my automatic seal of approval," Owen stands up. "And Dom... ," I wait for him to continue. "I've never wanted to win a bet more than I do this one. For once in your life, prove me right, will ya?"

Owen laughs as he clears the table, and I take my time getting back to the butcher shop. We've always made bets with each other, but this one is going to be easy to win. It was one dream. Yes, Micha is an attractive guy, but I won't be getting involved with anyone in less than a week.

Micha thinks I'm straight, anyway. He was nothing but kind towards me. He probably didn't even notice I'd been checking him out.

He's going to be a good friend for both Maggie and me. I enjoy being around him. And if he noticed I was looking, well, I'll deal with that if it ever comes up.

EIGHT

Micha

THE ENTIRE WALK HOME after meeting with Dominic I was conflicted. He's perfect for Maggie. She loved him right away, not like some people that met her. Dogs have a knack for sniffing out bad people, and she loved Dominic immediately. I knew she was best with him, but I had a problem.

Dominic is genuinely kind even in his own pain and he's centerfold handsome. Not to mention incredibly hot. Like I should wear oven mitts when I touch him hot. He's a perfect marriage of hard-working farmer body with sexy football player moves. Bulky yet graceful. Sexy but modest. The one tiny problem? He thinks I didn't notice he was checking me out.

When a sexy as sin man like Dominic checks you out, you notice. But the man was sending all kinds of mixed signals, which means I'm now in an awkward place. I'm technically representing the animal shelter; I really should keep things professional. But if he's thinking of switching teams and I'm the target, good god how do I turn that down?

I wrangled a deal to keep seeing Maggie, but unfortunately it means the temptation that is Dominic Morenzo will be there too. It's only a matter of time before I do something to screw things up and he doesn't allow me to visit anymore. I have the worst problem of falling for unavailable men. Men that have no genuine need for me beyond their own entertainment. The last one was married and got me kicked out of my own home. It's been years since then, but it doesn't mean I've forgotten how my actions always seem to bite me in the ass.

Dominic is still grieving for his wife. I should chalk up his attention to me as nothing more than loneliness. That's why he's getting a dog in the first place. I need to remember that. He's lonely, not gay.

Repeat after me Micha, he's a friend, not a lover.

I reach the house and the lights are off. Roberta left me a note that it's bridge night and she'll see me in the morning. I crumple the note and call for Tux.

"Here Mr. Puss!" I hear a thump as he jumps off of wherever he is and comes padding over to the door.

Meow, meow.

"Sorry I'm late, little man." I scoop him up and carry him downstairs to my suite with me. "Shall we dine together tonight? I do believe there's a can of tuna cat food for you somewhere."

Tux thinks that's a great idea and wiggles out of my arms to run to the food cupboard, meowing loudly.

"Calm your self dude. It's just the regular cat food. I'm not giving you fresh tuna or anything extra fancy."

I scoop out his food and he dives in like he hasn't eaten in a week. I poke around my cupboards and find nothing except microwave popcorn and packages of ramen noodles. After a moment of consideration, I pull out my phone and call Travis.

"Micha! What's up?"

"Are you busy tonight, or do you have time to join me and Tux for a rave in my apartment? All the cool kids will be here."

"Oh... that kind of night, is it? You, okay?"

"Truthfully, I want you to bring some home cooked food. But I also want to talk to my bestie. I have... issues."

Without missing a beat, Trav gets me. He knows there's something I need him for. He could be knee deep in his own problems and he'll be there for me.

"You want me to get your usual from the diner?"

"I'd love you forever. I'll call it in now."

"See you in about twenty, Micha."

I change into a pair of lounge pants and an old T-shirt after I call the diner and flop onto my couch to wait. As I tend to do when I have the time, my mind wanders back to a time in my life when I thought I had it all together. I had it all, and

I knew what *it* was at the tender of age of nineteen. Banging a married man and being kept a dirty secret was not the highlight of my life. Nor was it a highlight when my father found out the married man was one of his law partners. Did I mention he was married to a woman?

Tossed out like a piece of trash by both of them when the shit hit the fan, I made myself a promise to be smarter and chose someone that needed me just as much as the air they breathe. I needed to not be someone's toy or newest infatuation. Everyone I thought I could trust betrayed me. I couldn't have fucked up my life any harder if I tried.

I flop my head back and squeeze my eyes shut. I make shitty choices. Simple fact. For the last four years, I've turned it all around and started over. I'm successful and I own a business. I have a cat. I have a place to live, that I pay for with money I've earned. I'm worth something. More than something, I'm priceless and nobody is going to make me feel anything less than fantastic again. I'm damn fabulous and nobody will dull my shine.

My phone buzzes, alerting me Travis is here, so I jog up the stairs to let him in. Opening the door, my most bestest friend in the world has a bag of amazing smelling food and a hug. He steps in and immediately wraps me in his arms. I squeeze him tightly back.

"Food and hugs make everything better. Thanks for coming."

Travis follows me downstairs and I unpack the generous portion of meatloaf, mashed potatoes and garlic glazed carrots from the diner. They make everything from scratch and serve enough to last you for two meals. Best food ever and I will fight anyone over this meatloaf.

"You going to eat some with me, or did you eat already?"

"I can eat with you. I left the clinic late, so I'm actually pretty hungry."

I take an extra plate down and we squeeze into my two-seater table to dig in.

"So, why were you at work so late? Everything okay?"

Travis shrugs. "Yeah, it's fine. The possible new vet showed up late for a tour, and we stayed back chatting."

"And? Is it a good or bad thing? Don't leave me hanging, Trav."

"Eh, it's probably a good thing. Jury's still out."

I fork some meatloaf in my mouth, and it melts on my tongue. I moan. It's seriously like sex for your taste buds.

"Mic, you need to stop moaning around food when you eat. That kind of shit can get you in trouble." He peers over his fork at me. "So, what's going on? You're not your usual sparkling self. What happened?"

"Damn, am I that easy to read?"

"For the people close to you, yes. So, what had me bringing comfort food over and an SOS call from my best friend?"

"Well, I told you I was meeting with a possible adopter for Maggie, right?"

"Yes! That was tonight! OMG, she's gone now and you're sad. That's it, right? Oh, sugar." Travis squeezes out of his space and tries to hug me, but I swat him away.

"Would you sit down, you big oaf! That's not quite the entire problem."

He chuckles and scoots back to his seat. "Okay, sorry. I got carried away. Let me hear it then."

I sigh. "He's perfect. She loves him."

"Since that's the whole point of you meeting and getting her adopted, I'm not connecting the dots, Micha. What else?"

I drop my fork and run my hands through my hair. "He's gotta be the hottest man I've ever seen. The *I would look fantastic on his arm* kind of hot. He would look fucking fantastic sucking my dick, hot." I drop my head back and stare at the ceiling. That image is fighting my meatloaf for my sole attention right now.

Travis giggles. "Always so dramatic Mic. So, what's the problem? He's hot and adopting your favourite dog." He keeps eating the heavenly meatloaf, oblivious to the fact I'm having a minor life crisis. "What's got you so worked up?"

I snap my head back up. "Trav, he's still mourning his deceased wife. He's lonely." I pause. "He most definitely checked me out, but I'm not picking up any gay vibes from him. He was probably just curious because I'm so damn fabulous, right?" I shovel potatoes into my mouth. "Why am I being tempted? Like, the last guy I fell for was married to a woman and now I want to chase another straight guy." God, this meatloaf is good. "What the fuck is wrong with me?"

"Wait a minute. Is this Dominic you're talking about?"

"How the hell did you know that?"

"He owns Wild Baloney. I've met him a few times when I pick up our lunch. He's super nice and the only guy I know around town that lost a wife recently. He's also major cute. So, what's the problem again?"

"Trav! I can't make a move on the straight guy. Not only have I already made that mistake, I need to be professional. He offered to let me come visit Maggie whenever I want. No way can I fuck that up. You know I love that dog."

MEOW.

"You know I still love you too, Tux." I scoop him up and he snuggles into me, kneading my chest as he licks my nose.

"Micha. You're helping him with a new pet. Besides, you wouldn't be the first person from the shelter to flirt or hook up with people they've met there. Is that what you're worried about? If you want to make a move to see if he's interested, do it."

"What do you mean, I'm not the first? I'm way out of the loop here. Spill it."

"I know for a fact Jacob has flirted with a few of the sponsors at our fundraisers. One was a hockey player and I suspect they hooked up, but I haven't confirmed it. So, if the boss is doing it, why can't you?"

I gasp. "You're telling me, my sweet, sweet Jacob whored himself to a sponsor? I'm shocked and appalled, Trav."

He laughs at my theatrics, finishes his plate and takes it to the sink. "It's not confirmed. You know Jacob doesn't say much. The point is, if something happened, he wouldn't be bitching you out over it. Nor do I think Dominic would do anything to hurt the shelter. He's not like that."

"So, you don't think I'm stupid if I flirted or tried to feel him out? Even though I'm travelling down the straight guy highway? Something I swore I'd never do again, I might add."

"It's your heart, Micha. Only you can truly know what it can handle. If you want to see if he's game, then flirt and see where it goes. Worst case, he turns you down."

"Nuh uh. Worse case is, he won't let me see Maggie." I put Tux down and he saunters off to sleep off his dinner.

"I bet if he checked you out like you said, he's more interested than you think. You should go for it. Who can say no to you? You're gorgeous."

I walk over and hug him again. "You're so good for my ego, Trav."

"You're welcome. Listen, if you're okay, I'm going to get home. I'm bagged and tomorrow will be a long day with the new vet."

I walk him upstairs and squish him with another hug before I lock up behind him. I clean up the dishes and flop onto the bed.

It can't possibly be as easy as Trav says, can it? Do I flirt harmlessly and see if he flirts back? Is that going to be wrong? He obviously still loves his deceased wife. But he's lonely. It's so plain on his face and his big brown eyes are just... sad. I know that sadness, that empty, alone feeling. I've lived it. He even said he wanted the dog to share his love with, to help him move on. Maybe I read too much into his gazes and I'm completely overreacting.

I snuggle down under my covers, but I can't sleep. Every time I close my eyes, I see Dominic and Maggie and my heart flops all over, like a freshly caught fish. What if I'm the one to take his sadness away? Maggie deserves a happy owner, right?

Maybe I should try to be his friend. He needs a friend more than anything. I can do that with my eyes closed, I'm the most fabulous friend you can friend.

Except when I close my eyes, all I keep seeing is the two of us as more than friends. And I don't know if it's a good idea or not.

NINE

Dominic

A T 5:30 P.M., OUT of habit, I slide into the table I usually have lunch at with Owen. My palms are sweaty, and I feel like I need to bolt to the bathroom.

I spent the rest of the afternoon at work in my butcher shop, looping my earlier conversation with Owen over and over. He thinks I'm going to sleep with Micha within a week. Arrogant ass. It was one night of my life I was thinking of another man and not Jenny. I'm not about to go through a huge life changing epiphany to discover I'm bisexual. Or Micha sexual or whatever.

Not that there's anything wrong with that if I do. It just feels too fast. I think. I don't know what to think, really. I know I can't ignore the fact that he shifted something so monumental in me. I finally stopped moping for one night. Attractive or not, Micha pulled me away from my sadness, something even Owen couldn't do. Micha did it without knowing and without trying. While I still feel guilt for not following my nightly remembrance routine, the unexpected relief of knowing it's possible to move on again has left me hopeful that one day I will.

I drum my fingers on the table, wondering if I should preorder a snack for us. Decision made; I approach the cash register.

"Hi Dominic, your usual?"

"No Paige, I'm meeting someone, and I'd like to preorder if I could?"

"Absolutely. What would you like?"

"A piece of coconut cream pie, two forks and two café mochas. Could you make the little designs on top too?"

She chuckles. "I can. Any requests?"

"Can you make paw prints?"

"I'll do my best, Dom. I'll bring them over when your date gets here."

"He's just a friend. But please do that."

While I wait, I sit back down and scroll through my phone. I do little on social media. That was Jenny's thing. I only recently moved to a smart phone, because I smashed my old flip phone by accident. As I scroll through the Facebook feed, I never go on, there are a few tags of me, so I check them out. A friend from college has tagged an old photo of a group of us at some party. I smile softly and enlarge the photo. That was a good night. Jenny had too much to drink, and I physically carried her home. I huff a small laugh. She swore she'd never do shooters ever again, but she did.

There're more photos I've been tagged in but never noticed. One was with Jenny at a semi-formal in our last year of college and my fingers freeze from scrolling. It's amazing to see our faces so young and carefree after all we've been through since then. The smile hasn't left my face though because we had such a good time that night.

I'm so lost in my memories, I don't notice Micha until he clears his throat.

I drop my phone on the table and I forget how to say hello, because Micha is... breathtaking. A man should not be as beautiful as he is. I hastily stand up to greet him and pull out a chair.

"Hi Micha. Sorry I didn't see you come in." I gesture at my phone. "I was lost in memories." I motion for him to take the seat, and he does. "That was rude for me to not notice you there. You look great."

Why the hell did I just compliment him?

"Well, I know how to make an entrance, I'm told. Although I'm usually not waiting for the other party to notice me standing there for so long."

"Oh god, I'm sorry. How long were you standing there?"

He pulls out a folder from his laptop bag. "Maybe a minute. You looked like you were having a moment. I didn't want to interrupt."

When I spin my phone, I can see Jenny's face smiling back at me. I slide it over to Micha.

His hand goes to his mouth with a quiet gasp. "Oh Dominic, is this Jenny?" I nod with a proud smile, and he raises the phone for a closer look. "She's beautiful. I love her eyes, so full of happiness here. What were you doing?"

He passes the phone back to me and I close the screen. "It was the semi-formal in college. Almost ten years ago now. And thank you, she was beautiful."

"Not was Dom. She is and always will be. That's never going to change."

My mouth goes dry as I stare at this man. The only person who's pulled me away from speaking about Jenny in the past tense because he's right, she always will be beautiful, and he wasn't afraid to come out and say it. No tip toeing around, wondering if he might say the wrong thing to me. He so freely speaks his mind, even in the face of grief. It's a refreshing change from how most people speak to me about her. I definitely like it.

"You're right. She is."

Micha reaches over and gently squeezes my hand. "Thank you for sharing her with me." His smile is warm and genuine as he removes his hand and flips open the folder he brought with him. "We have a few papers to fill out, but it won't take long. You can take Maggie home tonight if you want to."

I wasn't expecting that. I thought we had longer. This is the only actual night I'm going to have with him. Why is that my first thought and not the fact I'll have a dog in my house soon?

"So soon?" My voice is higher than I intended and Micha stills. "I mean, I thought you had to do a home visit and all that stuff. Check out the yard. Make sure I pass a test of some sort." I rub the back of my neck. He's going to think I'm some pathetic man that needs hand holding.

"Um, well. You can wait for another day if you need it. Why don't we see how things go tonight and go from there? I don't think you need me to make sure you pass a test. You passed the only test I had; Maggie liked you."

I'm about to respond, but Paige comes over with my order.

"Hi, gentlemen. Here are your café mochas and coconut crème pie, two forks. Enjoy."

She places a mug in front of each of us and the pie in the middle. Micha's eyes twinkle as his face splits in a wide smile. My heart flops around, knowing I put that smile there. "You ordered me a mocha... with a paw print?" He brings his hand over his mouth again, but his smile still pokes out. "Dominic, this is so thoughtful, thank you. I love mochas. The paw print is totes adorbs. Gah, I'm all marshmallow right now."

I chuckle. "I have no idea what you just said, but I think it's good, right?"

"Yes, it's very good Dom." His laughter is light and all the anxiety I was feeling before he showed up melts away. "Okay, let's get some things signed."

He sips his drink as he flips back into the folder, and I watch with far more interest than necessary as his tongue peeks out to remove the frothy milk from his lips. Oh boy, I shouldn't be noticing things like that. I need his help with Maggie. I need to focus and get through tonight.

"Yes, let's get to it. What do you need?"

He hands me a pink, sparkly pen. It's covered in paw prints and cupcakes and has to be the cutest thing I've ever seen. It's show stopping and memorable, just like Micha. "I guess nobody will ever steal your pen if this is what you always have on hand, right?"

He snorts. "You'd be surprised how many people want that pen. I think this is my sixth one." He shuffles some forms. "Why get bent out of shape if someone wants my pen? If it makes them smile, then take it. Life is too short to sweat things like stolen pens."

He explains the forms to me and what I need to do. As I'm filling it in, I feel his eyes on me and a bead of sweat breaks my brow. I look up and meet his eyes. The pretty ones that he's lined with a purple eyeliner today and not black.

"What? Did I do something wrong?"

"Not really. I'm just wondering if we're sharing the pie since we got two forks, or is one a backup in case you get clumsy?"

"Do you mind if we share? It's always such a giant piece and I can never finish one myself." I pause. "Unless you think it's weird to split a dessert with me?"

He bites his lip. "No, not weird. That's what friends are for, right? To share things with?"

"Absolutely. It's coconut cream. Shit, I hope you don't have any allergies. I didn't even think of that."

"You're safe there. I'm only allergic to broken hearts and high school gym class." He grins before snatching a fork and slicing off a chunk of pie.

"Oh. Em. Gee! This is fantastic." He closes his eyes and licks his lips with a low purr, and my cock notices. No matter how hard I tell it to go back to sleep, it likes the sights and sounds of Micha more and more. Which is not helping the whole *he's just a friend* mantra in my mind.

I decide to ignore it and plow through with conversation. "You didn't like gym class?"

He laughs until tears escape. "Uh, that's a giant N-O, Dom. When you're scrawny and look like a girl, you get picked on and left out of all the team picking and what not. That kind of thing gets old after awhile, you know?"

He takes another scoop of pie and the shadows that fall across his face disappear just as fast as they appeared. "I'm sorry. It's their loss for not getting to know you and giving you a try."

"Funny, I say the same thing about the boys that never wanted to date me too. Not everyone appreciates my extra-ness, you know?" He pauses, hesitating. "Thank you for accepting me the way I am and letting me help you out."

I sit up straighter, appreciating that Micha just allowed me a glance into the real him and has a vulnerability like everyone else. The mood needs to be lightened, though. "I couldn't think of anyone else I'd love to share a cream pie with." But as the words pass my lips, that was the wrong to thing to say and I can feel my ears burn with embarrassment. "That sounded a lot better in my head. I'm sorry."

Micha's eyes sparkle with mischief. "Well, don't apologize." He takes another fork full of pie and makes a show of licking it off his fork. "I'm flattered I fall into such an esteemed category. But tell me Dominic, do you prefer the heavy cream on the bottom or the light fluffy cream on top?"

My entire body is aflame with the images his words are painting in my mind. My throat is dry, and my voice is croaky despite having my mocha next to me. If this is Micha playfully flirting, I don't know what he'll be like when he turns it up all the way. I also don't know the answer to his question, so I play it safe. "I like them both together, I think. I've never tried one without the other."

As quickly as he started his flirty banter, he shuts it down and goes back to business talk; leaving me with a mild case of whiplash and wondering what the hell had just happened. "Okay, let's finish the forms and we can go over the shopping list. You still want to go to PetSmart? It's at least a thirty-minute drive there."

I take his abrupt change of topic in stride. "Is that okay with you? I have the time, if you can spare it."

"Absolutely! I need to buy Tuxedo some presents while we're there too. Do you mind if we stop by my house first before we go?"

I drain my coffee cup and stand. "Not at all. Let's get going and we can talk while we drive."

Micha gathers the forms and folders and places them in his laptop bag. I let him walk ahead of me over to my truck parked at my shop, and I know I have exactly thirty-two steps to get my mind on task and away from any more flirty talk.

I want him to be a friend, and I need his help. But I'm also very attracted to him.

And even if he becomes more than a friend, I can't let Owen win that bet.

I had no idea adopting a dog was going to be this hard. Pun intended.

TEN

Micha

WHAT THE HELL DID I just do? From the moment I walked in and saw Dominic lost in thought, looking at his phone, I knew I was going to say something epically Micha. I did not disappoint. Although I didn't expect myself to throw out a cream pie joke this early in the game. That's gotta be a record, even for me. In my defense, he started it. He also commented on how nice I looked first, and it threw my brain out of gear.

Dominic showed me a picture of his wife, and that was the last thing I expected to happen. She's exceptionally beautiful, feminine and delicate, and even from a photo, I can tell she has a heart as big as Texas. No wonder he's been having such a hard time moving on with his life. When a guiding light goes out, it sure darkens the rest of the way for you.

I climb into his truck and as we buckle in; I give him my address.

"452 Marigold Lane, is my place. Do you know where it is?"

He stares at me. "Of course, and I think I know the house. Do you rent?"

"Yes, I rent a room from a lovely lady named Roberta. Do you know her?"

His face splits into a beaming grin. "I do. She's good friends with my mom. She's older than her by a few years, but they used to work together. Nice lady."

He puts the truck into gear and points us the few blocks up to my place. "She is a nice lady. She saved my life."

"Really? How?"

I hesitate. He did show me his wife's picture. Maybe I can allow myself to open up to him a little in return. "She sat beside me on a park bench one day in the city and started talking to me. I was homeless, and she wanted to help. She got me in her car and drove me here to the shelter. If she hadn't of done that, I might not still be alive today."

I'm not sugar coating my situation because that's only for bakers. It's the most truth. I had run out of money and pimps had been getting closer, hoping to lure me into the sex trade and I didn't want to go down that road. The sad reality was, I was hungry and alone and the choices were running out for me until she showed up. They were like sharks circling a wounded seal, and her timing alone saved me from a far worse fate. I risk a glance at Dominic as he turns onto my street. His jaw is set, and I can't tell if he's upset with what I just told him, or if it's something else.

He pulls into my driveway and when he puts the truck in park, he immediately grabs my hand. His eyes shimmer with unshed tears and my chest constricts. "I'm so sorry I couldn't be there to help you. That had to be a hard time for you. Thank you for telling me."

I squeeze his hand before unbuckling. "You didn't even know I existed yet at that point, Dom. But thank you for not judging me."

I slide out of the truck, and he follows me inside the house. When we enter, Roberta is out again, leaving me a note. She doesn't have to leave one, but she knows I'll worry if she doesn't.

Micha,

Went to the casino overnight with a friend. I set up the coffee pot on a timer for you, so don't worry, the coffee will still be waiting. See you tomorrow.

Roberta

"Looks like Roberta is away for the night. I rent the basement. Come on down, I just want to change my shirt and feed Tux before we go."

I bounce down the stairs, and Dominic follows. It's surreal having him in my little chunk of home, but when he sees Tux come running and scoops him up without a second thought, my heart turns into a pile of goo as he snuggles with my little man.

"Hi there, fella. You must be Tux. Aren't you handsome? You've got pretty eyes, just like your daddy."

The world just stopped spinning or I just started. Either way, when the words cross Dominic's lips, reality has warped. Two compliments in one night, neither of them provoked. My heart is hammering behind my ribcage, and I fear it might throw itself across the room at any moment. Our eyes meet and neither of us looks away. He continues to scratch Tux under the chin. His voice is gruff. "I'm sorry. I didn't mean to make things awkward."

Awkward? The only thing that's going to make this awkward is if he didn't mean it. I step closer and pet Tux while he still snuggles into Dominic, and I've never been more jealous of a pet. Wait, not true. When he hugged Maggie and told her he couldn't wait to make her his girl, I was jealous then too. Man, I have more issues than I thought if I'm jealous of animals.

"It's only awkward if you didn't mean it. I'll allow a pass if you were overcome with this fella's cuteness. He has that effect on people."

Jesus, I think the temperature in the room just went up a thousand degrees. Dom eases Tux on the floor and steps closer to me. He only hesitates a moment before he cups my cheek with his hand. "You do have pretty eyes. It's one of the first things I noticed about you."

I place my hand over his and step closer. "What else did you notice if my eyes were the first?"

His chest rises and falls a little quicker, and he trails his hand down my body to stop at my hips. "The back of you. Your hips. Your ass. Your shoulders." His breath stutters. "When you turned around, it was your eyes and lips." He brushes a thumb over my lower lip. "I thought you were a woman. Even when I knew you were a man, I still thought you were breathtaking."

Holy mother of God. I'm going to die. Right here. Right now.

How is this happening? How am I still hesitating with how I want this to go? This is a no brainer for me. I want to jump on the hedonist train, right fucking now, and do all the things with this man.

"How does that make you feel? To know I'm a man and you still liked what you saw?"

Please God, let him be okay with it. I will go back to church if he's okay with this. Okay, well, not that far, but I might walk by it on the same side of the road next time. That's a suitable compromise, right?

He leans down until our foreheads touch and at any minute; I think I'm going to spontaneously combust. Our ragged breathing fills the room, and I know I need to put a stop to this. I want to feel his lips on mine in the worst way, but for once in my life, I have to think of the consequences. His breath whispers across my face. "At first I was confused but... I can't stop thinking about you."

MEOW!

An insistent wail from Tux causes us to jump and look in his direction as he waits near the food cupboard, with the put off expression of a cat that hasn't eaten in a few hours. Since he's one of the reasons I asked to come back here, I release my grip on Dominic and gently nudge him away so I can feed the suffering feline.

My hands are shaking as I scoop his canned food into a separate bowl next to fresh kibble and refill his water dish. I press my palm into my groin and will the mother of hard-ons to go away as I take a drink of water. Dominic stays silent and I'm afraid to look at him, but I can't ignore the magnetic pull he has on me, and I turn to face him.

Dominic doesn't look like he regrets a thing. If anything, he looks like he wishes we weren't interrupted. For the first time in a very long time, I have nothing to say. Not that I don't have any thoughts on the matter, I just don't know where to start. So, I do what I do best, avoid like a champion.

"I'm going to change real quick and we can still get going if you want to."

"Of course, I still want to, don't you?"

"Absolutely. I need to set up our girl properly and spend her daddy's money. Make sure she has all the things." I smile when he laughs, and the awkwardness dissipates. "Just give me a few."

I duck into my bedroom and take a moment to compose myself.

I root around and find a fresh shirt while I deep breathe to get my heart rate back to normal. This whole, only be a friend thing, just got a lot more complicated.

ELEVEN

Dominic

WHEN MICHA DISAPPEARS INTO his bedroom, I take a moment to get myself under control and have a seat on his sofa. Well, it's pretty tiny, so let's call it a love seat. I didn't mean to almost kiss him. Well, I meant it, but not tonight. Not so soon.

I can't say I'm mad about it though. I learned two things tonight. First, I'm into this man. It's not a question anymore. I've confirmed it. I'm one hundred percent attracted to this ridiculously funny, over the top, kind and beautiful man. The second thing is, he's feeling the same thing I am. So where do I go from here?

A little paw taps on my leg, and I look down to see Tuxedo blinking at me with curiosity.

I pick him up and he immediately starts purring. "You really are a pretty cat, you know. I wasn't joking." He butts his head right into my nose and I laugh. "Don't worry, I'm not a threat. You don't have to hurt me. Micha is still your daddy." Tux keeps purring and slides out of my arms to knead a circle on the cushion next to me and flops down. I continue to pet him, and he revels in the extra attention. He sure is a snuggly cat.

I hear movement and see Micha leaving his room. He's changed his shirt and his cheeks are flushed. His lips have a fresh coat of lip gloss, and I wonder if his gloss tastes like the root beer I could smell when we were so close.

I stand up, being careful not to disturb Tux, and shove my hands in my pockets. I shouldn't try to touch him again so soon. We have things to do and a lot to talk about. He leans against the door frame, looking so damn cute.

"Hi."

"Hi." He smiles back at me, but stays where he is.

I run my hand over my face. "Listen, Micha. I don't want you to feel like you're obligated to be more than a friend or to ah, be physical with me just to see Maggie."

Which is true. I know he loves the dog and I still want him to visit if he ever wants to. I'd feel terrible if I somehow made him feel uncomfortable about it. Even though I'd be more than happy if he said he felt no obligation and wanted to do it, anyway.

"Pfft, come on Dominic. It was an almost kiss. We let ourselves get caught up in it, that's all." He slings his messenger bag over his lithe body and his T-shirt rides up, giving me a glimpse of his pale smooth skin. I close my eyes to wash the sight from my memory as he crosses the room to speak to Tux.

"I'll be home late tonight; you behave while I'm gone. I'll spoil you with treats and a new toy though, okay, buddy?" He cuddles him like a baby and the cat loves it. It's adorable to see Micha be affectionate with him. I wonder if I can do that with Maggie?

"Okay Dom, we have a dog to prepare for and a cat to spoil. Let's shake a leg, so we get home at a decent hour."

Once we settle into the truck and start our thirty-minute drive to the city nearby, the air is thick with tension. He brushed our encounter off as insignificant at his place, but it was a big deal. I almost kissed him. I feel we need to have a discussion and find our footing again, or it's always going to be awkward between us. He's watching out the window as we drive and even though he's in the seat next to me, he couldn't feel farther away.

I clear my throat. He's the only person in the last two years that has made me feel comfortable with myself. Like it's okay to love someone else. I owe it to him to let him know how he makes me feel. "I meant what I said at your place about not feeling obligated to do anything, Micha. But I want you to know, this is the first time I've ever been attracted to someone since Jenny. I want you to know that."

"You don't need to explain yourself, Dominic. It's fine. I'm used to being set aside after the first touch." His laugh is dark. "I never get to kiss the prince; this is no different."

He looks so sad. Not the bubbly Micha I already hold dear, because he is. He's something special and I don't know where he slots into my life just yet, but he's somewhere. What happened to him to be like this?

I make a snap decision and pull off the highway at a popular rest stop. His eyebrows scrunch when I park and turn the truck off. I turn to face him. "What's wrong? Why did you stop?"

"It's only fair, as your friend, you share with me why you think you can't be loved. I showed you my whole struggle the night at the lake, which I never do with just anyone. You already know me better than most of my friends. Why can't you kiss a prince?"

He studies his hands for a moment before he finally meets my gaze. "The last man I thought was a prince turned out to be the biggest toad of them all. He used me. He's the reason I lost my family and found myself here living in a shelter." For the first time since I met him, I see part of his confident image fall apart as a single tear travels down his cheek. He half smiles at me, "I know what you're thinking, Dom."

"You can't possibly know what I'm thinking right now."

Micha shifts in his seat, tucking a slim leg under him. "You're thinking there's no way I let someone else ruin my life when I'm so in control and seemingly confident."

I reach over to take his hand in mine. "Not even close. I was thinking, how can such a beautiful person be treated so badly, he thinks his own actions caused his life to be upended? It wasn't your fault this guy was an asshole and didn't see what was right in front of him. It's certainly not his fault your family left. That's on them. They should've been there for you." His breath hitches and he squeezes my hand back. "We all wear a mask to get through tough days. You're no different than I am. I'm grieving a wife and you're grieving a life you once had."

That's the full truth. Micha and I have more in common than either of us knew. I had no idea hiding under his effervescent self was someone truly suffering with a sadness few people can understand.

He sniffs and reaches in his bag for a tissue to dab his eyes. "It's nice to hear that from someone who doesn't even know the whole story. Thank you."

"I hope one day you might share the whole story with me. As friends. But not tonight. We have some animals to shop for and spoil. How about we take care of that first?"

Micha is smiling again, that impish, full of trouble smirk he has perfected, and I'm breathless over how one smile from him sends all my blood south.

I SHOULD NOT LEAVE Micha alone in a pet store. We have two carts piled high with pet food, treats, toys, beds and God knows what else.

He hands me an article of clothing. I think. Do dogs wear clothes? "What's this?"

He sighs. "Dom, it's a dog sweater. Fall is coming, she's going to be chilly when you walk her. And besides, look at all the cute pumpkins on it! Isn't it cute?"

"I guess it's cute. Does she need it?"

"Pfft, of course she doesn't need it. But she needs it. Trust me."

I add it to the cart that's already threatening to buckle under its load when Micha squeals so loud I fear for everyone's ear drums in a two-block radius.

"Dom! Dom! You have to get this!"

I turn around to see what he's talking about, and it takes me a moment to figure out what he's holding up.

I shake my head. "No damn way am I getting that."

"You have to." He pouts and I already feel my resolve fleeing. "You'd look so cute together. Maggie would love it."

"I'm not wearing a matching sweater with my dog. How is that even a thing?" Seriously, do people do this?

Micha is bouncing from foot to foot, holding a matching pumpkin sweater out to me. His smile and excitement over the prospect of me in a matching pumpkin sweater with my dog is all the convincing I need. I take it from him and confirm the size.

"I'm only doing this because it's worth it if you smile like that every time I wear it."

"Yasss!" He throws his arms around me in a hug, and I squeeze him back before letting him go. "You're the best. I can't wait to see you guys all matched up. It's gonna be so adorbs."

I shake my head at his over-the-top excitement and follow him along to the cat section. He chooses a few bags of different cat treats and laughs at all the zany cat toys, choosing a catnip filled fish and several little furry mice.

He pauses at the cat towers. "One day I'm going to get Tux one of these, he'd love it. I'll even live on a main floor somewhere and it can be right in front of the main window."

"I'm sure he'd love that. Why don't you get it now?"

He shrugs. "It's silly, but I see this tower as one of the last goals I have. To move out of a basement and rent or own on a main floor, it's a step-up sort of thing. A cat tower for Tux would be the ultimate celebration."

"It's good to have goals, no matter how big or small. It'll happen. If anyone can make it happen, it's you. You're amazing."

"You're right, I am." He winks and leads us up to the cash register. "Let's burn up your credit card and get home. I want to see you try on the sweater." He snickers and I roll my eyes.

Looks like I'm going to need to pull off wearing a pumpkin sweater sooner than I thought.

TWELVE

Micha

"I'M HELPING YOU LUG all this stuff into your place before you drop me off. It's the least I can do, for getting you to buy all of it."

He snorts as we travel down the street to his place. While I live downtown in an older area of Bloomburg, Dominic lives on the hill where the more affluent homes are. Most of the houses up here have views of Dogwood Pond, some even have waterfront property. It's a gorgeous area.

Dominic pulls into the driveway of a gorgeous grey brick bungalow with a wrap-around porch. Even in the dark, I can tell its landscaping is beautiful. A giant bay window dominates the front of the brick house, and there's an apple tree in the front yard. There's even a porch swing out front and I giggle because the only thing missing is a white picket fence.

"What's so funny?"

"I was wondering where the white picket fence is?"

He laughs. "No fence. They're a bitch to deal with when you're moving snow."

We exit, each of us taking a few bags from the back of his truck, and I follow him up to the front door. Soft lighting in the front garden beds showcase freshly planted mums. I wonder if Dominic does all the yard work. We enter his home, and he disables an alarm system before stepping forward to drop the bags in the front entranceway. It's a gorgeous open area with ceramic tile flooring that includes a giant M inlay. A square mirror hangs above an entryway table and a coat closet is next to that.

"We can pile everything here and I'll deal with it after." He gestures to a space where he drops his shopping bags.

"You have a gorgeous home, Dominic. Do you do the gardening too?"

His cheeks flush pink, and he ducks his head. "I do. I like to plant things. I find it relaxing. It's been a real life-saver for me the last few years." He flips on a light to illuminate the back yard. With the open floor plan, I can see straight through the house into the back and it's stunning, even with the muted accent lighting.

"Wow. Maggie is going to love it out there."

"Maybe I can give you a tour sometime."

His eyes have dropped to my mouth and for a moment, I forget where we are and why I shouldn't give in. But thankfully, for once I don't dive off the end of the dock without looking and I move to the front door instead. "I'd love to see it. But let's finish unloading. It's getting late, and we both work tomorrow. Well, I do anyway. Lots of fur babies on the schedule tomorrow. I should be rested."

My heart is hammering so hard I can hear my blood rushing in my ears. He clears his throat. "Right, yes. We should, ah, just get everything inside before we go to bed. I mean sleep. Before we both go to sleep. Separately."

Okay then. Glad we're both fighting an obvious attraction for... what was the reason again? Oh right, I want to visit the dog without awkwardness. That seems to be going well for me so far. Nothing awkward at all if you forget about the almost kiss, the cream pie joke and the thoughtful discussion on the way to the pet store. Oh, and the fact he was staring at my mouth, ready to go at it a moment ago before I flipped the switch. That's just off the top of my head.

He follows me outside and we each lift a giant bag of dog food from the truck. I feel a tad guilty for having him buy all this dog stuff. I might have gone a teeny tiny bit overboard. But he enjoyed every minute of it. And the pumpkin sweater. I smile to myself with the mental image of them in matching sweaters. That's going to be a hoot and Dominic will be so adorable.

"Are you okay to drop me at home still? I can call a cab if you want."

"God no Micha. I'm taking you home. You're not calling a cab. I need to make sure you get home okay."

"I don't want to put you out anymore than I already have, Dominic. I should've had you drop me off first."

He nudges me out the front door, and we get back in his truck. It's maybe a ten-minute drive to my place, but the walk would likely take me closer to an hour. The cab of the truck is back to being full of awkward silence and I don't know what I did to make it that way again. I'm fucking everything up without even trying this time. Maybe it's just as well. He only thinks he wants me. I'm just a suitcase full of drama. He doesn't need that baggage in his life. Not when he's finally getting over his deceased wife and moving on.

He parks in my driveway and meets me on the passenger side. I have a single bag of cat things and shuffle awkwardly.

"Thanks again for letting me help you today. It means a lot to be involved with Maggie's adoption."

"I'm the one that should be thanking you. You were a great help today, Micha. I mean that. I had fun and I feel better about the whole dog thing."

"Well, we can agree we're both thankful then. So tomorrow will be the big day, if that works?"

"Yep. I'll come over after work to pick her up." His warm brown eyes meet mine. "You're going to be there, right? So, we can get our picture together on the adoption wall?"

My breath hitches at his sincerity over wanting me to be there. "Of course, I wouldn't miss it for the world. She's my girl. I need to say goodbye." And now my eyes are watering at the thought of no longer taking Maggie for a walk at night after work or popping by at lunchtime. I had allowed myself to think of her as mine, and that was a huge mistake. What is it with me being attached to things I can't have?

I clear my throat, but my voice still sounds thick and sad. "I should get inside and see Tux. See you tomorrow. Thanks again Dom."

I spin to walk up to my front door, but a strong hand wraps around my wrist and yanks me backwards. I drop my bag and brace myself against Dominic's warm chest as I crash into him. What the hell?

His other hand flutters to my cheek. "Micha, this is stupid. I can't stop thinking about kissing you. For the love of God, I need to kiss you." His face hovers near mine. His brown eyes are now black pools of desire, causing my rational thought to fly away faster than confetti in a windstorm. I only manage a nod before his mouth is on mine.

His hands slide in my hair as his tongue seeks entrance and I'm a pile of goo in his hands. A sigh escapes me as his tongue licks my lower lip before dancing with my own. Hot damn, the man can kiss. Why have I been so resistant to this? My hands clutch his shirt as I allow him to devour me. A car passes down the street, headlights flashing across us, but Dom doesn't stop. He presses me up against the side of the truck and I gasp as my T-shirt rides up to expose my back to the cold metal.

He briefly pulls away, staring at me with wide eyes before his hands find mine, still clutching his shirt. He pins my wrists over my head and takes my breath away again, holding me at his mercy. On his next breath, his lips trail down my neck and I can't stop the lust-filled moan that escapes me. "Fuck... Micha." He bites my collarbone and I buck my hips towards him with a muttered curse.

When Dominic rewards me by pressing his own hips into mine, it's his turn to groan. Now that I'm suddenly a wanton harlot, I wrap a leg around his waist, drawing him closer and keeping him there.

"Jesus." He nips my lips, and we rut on each other, in the driveway against the side of his truck, and I couldn't care less who might come by or see us. Or how this is going to change things between us. That's a problem for future Micha.

"I knew you'd taste like root beer." He breathes over my ear and my whole-body shivers, stretching itself to meet him.

"Is that a good thing?" I pant.

"I fucking love root beer." He growls before kissing me again, and he finally releases my wrists. So, I do what I've been dying to do. I jump up and wrap my legs around him, spearing my hands in his hair. Dominic doesn't miss a beat and palms my ass without taking his mouth off me.

I've never been so lost in a moment with a single kiss. I'm burning up with pent up lust and frustration and I want to ask him inside, but I also want to stay like this forever.

Honk, Honk, Honk.

We both separate with a jolt as his car alarm goes off. He lowers me to the ground and searches his pockets for the fob to silence it. When we're plunged back into the nighttime solitude, we're left panting and staring at each other. He's so fucking gorgeous with his kiss swollen lips and warm brown eyes. I glance down to see his erection is just as insistent as mine, so that's something. But remorse fills me by allowing this. He's not ready and neither am I.

He runs a hand through his hair and blows out a long shaky breath. "We should get some sleep. Big day tomorrow."

Okay, so he wants to avoid talking about it. Got it. I clear my throat. "Right, big day." I move past him to pick up the bag I dropped. "I'll see you tomorrow then." As I walk up towards my front door and find my keys with shaking hands, I know he's watching me. I can feel his eyes on me, just as much as his hands were earlier.

When I dare to peek over my shoulder, I'm hopeful with the expression I see on his face. It's longing and want, and his fists are still clenched at his sides.

With a small wave, I close and lock the door behind me, before finally allowing my boneless legs to give out and slide to the floor.

What have we just done?

Thirteen

Dominic

IT'S LATE AND I need to work tomorrow, yet I've never been so awake.

I kissed Micha, and I fucking loved it. I want to do it again. Closing my eyes, I return to the moment, reliving how it felt to have him wrapped around me with his ass in my hands and his root beer tasting lips on mine. My whole-body shivers with the memory. I need to do something other than lay here thinking. I toss the covers back and wander out to the living room.

The pile of dog things is still in the front entrance where we left them. Since I can't sleep, I may as well get them put away. I shove the bags of dog food in a coat closet and put the dog treats under the sink.

Taking a pair of scissors, I snag the bag full of dog toys and sit on the sofa while removing the tags. The ambient lighting is on in the backyard and it's always such a beautiful sight. My rosebush for Jenny glows in the moonlight and I pause in my tag removal, dropping a squeaky chicken on the floor with a soft wheeze.

I stand at the window and gaze into the yard I created. The yard I put my blood, sweat and tears into the last two years. A grief counsellor suggested to try gardening to work through my pain. I was skeptical, but nobody was more surprised than me to discover it worked. I took on project after project and transformed my backyard into an oasis. The mindless task of digging holes soon became a soothing therapy, and I poured all my love and grief for Jenny into choosing a pleasing landscape design. The plants, the garden borders and lighting, the covered gazebo and even the small shed in the back to keep all my newly acquired garden tools. I found comfort in turning the boring and drab yard into a thing a beauty.

But it still didn't bring back Jenny. It was an action to fill a void that couldn't be filled.

The rose bush is my pride and joy. It's flourished this past summer, and I even cut a few blooms once and brought them inside to enjoy. Now that the hard part is done, I simply do maintenance on the plants. I planted the rosebush for Jenny because she loved roses. It was the flower at our wedding and the flower I brought home to her every time the occasion called for it.

I pass my hand over my face and let a small laugh of disbelief escape me. This is the second night in a row I haven't sat here with my drink and stared longingly at a rosebush, hoping it would do... I'm not sure what. It's not lost on me that the reason I've broke my routine twice now is Micha. I resume my place on the couch, removing tags and not for the first time, I wonder what it is about him that has me so entranced.

He's funny and outspoken. He's confident, but has also shared his vulnerability with me. He loves animals and wants to help people just as much as pets. And he's beautiful. Micha has the prettiest eyes I've seen, dark brown with flecks of honey, and his eyelashes are so long and thick, they kiss his cheeks when he blinks. Then he wears eyeliner that makes me want to stare into them even more. I press my hand against my dick as it reminds me it's still there, and it really likes where my thoughts are going.

Finishing with the tag removal, I jam the metric tonne of dog toys back into the bag. I leave it at the end of the sofa because I'm not sure what else to do with them. I think Micha went overboard wanting to spoil Maggie, and that thought makes my heart swell at his want to make her happy. Sure, he spent my money doing it, but he had fun with it. That brings me just as much joy, knowing such a simple thing like picking out squeaky toys makes him smile.

There are now three dog beds to deal with. I take the tags off and place one in the living room, one in my bedroom, and leave the third one in the bag. I don't know why he said I needed three. With a shrug, I clean up the garbage before placing the new leash and collar on the side table near the door. I'll need to take that with me tomorrow to pick her up.

It's almost 1 A.M. and I feel no closer to sleep. My heart and my brain are at war. My heart is feeling lighter, and it wants to go down a fresh path, but my brain keeps saying, *"what about Jenny?"* It's too late for me to call Owen. He has to work even earlier than I do. It's too late to call anyone. So, I do the only thing I can do. I climb back into bed and stare at the ceiling, hoping to either fall asleep or morning will miraculously be here immediately, so I have something to do.

My eyes finally grow heavy, and rather than fight the guilt that seeps its way in, I let them close, and I welcome the sight of Micha in my dreams.

THE MORNING CALLS FOR massive caffeine and even after I've had one before leaving the house, I walk over to The Screaming Bean to grab one for Jade and me before I start work. When the doorbell chimes, it's not Owen at the front though, it's Paige.

"Hey Paige, is Owen here?"

"Oh hi, Dom. Yes, he's in the office if you wanted to head back there, I'm sure he wouldn't mind."

"I won't keep him long. Can you have two large double doubles ready for me in ten minutes? Oh, and is it too late to reserve some cupcakes for tonight?"

"Not at all. Parker will bake most of today. We'll make it happen, Dom. What would you like?"

"Nothing crazy, just six vanilla cupcakes with pink frosting. Oh, and if you can make them sparkly even better."

"We can do that, Dom; they'll be ready at 5 P.M. for you."

"Awesome. I'll be right back for the coffee."

I walk down the back hall to where Owen's office is and just as I get there, Parker comes storming out, narrowly missing slamming into me.

"Whoa. Keep your head up, Parker. That could have ended badly."

He scowls and mutters sorry under his breath before speed walking away. I knock softly on Owen's door before poking my head in. "Hey O, is this a good time?"

He gestures to the other chair in the room for me to sit. "Of course, come in. What's going on?"

"I should ask you that. Parker just stormed out of here like his ass was on fire. What's up with that?"

"His ass is on something that's for sure. He'll be fine. But tell me what's up. It's dog day today, right?"

I chuckle. "It is. I'll let her get settled tonight and hopefully you can come meet her tomorrow. But that's not why I'm here." I glance at my watch. "Listen, it's not bad if I've met someone I think I like and want to move on, is it? You don't think it's too soon or anything?"

He sighs. "Dom, it's been two years. It's time. I've told you this. What's going on?"

"Funny thing, actually. I kissed Micha last night." I count, ticking off each item with my fingers. "For the second night in a row, I didn't do my stare at the rosebush thing, and I couldn't sleep, because I'm torn between wanting him and not thinking of Jenny." I register his raised eyebrows and smile. "I'm having a hard time coping with all the conflicting emotions, and I wanted to run it by you."

"Jeez Dom, it's barely 9 A.M. That's a lot to lay on me." His face softens. "Listen, I know I made you a bet and I can see that might have been the wrong thing to do now. I can't take away your guilt because I don't know how. But I hope you believe me when I say nobody thinks less of you for moving on. Nobody thinks less of you for not thinking of her every night like you've been doing." He stands up to walk around his desk and I rise to meet him. "If you need permission, if you need to hear from anyone, I'm spelling it out to you and giving you permission to move on. With Micha or someone else. It's time."

I don't know why I need to constantly seek approval for attempting to keep moving my life forward. It's a hard struggle, but hearing Owen back me is a step in the right direction. Jenny is always going to be part of me, but there's room for her and someone new in my heart. I have to acknowledge this attraction to Micha.

Owen crushes me with a hug and walks me out front. "Thanks O, I'll keep you posted."

"Damn straight you will." He snorts. "Wait, maybe that's not the right word anymore."

That earns him a snicker. "Ha, ha Owen. Laugh it up." I take my coffees off the counter. "Just for that, I'm not paying today."

"You never pay, Dom."

"It's the cost of keeping me as a friend!"

Owen laughs and walks back to the kitchen, waving over his shoulder on his way. I smile and walk over to Wild Baloney, feeling slightly better over the whole thing. Tonight, I officially become a dog dad and I hope to celebrate with Micha. It's going to be a great day.

FOURTEEN

Micha

THIS IS GOING TO be the shittiest day ever.

I had zero sleep because all I kept thinking about was how I screwed things up by letting Dominic kiss me. That man knows how to kiss. I shouldn't have let it happen. Everything is going to be awkward again and just yuck. I was supposed to keep him in the friend zone and I'm already failing. Yay me for choosing the worst time to be an overachiever.

The only positive about today is I don't have to fight with my alarm clock and I'm already awake early.

Meow.

Tux sits like he does every day on the floor by my bed and waits for me to pick him up. He jumps on everything, everywhere, but refuses to jump on my bed.

"Hello handsome. Did you get some sleep last night or did you have a gorgeous hunk of a man running through your head all night, too?"

Meow?

I chuckle when Tux cocks his head, like he actually understands what I'm talking about. I sit up with him in my arms and his instant purring starts. "Tux, I don't understand what I'm so afraid of." I scoop his morning food into a dish and change his water while he ignores me during breakfast. Dominic is interested. I should take the offered goods with both hands. Old Micha would have jumped back onto him after the car alarm without another thought.

New Micha is cautious. Afraid to get hurt and lose everything, no matter how little, I've built back for myself. I miss old Micha; he had a lot more fun. But can't I combine old and new Micha? Can't I proceed with caution and enjoy the opportunity?

I run through my morning routine, a little slower this time because I'm not racing the clock. I pack extra clothes to take to work. It's adoption day and I want to look nice for Dominic. It'll be my last photo with Maggie, too. I need to stop thinking about how she won't be there. This is what every pet dreams of, their fur-ever home. It's what's best for her. Dominic will love her and care for her. So why can't I let myself be happy about that?

I tuck my favourite root beer lip gloss into my front pocket, grab my bag and amble up to get my coffee. The timer came on as Roberta said it would, and I breathe the smell of fresh brew in. It's heavenly and gives me a tiny jolt before the first sip. I pour my coffee into my travel mug and mix it how I like before I walk to work. The mornings are getting darker and chillier. Fall is just around the corner. My breath hangs in the cold air as I walk, and I use the time to ground myself. I don't want to keep letting my mind get wound up over things beyond my control. I want to enjoy this peaceful morning with my coffee before my day erupts into nonstop fuzz making.

Today will be a busy one, but I love what I do. A pet groomer may seem like a boring job to many, but it was a natural calling for me. I love animals and I love making them pretty. Everything should be pretty. It was a no brainer, and to own my business was a dream I never thought I'd achieve. As I walk by The Screaming Bean, I debate if I should go in for a refill, but I see Dom's truck is in his lot already. He might be in The Bean with Owen. I don't want to interrupt or intrude if he is. He might be just as scrambled as I am and needing a friend to talk to.

I open the doors to Fuzzy's and disarm the alarm. I haven't even started my computer yet before Travis is knocking.

"What's the emergency Trav? I barely got in the door." I unlock the deadbolt, and he closes the door behind him.

"I have to be quick." He has an actual notepad with him and poises his pen over it. "We need to have a Fall Fling, final organizing meeting tomorrow night. Jacob wants to know if you're good with that."

"Yes, of course. I have no life, remember? I'll be there." He trails after me as I hang up my bag in my office.

"Awesome, second thing. Can you check your schedule and see if you have time to groom a Newfoundland this week? Any day or time, we have a client that's desperate."

I open my scheduling app on my phone since I didn't get to turn on the computer yet. "I can do Thursday 1 P.M. but warn her he might still be damp when she picks him up. What's the name?"

"Pork Puff."

I snort. "They named their dog, Pork Puff? Is he gonna fit in my tub?"

"Oh, ya he'll be good. I can come help lift if you have issues." He scribbles it down on his pad as I enter it on my app. It will sync with my computer once it starts up. Travis lingers, and I raise an eyebrow.

"You have something else on your list, Trav?"

He tucks his notepad into his lab coat pocket and leans on the counter. "Did you go to PetSmart last night?"

"I did. Why?"

"What time did you get home?"

I narrow my eyes. "I'm not entirely sure. Maybe 11 P.M.?" I put my hands on my hips. "What are you getting at?"

"You're really not going to tell me?"

"I can't tell you anything if I don't know what you're talking about. We went to the pet store; bought shit and I came home. What more do you want to know?"

Travis isn't usually like this, and I was going to talk to him about what happened with Dominic, but he's being super weird.

He crosses his arms and stands back up. "Micha, I drove by."

"And? People drive by all the time, Trav."

He puffs out a breath and runs his hand through his hair. "For the love of God, Mic. I saw you and Dominic in the driveway. It wasn't a goodnight kiss because the last I checked friends don't pin friends against vehicles and grind on them. Why didn't you tell me?"

I remember the car going by vaguely and how late it was. I say vaguely because that wasn't a top ten highlight to remember from last night. Being pinned down by Dominic was worthy of remembrance, though. Wait, Travis is never out after 9 P.M. "Before I fill you in, what were you doing out so late? And I was going to tell you today. Last night, I needed time to process." I cross my arms and give him the same look. "So why were you out in my neighbourhood so late?"

"I asked you first. What happened with Dominic? Other than a hot make-out session where anyone driving past can see."

I check my clock, and my first appointment should be here in ten minutes. Not nearly enough time to get through everything I want to talk to Travis about. "He kissed me, Trav. We had this back and forth all night. I told him about my ex." I walk to my washing area and put my apron on while Travis follows. "He was the one that started it. I should never have let it happen."

"What? Why? I thought you said you'd flirt and be okay with it?"

"You're right, I did. But as much as we seem to have this connection or pull or whatever you want to call it, I don't want a repeat of Robert."

I can't let myself ever feel so worthless again. I can never open myself up for that again. If I'm a lonely cat man, instead of a cat lady, then so be it.

"Aww, Micha. I wish you wouldn't be so afraid to take a chance. Not everybody is like him." He hugs me quick and turns to go back to the vet hospital. "I'll see you tonight at the adoption. I'll be there for you." He leaves through the shared door, and I flip the deadbolt behind him.

My door chimes when my first client of the day arrives. A standard Poodle named Marbles. She's a sweetheart and her owner is one of Roberta's friends. "Hi Mrs. Marcus, you look lovely today." She passes me Marbles leash and leans in to give me a hug.

"Thank you, Micha. You're a doll for saying so. I look dreadful."

No, she doesn't. She's more put together than anyone I know. Always matching outfits and handbags, accessories to match. Never a hair out of place. "Stop it. You're fabulous and you know it, girl." She giggles and swats my arm.

"I'll be back at lunchtime to get her, Micha."

I walk Marbles to the back and put her in the kennel while I finish setting up. Travis' words are sitting like lead on my chest. *Don't be afraid to take the chance.* He's right. I need to shake this, whatever it is. I need to get back to life. It's been four damn years.

The water is warm, and I lead Marbles up my ramp into the tub. She's good that way. No fear of trying something new when I introduced a ramp to ease up on my back. She walked right up and stepped into the tub, preened with pride and never looked back. I click her to the tether and move the ramp out of the way.

"Marbles love, I wish you could talk. You're the only dog I've had in here who doesn't even hesitate to try something new. Why can't I be more like you?" She snorts, spraying me with dog slobber and soapy water. "I mean, if you can do it and not be afraid, surely I can, right?"

The best thing about working with animals by yourself all day is cheap therapy. Sometimes I can work out my problems by talking out loud to something that doesn't talk back. Animals are great listeners. I massage shampoo into Marbles' coat, and she groans with appreciation, so I spend more time in the spot she likes. "Do you think I should finally try something new? Is it time, you think?" She stretches her neck and licks my face. "You're right, kisses *are* good. Especially when you get them from a person you really like."

Woof!

"Don't worry, I'll always love your kisses, but I don't enjoy your tongue in my mouth, you know? It's nothing personal, love." I smooth her ears back and kiss her nose. "I prefer my tongue kisses from other men, if you know what I mean."

By the time Mrs. Marcus returns to pick her up, I've had enough time to analyze myself and come to a conclusion.

I'm still afraid to get my heart broken, but it's time to take a chance.

Fifteen

Dominic

"**Y**OU'RE OKAY TO LOCK up, Jade?" I hang up my apron and come out to the storefront.

"Of course, boss. You go do what you need to, and I'll take care of everything." She rubs her hands together. "I can't wait to meet this girl."

"Maybe I'll bring her by tomorrow. I hate having to leave her home all the time, but I can't have her here with all the food." Which was one thing I didn't even consider. No way would anyone want a dog in a meat shop. Hello health code violation.

"It's gonna work out, Dom. I can feel it." She shoves me towards the door. "Now get going."

I walk over next door first to get my cupcakes. At the door chime, Paige looks up and smiles. "Hey Dom! I have your cupcakes ready." She pulls out a white cake box and opens the lid for me to see. "What do you think?"

A grin paints my face. "These are fantastic and more than I expected. Just perfect." I pay for the cupcakes, and with a newfound lightness, I take them back to my truck and make a quick drive home before heading to the shelter.

When I walk up to my door, there's a small bag hanging on the doorknob. I pluck it off the handle and take it in with me. I place the cupcakes in the fridge and return to open the bag. It's from the gift shop in town called Curiosities. There's a card with my name on it and I open it first. I laugh when I see it's from Owen, and he left a note.

Dom,

I didn't want to drop this at the shop. When you get to the bottom of the bag you'll see why.

I wanted to let you know I'm proud of you, and you're doing the right thing. Can't wait to meet my new dog niece and hopefully the person who has you looking forward to life again.

Have fun tonight, buddy, and I'll see you tomorrow.

O

I remove the tissue paper and find a T-shirt that says 'Dog Dad" on it. Laughing, I hold it against me and look in the mirror before taking my shirt off and putting it on. My grin still hasn't left my face. It's the perfect shirt for picking up my new dog. A glance at the clock says I have a few more minutes before I should leave. I remove more tissue paper and freeze when I see what Owen included on the bottom.

Condoms and lube. My breath leaves me with a whoosh as the possibilities of what might happen with Micha tumble through my mind. Thank God Owen had enough sense to prepare me for this. When you've been out of the game for this long, you tend to not think of being prepared for sex. A shudder runs through my body as I replay our kiss last night. I had no idea a body could burn as hot as mine did once I had a taste of his root beer flavoured lips. I don't know how long that kiss lasted, but it felt like I could do it all night and still not have my fill.

I thought of Micha a lot today while I was working, and I made a discovery. After seeing Owen and having him confirm it was okay to move on, I found my guilt slipping away. It was still there, but it wasn't as gripping as it once was. Many people have been giving me the nudge to get back into living a life and finding joy. It started with the garden and it's turning to a dog. But it's including Micha. I can't ignore how much I think of him and how he makes me feel. I've finally accepted the repeated mantra that Jenny would want me to be happy.

I sweep the room to make sure it's acceptable for when Micha comes back, and I hope he accepts my invite. He thinks he's losing Maggie, but he's not. I really do want him to be involved. I'm ready to feel alive again.

When I arrive at the shelter, there's several people there I wasn't expecting. It looks like half the staff is here, and my steps stutter as I enter the building.

"Dominic! Happy adoption day! How has everything been? Has Micha been helpful?"

Jacob's friendly face smiles as he extends his hand to me. "Um ya, of course. He's great. I mean, he's been a great help." I rub my hand on my neck. "What's with all the people? I thought there would be like three of us."

He tugs me by the arm and leads me over to the small group. "These are a few of the shelter volunteers. We all love Maggie and wanted to see her off." A tall, lanky guy with black hair who seems familiar extends his hand. His grip is tight, and he stares me down. "I'm Travis, Micha's best friend. Nice to formally meet you."

"Oh! You come to the meat shop a lot, right? The charcuterie lunch board for two most days, if I remember."

He relaxes his stance. "Yep, that's me. Love that stuff." He turns to the man next to him. "This is Kody. He's a new vet filling in here, while we have one on maternity leave."

"Nice to meet you, Kody. Thanks for coming to the popular event of dog adoption."

His giant paw of a hand engulfs mine. "It's a big day for you. I wanted to see how the shelter does things. I hope you don't mind."

"Not at all. I just wasn't expecting a welcoming committee." Parker pokes his head around Kody. "Hi Dom.

I just happened to be here today, so thought I'd stay for the celebration."

"Hi Parker. The more the merrier, right?"

The guys are catching up on their day, engaging in the normal small talk, and Micha still isn't here. I tap my fingers against my leg and wander over to the photo wall. My heart is beating faster as the moment gets closer, and Micha hasn't arrived. I can't explain the bone deep ache to have him here. I'm not doing this unless he shows up. He needs to be in this picture. It's important to him. How am I going to handle this if he doesn't show up?

There's a tap on my shoulder, and when I turn around, it's Micha. My cheeks hurt with the smile that breaks my face to see him.

"You're here." I breathe. I want to hug him, but I'm not sure if he's comfortable with that in front of his friends. I shove my hands in my pockets instead.

"Of course, I'm here. I wouldn't miss it." His eyes flick to my shirt and a smile graces his beautiful face. "Dog Dad. Maggie is one lucky dog to call you Daddy."

I lean in closer. "Are you feeling left out? Did you want to call me Daddy?"

His nostrils flare as he swallows. "I'm not really into the *Daddy* thing." He takes a step closer and stretches up on his tiptoes. His breath whispers across my skin and I shiver. "But I can call you whatever you want me to, if it makes you look at me like that."

"Like what?" I turn my head slightly, and I know he has that same lip gloss on. I can smell the root beer from here and I want to taste it again.

"Like you want to pin me up against your truck again."

"Ahem." We both stare at each other for a beat before Micha slowly turns around to face Jacob and nobody else. "Sorry, I sent everyone else out. It looked like a private moment."

"Shit. I'm sorry Jake. It won't happen again."

"You're not gonna talk sexy to the handsome hunk who's clearly into it?" He lifts his eyebrow. "Micha, it's fine. As long as you aren't having orgies in the kennels, you're allowed to have a relationship. Did you think I'd be mad?"

"I was worried you'd think it was unprofessional. I'd never want to disappoint you."

Jacob throws his head back in laughter. "Oh Mic, the only thing that would've disappointed me is if you turned him down."

The doors to the back open and Travis returns with Maggie. When she sees Micha, she takes off, wagging furiously and stomping her feet in front of him. Just like he did before, he drops and hugs her while burying his face in her neck. My heart gets all flip floppy seeing them like that. I crouch down next to them, and I'm stunned to feel tears threatening. I blink them away as Maggie spins to me and licks my face making me laugh.

"Hey pretty girl. Are you ready to come to your new home? I'm really excited to have you there." Maggie is definitely excited, although I'm not sure if it's because of me or Micha.

"Well then, let's get the adoption photo for our wall of happiness, guys."

I pick up her leash that she has trailing behind her, and without even thinking about it, I reach for Micha and take his hand in mine to stand where Jacob wants us. He doesn't miss a beat and squeezes back while following me to the photo prop.

"I'm going to take one with the Polaroid for you to have right away. Then I'll take a few digitals. I can print one for you when I do the copy for the wall."

He motions me over and I tug Micha with me. "You made this happen. I want you in all of them."

He smiles at me, the most loopy, goofy grin and I beam it right back.

Click

We both turn and catch Jacob with a knowing grin. "I'm no professional photographer, but that's gonna be a keeper." He shakes the pic before setting it on the desk and having us pose properly with Maggie in front of the adoption back drop. He snaps a few pics, and it's all over.

"I may be speaking out of turn here, but I'm going to say this." He hands me the Polaroid. "That photo is a thing of beauty." He wags a finger back and forth between Micha and me. "You two are lost in each other. Look at Maggie too. She's gazing at you both like you hung the moon. I've never seen a happier picture."

It's amazing. The looks on our faces, captured at just the right time, are full of hope, trust, and happiness.

Happiness. I can see it on my face, and I haven't felt like that for a very long time.

"You're not out of line, Jacob. Thank you. It's a beautiful photo, and it's going on my fridge."

Micha giggles. "Really? The fridge? What are you, fifty?"

"Well, won't fit in my wallet so that's the next best place of honour." I take his hand again. "Will you come home with Maggie and me right now? I thought we could have a celebration in her new home with you."

Micah stares at me and I'm thinking I made a mistake inviting him. His voice is scratchy and raw when he finally responds. "I'd love to see her home. Thank you for including me. Let me get my things and we'll go."

He exits to the back and Jacob is left, regarding me with an expression I can't quite read.

"Um, he's not going to be in trouble with you, is he? For, um, maybe being with me? I know you said no earlier but, you're close to him. I don't want to cause any waves."

He scoffs. "No, he's not in trouble, and I have no idea why he keeps thinking he would be." He pauses. "Dom, just be careful with him, okay? Don't hurt him. He's been through a lot."

"I never want him to hurt again. He... woke something in me that's been dead for a very long time. He's something special." I reach down and pet Maggie. "I know this dog is special to him too, and I don't want him to think she's gone forever."

The doors swing open and Micha re-enters. "Okay fabulous people, let's get this threesome started!" He chuckles. "Well, not that kind of threesome, but that's a topic for another day."

Jacob waves us off and we exit the shelter to climb into my truck. Maggie sits in the back seat with her head out the window and I can't wipe this stupid smile off my face.

Have I finally found a way to move on?

Sixteen

Micha

I CAN'T BELIEVE THIS is happening. First, he kissed me, now he's inviting me back to his place. Straight guy has crossed the line. I don't even care about the blatant flirting in front of the crew. I'm going to be endlessly questioned about this tomorrow. But all that aside, I'm happy. No, more than happy.

Elated? Jubilant? Whatever it is, I'm high on it.

I catch sight of Maggie in the side mirror, ears in full flap and tongue to the side. Pure doggy bliss.

"Do you think you'll take her for rides much?" I turn to Dom and his own shaggy brown hair ruffles in the breeze, making my breath hitch in my throat. He's stunning in a carefree way that's been buried for too long.

"I want to take her wherever and whenever I can. She's my sidekick. My leading lady. I want her to be happy for the rest of her days." He looks in the mirror and grins when he sees her in the mirror like I do. "There's no happier look than the one on the face of a dog with its head out the window is there?"

I laugh, light and happy. "I think we both have the same look on our faces to be honest."

He pulls into his driveway and Maggie perks up. I step aside and motion for him to let her out since she's his now. I'm just here for the ride, as long as it lasts.

He opens the door and clips the leash on her. She bounces out and immediately sniffs around the yard while bouncing back to Dominic after each new discovery. It's adorable. It reminds me of a small child showing a parent each new toy on Christmas morning.

"Let's go to the back, Micha. I'll show you the yard before it gets too dark." He takes my hand in his, like it's the most natural thing in the world, and leads me through a small gate into his backyard. He unclips Maggie from her leash once the gate is latched and she takes off into the green space.

"Wow, it's like a private oasis out here." I walk down the flagstone path that curves around the corner of his house and ends in the luscious green lawn. A six-foot privacy fence encloses the backyard and at every large fence post, he has hanging planters filled with Boston ferns. Flower beds border two sides of the yard, and even in late summer, is still full of colour and manicured shrubs. A tiny red garden shed sits in the far back corner of the yard, and it resembles an adorable barn. Across the back of the house, a sprawling multi level deck holds pride of place. A covered wooden gazebo has a free-standing hammock inside, and there's a large patio set for entertaining on its own level. Various free-standing planters litter the deck, filled with various colours of fall mums. It's breathtaking, and I'd be happy to spend all my time out here when I'm away from work.

"It's really pretty when I have the lights on. I hard wired them all and connected them to a switch. I'll turn it on soon so you can see it."

Maggie flops down with a groan and starts rolling in the middle of the grass. My heart bursts to see her enjoying this yard. She loves it. She bounces up and sits in front of Dominic wagging and smiling, and he looks at me. "What does that mean?"

I chuckle. "Well, I think she's happy and wants to play. Where did you put the tennis ball we bought?"

"Oh! I'll get it quick." He races inside and comes back triumphantly with a ball in his hand. When Maggie sees it, her eyes light up and she races after it when he throws it.

"Oh my God, this is so fun! I had no idea this was what she liked." She returns and drops the slobbery ball at his feet, and he throws it again, his eyes dancing like a child as he plays fetch with her. I take a seat on one of the patio chairs, content with watching these two bond. Maggie is panting hard now, and I think Dominic's arm is getting tired.

"Do you have her dishes ready? I think she needs water, after all that."

"It certainly looks like it. Let's go Maggie." He opens the sliding patio door, and she waltzes in, sniffing around and exploring while he takes a dish out from under the sink and fills it with water. After placing it on the most adorable feeding mat, covered in paw prints and hearts I insisted he buy, he calls her over. She drinks half the bowl, and the other half splashes on the floor. Dominic looks slightly put off and I laugh.

"She's going to make slobber messes at the dish. She's a big dog, floppy lips." I squish my cheeks together to demonstrate.

"I guess I'll get used to that part." He wipes the mess with a paper towel and washes his hands.

"Um, listen. I invited you here because I wanted you to see Maggie in her place and... I got us something."

I bounce up and down. "Ooh, I like presents. Is it presents?"

"No, but it often goes with presents." He turns to the fridge and takes out a white box.

I clap my hands. "Please tell me it's more of that delicious pie. That was so good."

His face falls. "Shit, I didn't even think of that. Well, I thought of this at least, and maybe you'll like it better."

He spins the box towards me and inside are six cupcakes with pink sparkling icing. On each cupcake sits a cookie in the shape of a dog bone. "Dom... I love these and I haven't even tasted them. You did this for me?"

"I did it for us, but mostly for you." He inhales. "I wanted a vanilla cupcake because vanilla is strong, predictable and loved. It's a solid base. I asked for pink frosting with sparkles because the outside dresses what's underneath. It's usually showier to make up for what lots of people think is boring or plain." He pauses before raising his eyes to meet mine. "And I created this because it perfectly represents you."

"You think I'm a cupcake? I don't know how I should take that, to be honest." I know exactly how I'm going to take it. Swooning off my feet, because he just described me perfectly by comparing me to a beloved confection. Although I've never considered myself boring, I can follow his logic.

"No, I don't think you're a cupcake. I think you're someone like me. Someone with a lot of layers, pretty and sweet on the outside while solid and fulfilling on the inside."

"Hmm, you think I'm sweet?" I step closer to him, and he smiles down at me.

"I do."

"Am I still sweet if I want to do this?" I swipe my thumb through some frosting and brush it across his lips. His tongue darts out to taste it, but I stop him with my thumb. "Let me." I stretch onto my tiptoes until my mouth is close to his. With the tip of my tongue, I lick the frosting from his lips. I've never tasted anything so good. "Mmm. That tastes much better on you than it does on a cupcake."

His nostrils flare as he reaches behind me and swipes his own dollop of icing. "I'd like to test that theory too." He smears a path of icing down the side of my neck, and I tilt to the side. He takes his time licking it off, nibbling and biting until my knees are jello and I'm panting like a racehorse after the Kentucky Derby. "You were right. It tastes much better on you." He swallows my moan with cherry flavoured lips and pulls me against his hard body. My fingers creep under his T-shirt and I slide it up, pressing my palms into his burning hot skin.

He breaks away to pull his shirt over his head before kissing me again and backing me into the opposite counter. My hands can't stop feeling his skin, memorizing every dip and valley. He peppers kisses down my neck again, before licking a stripe across my collarbone. Large hands find their way under my shirt, and we separate again as he pulls it off me, tossing it somewhere over his shoulder. His fingertips graze my flesh, leaving a trail of goosebumps in their wake.

I slide my hands into the back of his jeans, and he gasps. "You okay with that? I should've asked." He responds by pressing into me even farther.

"It's okay, just shocked me." I chuckle.

"Dom, that's not even close to shocking. I'm capable of much more."

He raises an eyebrow. "I didn't say stop, did I?"

Boldly, I grasp the top of his jeans and flick the button open. I take the zipper between my fingers and look him in the eye. "No regrets?"

His voice is rough as he slowly shakes his head. "No regrets." He covers my hand with his and presses it into his erection. I continue to unzip and peel open the front of his jeans, and I'm pleased to see a wet patch blooming through his boxers. I lick my lips, hoping beyond all hopes I can taste him. Before I can drop to my knees and do that, he gathers my wrists, pinning them over my head to the overhead cabinet, forcing me to arch into him.

His other hand deftly unfastens my pants and finds my hard cock, waiting for any kind of attention. He presses his groin into mine and slowly grinds, while sucking a spot on my collarbone.

"Fuck, Dom." My head falls back with a thud on the cabinet door and a whine escapes me as he cradles my balls with a gentle squeeze. "Let me touch you, please."

"If I let you touch me right now, I'm going to go off in a nanosecond." His hand creeps up and fingers dip into the waistband of my boxers. He pauses and releases my wrists, but before I can do what I want with my free hands, he has both of his tearing my pants and boxers down to my thighs.

His lips press into mine once more as his warm hand closes around my dick and I spear my hands into his hair. He's not shy, nothing about his touch is tentative. If he had any reservations about hooking up with another man, he left them behind because he knows how to work my hard length, and if he keeps it up, this is going to be over far too soon.

I wrap a hand over his. "Give me a minute." I breathe. "I don't want to come yet and I haven't even gotten to touch you."

Dominic rests his forehead against mine. "Sorry. I just wanted to make you feel good." He feathers kisses on my eyes. "I wasn't thinking about myself." No. Just no. What did I do to deserve a hot man ravaging me with no regard to his own sexual satisfaction? I know people get off on their partner getting off, but why did he pick me? Placing my free hand behind me, I want to push off the counter, but instead, I crush my hand into a bag. I want to ignore it and get back to the hands on my dick, but I recognize the feeling of the square packet under my hand.

"What's in the bag, Dom?" I release my hand over his and use both to look inside. A sly grin crosses my face as a blush spreads down his neck. I peek inside the bag and my suspicions are confirmed. "You little boy scout. Do you always keep condoms and lube in your kitchen, Dom?"

"Owen left them for me with my T-shirt. I forgot about the bag when I rushed out to the shelter."

I quickly remove the packaging from the lube and pop the cap. "Do you trust me?" He nods. "Good. Because I'm going to solve your problem and make us both feel good." I gently nudge him back from me. Shirtless, his pants hanging open and chest heaving, his cock begging to be released and his eyes molten pools of lust fixated on me; I've never seen anything hotter in my twenty-four years of life. Plunging my hands down his pants, I first yank his jeans to his thighs. Running my hand over his shaft, his breath hitches as I peel his boxers down, and his cock springs into his stomach. Goddamn, he's a beautiful sight.

I grab his wrist and tug him back to me, relishing the feel of his heat against me. "Kiss me." Dominic complies and his kiss is laden with so much passion, I'm dizzy. I reach back to find the bottle and squirt a generous amount of lube into my hand. No time to warm anything up, but that's not going to matter. The temperature between us is nearing boiling point and a bit of chilly lube won't be noticed. I wrap my hand around him and I'm rewarded with a guttural moan.

His lips rip from mine as he looks between us to watch. I add my own cock, gripping us together and rocking slowly. "Jesus Micha... I've never... " He doesn't finish his sentence because I smash my mouth over his and slide us together faster. I can feel myself on the precipice of an intense orgasm and Dominic isn't far behind me.

"Come baby, I want to feel it." He detonates. His whole-body shudders as he braces a hand against the counter and I come with a loud moan, spilling so much cum between us, I can hear it splatter as it overflows my fist and hits the floor.

"Fuck, Micha." He kisses my neck. "This was... hot. Incredible. Hot."

I chuckle. "You said hot twice."

"My brain melted, and I couldn't think of other words."

We pant against each other, trying to return to a normal breathing pattern. He fumbles behind me and produces a roll of paper towel.

"It's not the best, but we need to mop this up before either of us moves, I think."

It's rough but does the job as he said and he's overly gentle as he swipes off the cooling jizz that's puddled at the root of my dick. When he's satisfied with the cleanup, he washes his hands and I join him. Both of us, shoulder to shoulder, pants undone and dicks still hanging out.

He jolts. "Oh fuck! Maggie!" He hitches his pants up as he tries to jog around looking for her, distressed he'd forgotten she was even here.

"Micha, come down the hallway. Last room on the left."

I finish washing and do the same scurry while pulling up my pants walking down the hall. Dominic is leaning against the door frame with a giant smile on his face. He wraps a hand around my waist and pulls me against him while pointing into the room. Maggie has made herself completely at home. She found her dog bed in Dominic's room and has a stuffed octopus with her. She's curled up fast asleep without a care in the world.

"I don't think you need to worry about if she'll be happy here or not. She's obviously completely at ease."

He peers down at me with sex satiated eyes. "Are you at ease here?"

The truth is, I've never felt so alive and complete as I have since the moment we left the animal shelter together. "I'm very at ease with you. You see me more than anyone ever has." That's the honest truth. He's not judged me for the outside appearance. He's not turned his nose up at me being a homeless gay man only a few short years ago. He's figured me out quickly and the invite to come here for Maggie's first night was another measure of his thoughtfulness. A man I am falling for the longer I spend time with him.

"Completely." I peck a kiss on his cheek.

"Awesome. Will you spend the night with me?"

SEVENTEEN

Dominic

I WASN'T EXPECTING TO ask Micha to spend the night. It wasn't on my agenda at all. But as we watched Maggie sleeping, and I was still drunk on the post orgasm feeling, I realized I didn't want him to go.

I didn't think we'd do... whatever you call what we just did, in the kitchen. I know for certain I'm never going to look at cupcakes the same again, and we didn't even eat them yet.

From the minute we left the animal shelter, to the moment he smeared pink, cherry flavoured icing across my lips, to the two of us at the sink washing our hands with our junk hanging out; it felt natural and filled a chasm in my heart. One that had been steadily growing bigger, and until now, I felt powerless to stop it. Somehow, this 5ft 10inch blond, a man sparkling and oozing attitude, has flipped my entire world on its head.

A fire in me that's been long extinguished has reignited, and it feels amazing. I don't want it to go out again. Micha chews his bottom lip, contemplating his words. A bead of sweat breaks my brow while we silently watch Maggie doze away on her dog bed.

"Are you sure about that?"

"About you spending the night?"

He turns to me and snuggles into my chest. My fingertips caress his back, and his body shakes gently, like he's trying not to cry. "Yes." He squeaks.

I squeeze him closer. "I want to wake up with you in my arms and not care about the past. I want to live again. You make me want to do that." I rest my chin on his head. "I don't know everything about why you're so scared, Micha, but I would never hurt you. If you aren't ready to stay, I can take you home. Just tell me you want to take it slow. I couldn't handle it if you wanted to walk away after tonight."

Micha steps back and confirms my suspicions. He's crying. His face is red and blotchy, his beautiful long eyelashes are wet and matted. I wipe his eyes with my thumbs and kiss his forehead. I swallow down the lump sitting in my throat as I brace myself for his answer.

"You won't be mad if I say no?" He whispers.

"I'm not mad. Disappointed, but not mad." I brush my lips across his. "But it's not a no forever, right?"

A smile breaks across his face. "Definitely not forever. I just need some time to process it all." His hand cups my cheek.

"I have a hard time accepting when good things happen to me. If you can be patient... I'm not going anywhere."

My shoulders sag with relief. He's not bolting completely. "I can wait as long as you need me to, Micha. Now, let's find our missing clothing and I can get you home. You probably want to see Tux before you get to bed anyway."

"I sure do, but I..."

I brush my hand up and down his arm. "It's okay. You can say it."

He's so breathtakingly gorgeous, I can't take my eyes off him. "It's not what I want to say, it's what I want to do." He loops his arms around my neck and kisses me long and deep. My fingers flex on his hips, wanting to keep him molded to me forever, but knowing he's not ready to stay yet. I take what he offers, and I relish every moment of it. When he finally steps away, he ducks his head. "I'm not always good with words." He rasps. "I hope you figured out what I was trying to say."

I brush his hair off his face. "I think so. Gotta say, it's okay if you don't want to use your words and talk to me like that instead. I'm down."

He giggles and tiptoes over to Maggie, dropping a kiss on her head. "Goodnight, my sweet girl. I'll see you again soon."

We found our shirts and actually ate a cupcake before we left. We chatted about his upcoming workday and how he had a meeting to attend the next night for the shelters. He wasn't sure if he'd be able to see me. It was a domestic scene I could grow to love. Complete with mopping spilled cum off the floor, like it was a perfectly normal activity as we talked.

When I park in front of his house and turn to him, he's already stretching over the console to kiss me goodnight. He still tastes like cherry frosting, and my dick perks at the memory. I'm going to have to keep some of that in the fridge all the time, I think.

"I'll call you when I'm done with the meeting. If it's not too late, maybe we could take Maggie for a walk together?"

"I think we'd both like that."

I watch from the truck until he unlocks his door and is safely inside, then I linger a few minutes longer, just because I miss him. When it feels like I might cross into creepy stalker zone, I reluctantly return home.

When I enter the house, Maggie rouses from her sleep to meet me. Wagging and smiling, I scratch her ears and let her out the patio doors for a pee. She bounces and sniffs around, reluctant to come back in, but eventually does when I shake the box of dog treats. I give her two because she sits so darn nice without asking.

"You're a good dog, aren't you, girl?" I rub her head and flop on the couch. She collapses at my feet with a groan, stretching out and thumping her tail as I rub my foot along her back.

It's nearing 11 P.M. and I should really get some sleep, but my mind won't shut off. Leaning my head back, I stare at the ceiling, wondering if I feel completely okay with what I think is a new relationship forming. I can't deny my attraction to Micha, and I can't deny he lights up my world like nothing has since Jenny.

I turn my head to stare outside, my eyes drawn to the rosebush. Maggie snores softly at my feet and only stirs slightly when I tell her I'll be right back. I exit to the backyard and walk through the dewy grass to what I've always called *Jenny's rose* in my head. Ignoring the wetness, I kneel in front of the rosebush and speak to the wife I lost far too soon.

"Jen, we weren't supposed to be here like this. You know I'm never going to stop missing you and thinking of you." I heave in a breath as a tear runs down my cheek. "But I think I've finally found another person to make me as happy as you did. You'd love him. He's super sweet and loves animals." I brush away a few more tears. "He's leading me out of the dark cave I've been in since you left. I've finally found something to keep going for and I'm tired of not enjoying life. I want to laugh again."

I take a moment to let my tears flow freely as I face the reality of letting my safety blanket of grief go. The one I used as my excuse for anything I could, as long as I could. Grief is a hard bitch to kick to the curb. Like a wheel constantly turning, you didn't know when the spoke carrying your pain would come around and kick you in the face. But with all my soul searching the last few days and talks with Owen, I've accepted this new reality. I can either feel like this forever or deal with it and be me again. Jenny will always live in my heart, but I can share it with someone else for the rest of my days.

"This isn't goodbye Jen. I'm never going to forget you or stop loving you, but I'm going to go on without you. Just like you wanted me to. I'll still be around occasionally. I just wanted you to know it won't be as often. Feel free to say hello though. If you ever get a chance somehow, let me know you're there."

I wipe the tears from my eyes and stand up. It's only talking to a rosebush, but to me, it's a direct line to Jenny, and that conversation was the final band-aid being removed from what was once a gaping wound. I walk to the house and wipe my feet on the mat before going inside. Maggie perks up when she hears the door, wagging when she sees me. "Come on, girl, let's go to bed."

She trots down the hall ahead of me and walks around in three circles on her bed before curling into a ball to sleep. I remove my clothes and chuckle that I still have crusty spots on my jeans and boxers from earlier and throw them into my hamper. I pull on a pair of sleep pants and crawl under my covers.

Sleep comes faster than it ever has, because when I close my eyes, I see Micha and me. If I sleep, morning comes faster. Which means I get to see him again.

Eighteen

Micha

T HE DAY BEGINS AS it always does, with me and my alarm clock fighting it out for extra minutes. I slept well though, it's just these pesky mornings I hate. Mornings like today when I have to wake up and hope last night wasn't a dream.

Talk about an unexpected turn of events. While we'd been flirting hard and Dominic was all in, I didn't expect us to rut like animals in the kitchen. To be fair, it was entirely my fault. How was I supposed to act when he compared me to a cupcake and was so accurate in describing me; the only thing I could think of doing was kissing him. Damn, I doubt I'll ever be able to look at a cherry frosted cupcake the same again though. I'm still swooning over it. Should that be a new thing? Pair your mate to a cupcake? Maybe that could be a dating game at a fund raiser one day? Or if you're really ambitious, develop a dating app. I should really write these ideas down somewhere.

Stretching out, I lie in bed a little longer. I really wanted to spend the night. Achingly so, but I couldn't do it. I couldn't let myself accept this beautiful man actually wanted me to stay and liked me. He said he'd wait and be patient, so I'm going to have to believe him while I work up the courage to let myself accept it. I wouldn't be Micha if I didn't analyze the shit out of everything and decide if the risk was worth me having a broken heart. When it comes to relationships, ever since Robert, I approach them with self preservation as my ultimate goal. I need to retreat, evaluate, and keep a distance until I decide what to do. Yep, solid plan.

Tux isn't here to pull me from my thoughts. I'll have to go on without him this morning. Roberta has probably given him tuna juice and he'll be glued to her for the day. Just as well, I'm still distracted wondering how I can jump in with Dominic like I've never jumped before. I really, really want to. I was sure Marbles told me yesterday to just do it. That's dogs for you. Do one thing and tell you another. I'll talk it out again today with another unsuspecting canine. Look for the consensus and all that.

After I shower and dress, I pack extra clothes for the Fall Fling meeting tonight. I frown when I notice how few clean clothes I have left. I'm going to need to do the laundry soon. Only a few boxers left before I have to raid the lingerie drawer and I'm not feeling up to that just yet. I leave Tux his dry food before I head upstairs for coffee, and just as I thought, Roberta gave him tuna this morning. He's curled up next to her on a fuzzy blanket and doesn't even give me the time of day. Traitor.

"You two look all lovey-dovey today. You bought my cat's love with tuna this morning Roberta, do you have no shame?" I pour my coffee as she chuckles. "Sorry, Micha, I was feeling sad, and I wanted him to snuggle with me today." I halt my coffee prep and walk over to her in the living room.

"Hey momma Berta, everything okay?" She's had some down days when I met her, usually when an anniversary rolls around, but a quick mental calendar check doesn't scream anything to me.

She smiles, but it's tired and my heart pangs. "I couldn't sleep last night, and when I got up to watch T.V. for awhile, I remembered John used to get up with me and I missed him. But I'll be okay." She pats the hand I placed on her knee.

"If you need anything you let me know. You can borrow my freeloading cat any time if he makes you happy."

"You're a good boy, Micha." She eyeballs me and I wonder if I have something on my face, by the way she's inspecting me. "Do you have anything to tell me, my boy?"

She's a witch. That's the only explanation. "What do you mean? Happy Wednesday, thank you for the coffee. I don't have anything to tell you?" That didn't sound suspicious. Nope.

She cocks her head. "Do you think I haven't noticed everything about you since we met? Or how I know you so well, some mornings I meet you with a coffee ready and other mornings, like today, I know you can do it yourself?" Well then, maybe she isn't a witch and is using that mom intuition stuff. That's a more likely scenario and makes more sense.

"I don't know if there's anything to tell yet. Is that going to buy me some time?"

"I heard you come in last night."

"I'm sorry. I'll be more careful next time."

"Is there going to be a next time?"

"Maybe, if I can't say yes to stay over next time."

"Will Dom drive you home every time?"

"Yes, he said he'd —" She is a witch! Damn trickery with her questions. "Go ahead and preen. You got me. Hope you're satisfied."

She throws her head back, laughing. "I didn't think you'd fall for that." She slaps her knee. "Don't worry honey, I won't do or say anything if you aren't ready."

I walk back to the kitchen to finish with my coffee. "How did you know it was Dominic?" I ask over my shoulder as I glug some cream into the mug and stir.

Roberta follows me into the kitchen and points behind me. "Through the window. I heard you come in and go downstairs, but the truck stayed in the driveway for several minutes. When he pulled away, I saw the Wild Baloney signage on the side of the truck when he passed the streetlight."

I snort. "Okay, so not a witch, after all. Just good timing."

She chuckles again. "Micha, I know you're overthinking whatever is going on with you two." I open my mouth, but she holds up her hand. "He's a good man and if he wants to be with you, do it. Stop thinking about all the what-ifs for once."

I step over and kiss her cheek. "Thank you. I'll think about it."

"That's what I'm worried about."

I leave the house for my morning walk to work and chuckle over how much she's noticed and picked up with me living with her for the last few years. She really is another mom for me. She also echoed Travis, and I suppose Marbles, with the advice of, just do it. Easier said than done, as they say.

IT HAS BEEN A day at Fuzzy's. There's been constant late drop offs and pickups and my schedule is so out of whack, I didn't break for lunch as usual and I'm bordering on hangry. Nobody needs to see me hangry. Once I finish with this Pekinese named Carl, it'll be time to clean up before my meeting.

"Carl, do you ever wonder how people choose who they trust? Or even other dogs? How do you choose which dog at the dog park to butt sniff? Like, is it a built-in dog sense or what? Bark once if it's yes."

I pause with my scissors and comb as he peers at me with his buggy eyes.

Bark

"Thank you, because I think it could be that way with people, you know? Well, not the butt sniffing part, eww, but the built-in sense thing. I don't think I have that thing. That sense of knowing who to trust isn't easy for me."

I pause again and he eyeballs me, completely put out I'm talking to him.

Bark

"That's not very supportive, Carl." I turn the blower on him to get rid of all the tiny hairs from the cutting. "I mean, if you asked me if you should say yes to the cute Poodle across the street, I'd say hell ya, Carl. Go get some of that." I turn off the blower and brush him one more time before his mom comes. "But you're really not helping my problem. Do I say yes to Dominic, or what?"

"Would it help if he brought you a late lunch and a visitor?"

I whirl around, my hand to my heart, as Dominic's deep voice startles me. "How long have you been standing there listening?"

He ducks his head. "Long enough to hear you ask a dog about how he knows whose butt to sniff." He's biting back laughter. "Your doorbell isn't working, but I didn't want to interrupt such a deep and meaningful conversation." He can't keep his laughter at bay any longer and cracks up just as Carl's mom arrives.

I hold in my own laughter and embarrassment that he even heard me and take Carl out to Mrs. Warren. "He's been a doll, as always. But you better watch the Poodle across the street. He's been eyeing her." She giggles and passes me her credit card to pay. "Micha, you're the sweetest thing. Carl loves it here. I'll call you for his next appointment."

"Have a good day, Mrs. Warren." Dominic holds the door for her, then leans against it after she exits.

"You must be starving. You've been on your feet all day and didn't get lunch. Your meeting's in an hour. Are you up for some food and a visitor?"

"I would love some food. And if the visitor isn't you, but just happens to be black and four legged, then yes. I'd love a visitor."

He smiles wide and bright. It lights up his entire face. "I'll be right back." I sit on a chair behind my desk and begin closing out my daily sales and Dominic re-enters with a bag and Maggie. "So, your favourite fuzzy visitor told me she missed you." He drops her leash and she wiggle slides around the counter to greet me.

"Hey girl, how was your first day with dad? Did you like it?" I scratch her ears and kiss her nose before turning back to Dom. He brought me my favourite charcuterie board and a root beer. He laid a cloth napkin down and opened all the packages of spreads for me, as well as piled extra napkins to the side. My heart nearly explodes over his thoughtfulness and attention to details. Why did I say no to staying over last night? Right, I over think everything and deny myself basic happiness. I'm good that way.

"Thank you, Dom. This is... amazing."

"You're welcome and I'm happy to do it." I lean across the counter to him and kiss him softly on the lips as my heart packs a bag and jumps into his pocket.

"How did you know I loved root beer?"

He licks his lips. "Because that's what you tasted like when I first kissed you. I assumed you liked it if you wear it on your lips every day."

Is it hot in here? I clear my throat and focus on eating. "Very good assumption, then. Are you going to join me?"

"I'm going to clean up while you eat. Sit and enjoy it. Just show me where the vacuum is. That's what you do, right?"

I nod and point to my tiny closet with the cleaning supplies. I stuff my face and watch, because this is my idea of dinner and a show as Dom wrangles my giant vacuum and cleans up. He turns his ballcap backwards and I almost choke on my tongue at the increase in hotness factor. I continue to eat and ogle as he seamlessly switches from vacuum to mop. Without the racket of the vacuum we can talk.

"How did you know I didn't have lunch?" I sneak Maggie a piece of cheese and motion for her to zip and keep it our secret.

"Oh, Travis was in for his usual and when I asked if he was meeting up with you, he said you couldn't get away. But he and his friend were still going to make it for lunch."

"Oh, he was with someone else?" Interesting. Travis rarely has lunch out with anyone else these days.

"He only said he was meeting someone; I didn't see who." I watch his ass as he really throws his hips into swinging the mop across the floor and I sneak Maggie another piece of cheese. Shit, I'm a bad influence already.

"Do you need me to clean up anything else for you?" Dammit, Roberta is right. He's a damn good man.

"Uh, if you don't mind taking down the doorbell thing for me, I can change the batteries." When I do it, I have to borrow a stepladder from next door. Dominic has at least six inches of height on me. He doesn't need the ladder and if he's helping, I will accept with gratitude.

He replaces the batteries and secures it back in place. "Now you can't sneak up on me again."

I walk to my tiny office and dig out the clean clothes I brought. Dominic leans against the door frame with his hands in his pockets. His hat is still on backwards and there's a wicked glint in his eye. "Maybe I like to sneak up. You and Carl were in deep conversation about me. Get any answers?"

I pull my shirt off over my head, and his eyes darken as they roam over me. "I don't know. He had a lot of one-word answers. Hard to decipher." As he shifts his stance, I drop my pants and his breath hitches. I pull on my clean jeans, but I don't zip them up as I tug my clean shirt on. I walk over to him, toe to toe, and inhale his woodsy cologne. "He might have said something about, you only live once, so date the Poodle."

He raises an eyebrow. "I'm a Poodle? Really?"

"I don't work well under pressure. Poodle was all I could think of." I dust a finger across his collarbone. "But if you were a Poodle, you'd be a best in show champion for sure."

"I'm not liking you calling me a dog." He snatches my wrist to halt my collarbone caresses. It's a weakness. He has the sexiest dip at the base of his throat.

"What would you rather be called then?"

"I'd rather be called yours." He pulls me all the way against his hard body and just as we're about to have what I think will be the most life altering kiss, there's a giant retch and splat noise.

His eyes bug out and we both turn to find poor Maggie has barfed in my lobby.

Dom screws up his face. "What the hell is that?"

I look closer. "It appears the aged cheddar doesn't agree with her. You might want to remember that."

"You fed her cheese?"

I rummage for the clean up supplies to take care of it and give her a dish of water, which she drinks gratefully. "She was supposed to keep it a secret." Now that the mood is broken and I'm running out of time to make it to the meeting, I zip my pants and gather my things. "She'll be okay. Just don't feed her cheese again and she'll be fine."

"I didn't feed it to her. You did."

"Pfft, details." I peck him on the cheek and the three of us exit the building.

"Thanks again for dinner and the visit tonight. It means a lot to know you're thinking of me."

He leans in and I'm finally rewarded with the kiss that was thwarted earlier. "I never stop thinking of you. Now, get to your meeting and give me a call when you're done."

Carl is right, I need to date the Poodle.

NINETEEN

Dominic

I WATCH MICHA AS he walks around the building and down the street towards the youth shelter where his meeting is. His hips sway with each step and I need to tear my eyes away. I wish we could spend time at Dogwood Pond tonight. It's such a beautiful evening, but he has important things to do, and I respect him for it. I also have something to do. A glance at my watch says I better hustle if I want to make it to the town office before they close at 6 P.M.

"Let's go Mags. You're about to meet some new people."

We cross to the next street over, Main Street, and walk the three blocks up to the town offices. I need to buy a dog license and get her a tag. With ten minutes to spare, we step inside the large stone building. It's one of the largest buildings in town and it's a historical landmark. It houses the civil offices and the library on the main floor. Upstairs are business offices for the town council.

I lead Maggie into the small foyer on the left and her nails click on the smooth, polished tiles. As we approach the service counter, I find the two ladies that are a fixture in these offices as well as the town. Deep in conversation, heads tilted and almost touching, they're staring at something Janice is holding between them.

I clear my throat since neither of them has turned to greet me yet. Brandie waves over her shoulder, "We know you're there. Just be a minute."

I stifle the laugh building. These two are not what you'd call the picture of professionalism. They curse, tell off colour jokes and sometimes keep you waiting if they're in the middle of something like they are now. But they're two of the kindest women you'll ever meet. As long as you're a decent human, they'll back you on anything from fighting a parking ticket, to stepping up last minute and volunteering to serve Christmas dinner to all the boys at the shelter because they hate anyone to feel alone. With no children of their own, they mother anyone that lets them.

Laughter bursts out as they cackle together. "My god. Have you ever seen such a package? Where does he put it when he's not using it?" Most days when I walk in on their conversations, it's inappropriate. Today is no exception.

Janice turns to greet me. "Perfect timing! If it isn't the Sausage King himself." And that's why I assume it's always inappropriate. At that moment, Maggie sneezes and snorts and they both bend over the counter to look. Collective *awws* and *oh how cute,* pour out as they come around the gate and smother Maggie with affection. She eats it up, of course, and my heart swells watching them dote on her.

"You know I keep a good bone nearby for just such an occasion." Brandie removes a treat jar from a drawer and tosses a handful in front of Maggie. "Nothing like a good boning, right Jan?"

She snorts. "If that's what tickles your fancy. What about you Dom? You handle a lot of bones every day, don't you? Is there one you like better than the others?" They snicker together before finally getting back to dealing with why I'm here. Thank God there's not a waiting room full of people. I might be embarrassed otherwise.

"It's meat he handles, not bones. Get it right. How's the meat handling these days, Dom?"

I sigh as they both giggle and attempt to school their expressions. If I wanted to come here and not hear a joke about handling meat, sausage or bones, I'd have to come when they both retire, because it happens every single time.

"Business is good. I can't complain about that. This pretty lady needs a dog license. I just adopted her yesterday."

"Is she the one the cutie from the shelter always walks around the pond? What's his name? Micky, Marty... something with an M anyway." Brandie perches on the edge of her desk. "Did you adopt him too, Dom?"

"It's Micha, actually."

Janice peers over her glasses. "Hmm, but you didn't answer the rest of the question, love." I can feel my cheeks heat under her knowing gaze. "Interesting." She rummages for a form and a dog tag and begins filling it out while Brandie picks up on my embarrassment.

"Why ya blushin' Dom? He's cute isn't he? I just love his hair."

I'm not afraid of admitting how I feel about Micha. Hell, I want him to spend the night and possibly even more when we're ready. These ladies are judgement free; I might as well get used to saying I like Micha to people.

"He's very cute, I agree. He was a package deal. I took them both, but I don't need a tag for him."

Both ladies pause to stare at me. I hold their gaze. Brandie breaks into a giant grin. "Are you telling me the Sausage King really does like sausage? Cuz, honey, good for you. If he's the one to put that gorgeous smile back on your face, then you best be keeping him close."

"I'm never one to get emotional, Dom, but she's right. We've been missing you gobs. This lad is as good as they come, now c'mere." Janice rounds the counter and engulfs me in a motherly hug. Resistance is not an option, so I bend down to return it. "He's a much better choice than that Tara girl."

I straighten up. "What about her?" Tara's not one of my favourite people. I've allowed her to keep contact with me out of respect for Jenny and nothing more. Since Jenny died, she's always dropping by unannounced and inserting herself into my life. I've never given her the impression I was interested. At least I hope I haven't.

"Oh Dom, she was hoping you'd turn to her to fill your bed. That was as obvious as the day is long. I don't trust her one lick."

"What? No." That can't be true, could it? Is that what her motive is?

Both women raise an eyebrow and I'm floored I was so oblivious to Tara's methods. However, it makes a lot of sense now.

"Okay, well now I know. Thanks for the heads up. But you're right, he is a much better choice." My smile returns, and they both have hearts in their eyes over a love story emerging, but I'm not about to divulge any details. "Don't go asking me for your perverted details. A gentleman never kisses and tells."

"Ooh! So, you have kissed! I'd love to be a fly on the wall and watch that."

I sigh. "You really have no filter do you, Brandie?"

"That's a no." I look at Janice. "Pure and filter free all day long. No apologies."

I scribble my signature where needed, pay the fee, and pocket the dog tag to place on her collar when we get home. After a few more jokes about salami, I'm finally out the door and I lead Maggie back towards Fuzzy's, where I left my truck.

I've always enjoyed going to the town office directly to pay taxes or whatever business I have. Town business is the only kind I take care of in person and not online, because I love visiting with Janice and Brandie. But what they said about Tara has me replaying all our interactions since Jenny died, and I'm stunned to realize they were right. Tara was making a move, and I didn't see it. It's not uncommon for it to happen. People often lean on those close for comfort, but it makes me uncomfortable with any future interactions.

I wonder if Jenny's parents ever saw that with Tara?

Now that I'm thinking of them and I have time on my hands, I'm going to visit Jenny's parents and give them a heads up about Micha. They can meet Maggie too, they'd enjoy that. Just because their daughter isn't here doesn't mean I can't still say hello to them.

"Jump in girl. We have a visit to make."

I PARK IN THE driveway of Jenny's childhood home and a thickness settles in my throat. All the time I spent here as a teenager and a young man; those are times I'll never forget. Bonnie and Jack are like second parents to me. I still try to drop in a few times a year to keep in touch. I help them with any home or yard maintenance they might need too, because it's what I do, and they're good people.

I wipe my sweaty palms on my pants and lead Maggie up the walk to ring the doorbell. She sits beside me as we wait, smiling and happy as I reach down and give her a pat on the head.

"Dominic!" Bonnie rushes to hug me before I can even say hello. "Oh, you have a friend! Is she yours?" She scratches Maggie behind the ears and her puppy dog eyes close with ecstasy.

"Good to see you, Bonnie. This is Maggie and yes, she's mine. Is it a good time to drop by for a visit?"

"It's always a good time for you, Dom. Jack is out with the boys for wing night at the golf club, though. He'll be sorry he missed you."

I follow her into the house. "You okay with the dog inside?"

"Of course, she's always welcome. Would you like a drink? Can I get you anything?"

"Oh no, Bonnie, I'm okay. I just wanted to pop in and see you. I didn't realize it had been so long since I'd been by."

"You have a life to live, Dom. It's okay. We appreciate anytime you stop by." Her warm, sincere smile always makes me feel at home. I love this woman like my mother. She'll always be special to me. "You have something to tell me, though." She pats my knee.

I laugh softly. She knows me so well. "I do. The first of which is this girl here. I adopted her from the shelter yesterday at the suggestion of Owen." Maggie has laid down at my feet, at ease in yet another new surrounding. The butterflies start again in my gut, and I push them away. This is Bonnie. I can tell her anything. She'll be okay with it.

"I met someone." My voice is barely above a whisper as the words get stuck in my throat. It feels strange to be telling Jenny's mom I met someone when I proposed in this very room so many years ago.

"Sweetie, don't be scared. Do you honestly think every person who has lost a spouse has never found another partner?" I shake my head. "I can see the change in you already. You're lighter, more smiley." She beams at me and pats my cheek. "Jenny would want you to gift yourself to someone else because you brought her so much joy." She takes my hand. "She'll live forever right here." Bonnie places her hand over my heart, and I cover it with mine. "Honour her memory by providing someone else the happiness you brought her."

I thought I had dumped my burden the other night with my rose bush talk, but somehow another weight has lifted, and I sag in relief. "I don't know why that made me so relieved to hear, but I needed to hear it from you."

"If I knew you needed to hear it at all I would have said it a long time ago. If there's another person who lights you up like my Jenny did, grab on to them and don't let go. It rarely comes twice in a lifetime." She smiles again. "You'll always be like a son to me. I can't wait to meet her."

I chuckle again. "Well Bon, it's a good thing you're already sitting down because it's not a her."

Her eyes widen for just a split second before she grins again. "My dear, I love them no matter what they are if they put that smile on your face. I've missed your smile."

Missing my smile seems to be the theme of today and I didn't even know I hadn't been smiling that much.

TWENTY

Micha

WHEN I ENTER THE shelter and find a seat on the sofa, the inquisitors waste no time laying into me.

"I hope you ended up having a good time at whatever private party Dominic had arranged for you?" Jacob smirks. "Are you going to share with the group?"

"I'm not into sharing all the details of my life with you crumb bums." Of course, I want to shout it from the rooftops in reality, but I don't know if Dominic wants everyone knowing what we were up to. Also, kiss and tell is not flattering.

"We aren't asking what position you were in, drama llama. We just want to know what all that hot and heavy flirty stuff was about yesterday at the adoption." Travis settles beside me. "You two were oblivious to anyone else. We were all invisible. I wanted to watch, but Jacob made us leave." He fakes pouts at Jake.

"Which I appreciate. It should have been a private moment. Why were you all there anyway?"

Guilty looks abound as neither of them meets my eye or answers the question.

"Jake, you need to come clean with me, sweetie. What's the secret?"

He runs a hand through his hair before meeting my gaze. "No secret. I hoped you two would hit it off, but I didn't think it would be a home-run." He clears his throat. "I asked for the others to come just in case you were sad Maggie was leaving. I had no idea you'd be leaving with her."

That makes two of us. I didn't think things would escalate as quickly as they did. I'm in a room with two of my closest friends. They wouldn't judge me, and they most definitely would encourage me to chase my happiness. These are the people I can trust in the most basic sense of the word. Travis would bring a shovel and Jacob would drive the car to help me bury Dominic if he ever did me wrong.

"I talked to Carl today about it. I'm still on the fence, but leaning towards falling over and having Dom catch me."

"Who's Carl?" Jacob asks.

"Oh, he's a Pekinese I groomed today. Total doll."

Jacob blinks. "You asked a dog for advice? Did he, uh, answer?"

"Pfft, well not with words Jake, you know how I am." I pick imaginary lint off my pants. "I talk things through with animals because they can't say the things I don't want to hear. Carl is going after a Poodle, because you only live once, and Marbles has no fear, doesn't overthink a thing, just does it."

"Who's Marbles?" Jake says.

"Oh, she's a Poodle with no fear. Told me to just do it and don't overthink it. So, I did."

Jake sighs while Travis chuckles. Jacob doesn't see me every day like Travis does. He's obviously forgotten how bizarre I am with the dogs at the shop.

"What did you end up doing then?"

"Uh, well, first I let him kiss me in the driveway the other night."

Travis barks a laugh. "That wasn't a kiss, that was a make-out session."

"Wait, how did you see this Trav? Were you with him?"

I turn to grin. "He was driving by, he said. In my area, at 11 P.M. apparently."

Jacob shifts to look at Travis. "But you never leave the house after 9 P.M. because, and I quote, nine is the new midnight and you don't need to be up later than that to have fun."

"I thought we were talking about Micha." Travis sputters. He's flustered and I'm going to find out what's going on with him eventually. He's hiding something and then gives me hell, for not spilling my guts. It goes both ways, bestie.

Jacob puts his hands up. "Micha, are you going to tell us what happened last night or not?"

"I really like him. A lot." I drop my gaze to my hands in my lap. "I feel like I'm in a dream and it's going to end soon. Last night was fantastic and without giving you any dirty details... he asked me to spend the night."

The silence is deafening and when I raise my head, both of them have their jaws hanging open. "I know, I know. You thought he was straight. Let's just say we erased that straight line and he's so damn sweet, my teeth ache."

"Did you stay?" Travis asks.

I shake my head. "I couldn't do it. He drove me home because I didn't want to jinx it.

The last time I felt safe with someone I thought cared about me, he didn't stand up for me when I needed it and kicked me to the curb so fast, I barely had time to understand what was going on. I trusted him immediately since he'd been a lawyer and a friend of my father's. He had to be trustworthy. I thought, for sure, if anyone would help it would be him. Since I trusted him with my entire being and was betrayed in remarkable fashion, hesitation is always my go-to when things seem too good.

Travis takes my cheeks in his hands, smooshing them together. "Mic, stop thinking nothing good is going to happen with him. He's into you. I saw it with my own eyes, and before you say anything, I know he brought you food before you came over here today. The guy is not interested in a quick lay or an experiment or whatever else is going on in your head. He likes you. For the love of all things gay, say yes and be with him. You deserve it."

"Can ew le go my chicks?"

Travis releases his death squeeze on my cheeks, and I move my jaw around. "You're right. I'm going to go for the Poodle. I'll call him when we're done here." Scares the crap out of me, but I'm still young. If it fails spectacularly, I can spare another four years to recover.

"Yay! Now let's actually talk about the Fall Fling coming up and not compare our relationships to dogs." Jake flicks open his colour coded and neatly tagged notebook. The man is the most organized one I've ever met. His underwear is probably colour coded in his closet, too.

"We have the outdoor tent setup arranged and confirmed for next weekend. It'll be located at the end of the street in the community gardens like last year. We hit a giant snag today, though. I had a call from the caterer this morning. She needs to back out. The building she operates out of just sold and she only has the week to move her things. She doesn't have a suitable backup for preparation. We need to come up with a solution."

"We already checked with the diner, and she can't because of a prior commitment. What about the wedding caterer from Arpinville? She sometimes does a fast turn around?" Travis says.

I have an idea and it's even local. "We want casual, right? And food to allow people to mingle?"

Jake nods. "Yes, Austin and Logan and a few available players from the hockey team and modelling agency will be here. We want to move people along, so they aren't stuck at a food station or stuck in an autograph line."

"Okay, hear me out. Why don't we ask Dom if they can make individual charcuterie boxes or something like that? People could pick at their snack box and wander to the raffles and autographs at their leisure or even the other way around. They could take their snack box home since it's part of admission."

Jacob nods. "I like that idea. Do you want to ask, or do you want me to? I don't want you in an uncomfortable position." He chuckles. "Well, maybe you do want that kind of position, but I don't expect you to use a personal connection for our benefit."

"I agree, you should ask. But I'll bet he says yes." He has one of the kindest hearts I've ever known. If he knows the shelter is in a tight spot, he's going to jump through hoops to help us out. Not just because of me either, it's his nature.

"So, who are the hockey players coming? Has Austin told you yet?" Travis winks at me and both of us notice Jacob flush and duck his head.

"He, ah, hasn't confirmed, but sounds like two can make it. Bo Stayner, and um, the Swedish guy, Matts Anderson." Seems like Travis was right about Jacob and a certain hockey player. I don't think I've ever seen Jacob this flustered. "Logan's supposed to have one of his models come too, but he hasn't given me a name. So that's hopefully five celebrity names to draw the crowds."

Truth is, this town will come out in droves just for Austin and Logan. They don't need celebrity friends to have the support for the shelters, but it definitely helps bring in more money. Who wouldn't want a chance to meet someone famous that you might not otherwise meet? Bonus points if they're single and attractive.

We spend the next hour finalizing plans and dividing up tasks between us. Jake has a list for the kids at the shelter to choose what part they want to help with. With the current shelter residents, former residents like myself and many townspeople, we should have more than enough hands to make it all flow smoothly. The only cost for hired help will be for security.

Now that I've admitted to Travis and Jake, I like Dominic and I'm going to take the leap, I'm nervous as hell. My heart is racing so fast it feels like I should call an ambulance. I pull my phone from my pocket with shaking hands, staring at my contact list. Jacob slides up beside me, placing a hand on my shoulder.

"Micha, the regret of not jumping will feel worse than the fear. I know I can't promise nothing bad will happen. There's nothing certain in life. But believe me when I say regret is hard to live with." His eyes project a story he hasn't told, and I wonder what he's been keeping away from his closest friends. It's not the time to ask, though.

Instead, I wrap my arms around and hug with all my might, to thank him for offering me a shoulder and to also let him know I'm a safe place. When he pulls away, he got my message. "I'll tell you about it sometime. Now, stop staring at the phone and text that ridiculously cute butcher man to come pick you up."

Feeling my courage renewed, I open my phone and call.

Twenty-One

Dominic

I'M ABOUT TO LEAVE Bonnie's place when my phone rings. Glancing at the screen, I see Micha's name and my guts tumble over. Maggie is already in the back, head out the window and ready for a ride. I answer his call with a giant smile.

"Well, hello there. I'm hoping you're calling me because you miss me and couldn't go home without seeing me before bed."

His soft laugh crosses the line, making me miss him with a ferocity I wasn't sure was possible. "Part of that's true. Uh, the meeting went a bit late, and it's too dark for the walk, but if you want to, I'd love to spend the rest of the evening with you."

"I'd love to see you. Are you still at the shelter?"

"Um... no, I'm at home. Can you pick me up?"

"Of course, I'm on my way. Be there in twenty."

It's not the romantic lakeside walk I hoped for, but if Micha wants to spend the evening with me, I'm more than happy to pick him up. With the darkness coming sooner than ever as Fall approaches, I'll have to adjust the walk plans for the future.

"Ready Maggie? Let's go pick up our favourite pet groomer." Her tail thumps faster and I couldn't agree more with her excitement.

Jenny's parents live just outside of town in a more rural area, so it's a little farther to drive to Micha's place than if I was leaving from my own. The twenty minutes feels like forever until I finally pull into his driveway. I'm not even out of the truck and Micha comes running out of the house with a backpack slung over his shoulder and a gorgeous smile on his face.

Maggie bounces and whines when she sees him, drawing an even bigger smile from him. Before he can bypass me to see Maggie, I snag him by the elbow and pull him into my chest.

"Please tell me you weren't going to kiss the dog before me."

"Um, I was taught to never lie."

I chuckle, shaking my head with a grin at his cheekiness. "What am I going to do with you?"

"Anything you want." He rises on his tiptoes and presses his lips to mine before running over to the passenger side and planting a giant kiss on Maggie's nose.

God, this man is going to be the death of me, I swear.

"So, what do you want to do tonight?" I back out and point the truck towards my place.

When he doesn't immediately respond, I turn to see why he's quiet. Micha, my always forward and never shy, adorable man, appears embarrassed. "Micha, what is it?"

"Uh, you know how I was having a conversation with Carl, and you overheard?"

I chuckle. "Right, the little dog."

"Little dog, big attitude. Anyhow, he said I should just do it." He shifts in his seat and I risk a glance. He's fidgeting again. "So that's what I'm going to do."

"Do what exactly?"

I park in my driveway, and Micha still hasn't moved. I'm feeling itchy about what he wants to say. But he asked me to come pick him up so it can't be bad. At least I don't think it's bad.

"Is your offer still open?" He whispers. "Because I came prepared, if it is."

It takes me a solid minute getting lost in his eyes until I finally clue in on what he's asking me. "You want to spend the night?"

He pats the backpack. "I came prepared if you still want me to."

My breath leaves in a giant whoosh. Holy crap. He wants to stay with me. He picked me!

"Hell ya, I still want you to stay with me. I mean, I don't want to pressure you."

Maggie whines and sticks her head through the seats. We both laugh as she not so subtly looks for attention from both of us. Nosing each of us in turn, wagging and bouncing, eager to leave the vehicle.

"I guess we need to take care of the little miss first. Wouldn't want her feeling left out."

I let Maggie out my side, and she bounds to the gate for the backyard. I let her into the yard before leading Micha through the front door. As soon as the door closes, I gather him into my arms and brush my lips over his. "You're sure about staying? I don't want you to feel pressured, Micha. Never, on anything."

He slides his hands up my chest. "It's no pressure. I'm making this decision on my own. No animals actually influenced my decision to come here." He locks his arms behind my head. "It's mine alone and I want to be here. I want to be all in with you. Unless I misunderstood the other night, I think you want that too?"

I'm dizzy hearing these words cross his lips. I thought I might've scared him off by moving so quickly yesterday and asking him to stay. But he's not just a passing flavour. He's not a phase or an experiment. I need him in my life. Not just because of how he makes my body burn when he's close to me, but how he makes me enjoy the little things when we're together, like the taste of my morning coffee and the feel of the breeze through my hair with the window down. I'm alive and I don't want to let that feeling ever pass again.

I place a kiss on his neck. "I want you, Micha. The whole you and nothing less."

"There's nothing less about me, Dom. I'm extra with a capital E." He shoves me playfully away and walks to the patio door to call Maggie in.

I can't wipe the stupid smile off my face. Extra with a capital E. Something tells me life will never be boring with Micha.

AFTER SPENDING TIME WITH Maggie in the yard. Micha suggested we watch T.V. I never watch T.V., it's never been a draw. I always preferred books, but if it meant I got to have him snuggle next to me as we watched a show about sharks, I wasn't going to say no.

Maggie laid on the floor by my feet until she got annoyed. We kept waking her up, and she trotted off to the bedroom with a loud huff.

"Does it ever make you sad, knowing that cute little seal is going to be eaten and die a horrible death?"

I chuckle as I look down to find Micha with his hands over his face, peering through his fingers, but only barely. "It's the circle of life." I shrug. "Everything has to eat to survive."

He hides his face as the seal meets his maker. "Why did you put this show on if you don't like seeing it? It's sharks, it's what they do. They aren't vegetarians."

He sighs. "I know. I always hope it'll end differently and the seal eats the shark." A bark of laughter earns me a death glare. "Don't laugh at me. The underdog should win sometimes, balances things out."

I grab the remote and turn the T.V. off. "C'mere Micha." I tug on his arm to make him move to straddle my hips. "I feel like there's more to this. A seal will never eat a shark. Fact of life. You know this." I stretch up to meet him halfway and place a tender kiss on his lips. "What's this about?"

"Remember when you asked me to share my story with you at the rest stop?"

I nod. "I do. You said you never get to kiss the prince. Is that what this is about?"

"When I was nineteen, I was that seal." He swallows. "But the shark wasn't supposed to be like that. He was supposed to be, whatever it is that protects seals. Maybe a dolphin." I rub my hands up his back and wait for him to continue. "The shark's name was Robert. A charming, sexy, put together man in his forties. He wasn't always a shark though. That's why I always watch these shows and hope for a different outcome. It's silly, I know, but it's just something I do."

"It's not silly. It's how you deal with something that happened to you."

He snorts. "Well, it sure happened all right. Robert didn't have teeth in the beginning. He was kind, he told me I was beautiful. The man was going to leave his wife. He gave me gifts. I felt loved and cared for by him." Micha runs his hands into my hair and settles his forehead on mine. "Until my dad found out, and he grew all the teeth of a shark and then some. Robert said I was nothing to him, just a toy to pass the time, and I was his walk on the wild side, as they say." His lips whisper across mine and I can taste his root beer lip gloss. "He said gay wasn't his thing and if his wife found out, he'd ruin me more than he already had. It disgusted my dad to know I had a relationship with an older man. Not just any man, a trusted friend and colleague. He took that man's words over his own son's."

"Oh Micha... I'm sorry, baby."

"Don't be sorry. It happened. There was nothing you could do to help." His breath stutters. "That's what I meant when I said it's hard for me to accept when good things happen to me. I'm always afraid of the shark."

He collapses against me, burying his face into my neck, koala clinging to me and it's the best thing I've ever felt. Knowing he trusts me to put himself out there again and not be a shark, that's something I cherish and will never abuse. I stand from the couch, clutching his ass and he wraps his slim legs around my waist, plastering himself impossibly closer and making it almost impossible to walk. But I'm not a quitter.

Reaching my bedroom, I lay him on the bed and wait for him to let go. When he doesn't, I have to ask. "Micha, I'm not going anywhere. Can you let go, so we can get comfortable?" He reluctantly releases his hold and I straighten my back.

"How comfortable do you want to be?" His voice is thick as his eyes scan my body. While I cherish his disclosure of why he was so guarded, I couldn't hide the way I was feeling, having him so close to me. I've been wanting to get him naked since he told me he came prepared to spend the night.

I pull my T-shirt over my head. "I wouldn't mind having nothing between us."

His eyes darken as he scrambles to sit up and tear off his own clothes. Taking that as a display of agreement, I continue to strip naked while Micha watches me and trails a hand down his chest.

"Like what you see?"

"Yes, immensely." His voice is no more than a husky rasp.

I take my time returning the same inspection, allowing my eyes to map every inch of creamy white skin on display. "You're fucking gorgeous." I settle next to him, and he twines his legs through mine as I slide my hand up his thigh. "More than gorgeous. A work of art. " I tug the elastic from his hair and run my hands through it. It's soft and silky. "A masterpiece, inside and out." Ghosting my lips down his throat, I place tiny kisses across his collarbone and shift him onto his back.

I want to take forever with him. My hands continue to roam. I'm mesmerized with how he shudders and sighs with every slight touch. Every kiss elicits a tiny moan, every feathered touch a breathy gasp. I'm amazed I do this to him. It's heady to watch him squirm and moan under me, with only the lightest of touches and kisses. Growing bolder, I slide down his body and rest my head on his thigh, with my nose skimming the side of his cock. I didn't get time yesterday to really see it and it's just as beautiful as the rest of him. I sigh a breath across his hard length and watch as goosebumps race across his thigh. Fuck, this can be addicting. Watching all of Micha's reactions is an aphrodisiac. My dick aches, begging for touch, but I'm focused on the gift before me first. Nothing else matters.

His chest is rising and falling at an erratic pace. When I hazard a glance at his face, my breath stutters. Naked, raw emotion plays across his lust drunk face. His feelings are stamped for me right there. Awe and disbelief. I scramble up beside him and press my lips against his. "Are you okay? Did I do something wrong?" My thumb caresses his cheek and his eyes flutter closed.

"I'm okay." His voice is raspy as he grasps my wrist and presses a kiss to it. "Nobody has ever done this before."

"Done what? Taken their time to explore you, appreciate you, revel in your amazing body?"

A tortured moan leaves his mouth. "How are you real?" His fingers dance over my cheek. "No one, not that there's been that many to see me like this, but nobody has ever... worshipped me like this. I don't know how I'm supposed to feel."

"The only thing you need to feel is the pleasure it brings." I place a kiss over his heart. "Can I keep going?"

He nods and I slide back to my previous place. "Put your hands behind your head, baby." He complies and I indulge in my first taste of Micha. My tongue laps across his leaking cock and he cries out, arching his back off the bed. I've never given another man a blowjob before, but I may have done some research and I'm damn excited to have Micha be my first.

I take as much of him as I can in my mouth. Saliva flows faster than a rushing river, leaking from my lips. I'm drunk on his taste, and the weight of him on my tongue sends a shiver through my body. He tries to thrust, but I press him back down. I want him to lie here and enjoy what I do. I want him to know he's worth my undivided care and attention.

"Dom, I'm gonna come." His voice drips with pleasure and need.

"I want you to." I rasp.

"Oh, fuck... Dom." Salty, sweet nectar rushes over my tongue and I swallow what I can, letting the rest leak out and slide down my lips. Micha is stunning as he returns from his orgasm high. He's sweaty, flushed and moaning; and when his eyes find mine, he wordlessly passes the message we both feel but can't say.

Wiping my mouth with my hand, I scramble up the bed to kiss him. He's shaking as he wraps himself around me, never breaking his mouth from mine. When he finally stops shaking, I gently push him back and stroke the hair from his face. "Let me get you a cloth, sticky sucks."

He snickers. "It does, but what about you?" He reaches for me but stops when he notices my erection is no longer there. "But what... "

I chuckle. "I'm ah, pretty good, actually. Turns out having my boyfriend come in my mouth is enough to set me off." He looks at the bed and sees my mess and puts it together. "You came without me?"

"Uh, no, I came with you. I just didn't need you to touch me to do it."

"Wow, that's... so damn sexy. I did that?"

I laugh again at his shocked face as I find a cloth to moisten and wipe him up with. "You sure did." He continues to stare at me in awe while I clean him off.

Micha goes to the bathroom for his nightly routine, while I strip off the top comforter, toss it towards my laundry pile and take another one from the hall closet. When Micha exits the bathroom, my dick twitches. A switch has flipped, and the sex drive I had as a teenager is making a roaring comeback. I need to control my urge to jump him every time I see him naked, or we'll never leave this house, like ever.

I peel the covers back for him and he slides in. "You're okay with little spoon, right?" He giggles and snuggles back into me, nestling his ass over my groin.

"I love little spoon." He purrs.

"Why's that? I wrap my arms around him and drop a kiss to his head.

"Little spoon rubbing on big spoon, big spoon gets bigger. Big spoon needs a place to... deposit." He snorts. "What's not to love?"

"Nothing, you're absolutely right. Lucky little spoon. But let's stop talking about cutlery and get some sleep."

TWENTY-TWO

Micha

MY EYES BLINK SLOWLY awake when a giant, cold nose shoves itself into my face. Maggie.

Her bright eyes suggest she's happy to see me, but I can't be happy yet. It's too morning. I roll over and snuggle into the covers, hoping to snuggle into Dom, but his side of the bed is empty. I pat the sheets and find them cold. He's been gone for a while. I roll back over and find Maggie still looking at me, hopeful for more attention.

"Where's your dad? Why are you waking me up so early?"

"Wow, you really don't do mornings well do you?" Why does he always catch me talking about him to animals?

I feel the bed dip as Dominic drops beside me and presses a kiss to my cheek. "No, I don't. Mornings should be later. Like they shouldn't start until noon."

He chuckles. "Well, on weekends they can be later, but today we both need to work so rise and shine beautiful."

I groan and cover my head with the blankets. "Just five more minutes!"

"If you aren't up in five minutes, you won't have time to see Tux before work. I suggest you shake a leg, sweetheart."

"That's playing dirty! You shouldn't guilt me with my cat, Dom." I fling the blanket back, find a pillow, and throw it as he walks away, hitting him in the back. Shit, I didn't think I'd actually make contact. I normally suck at this kind of thing.

He calmly turns around and picks up the pillow with a raised eyebrow. "You sure you want to play that way, Micha?"

Dominic stalks towards me, and I gulp. Fuck, he's sexy in the morning with a playful gleam in his eye. He tosses the pillow on the bed and throws himself on top of me, pinning my hands over my head when I struggle to get free.

"Micha, I don't like to be late. Don't make me late." He nips my neck and presses his hips into mine. I groan and lift my hips, but he's already moved off me and back to the bedroom door. Such a tease.

"Five minutes, Micha!" His voice carries down the hall and Maggie trots after him. Reluctantly, I slide out of bed and shuffle to the bathroom. He said I have five minutes, but I need a shower. I still feel sticky after last night. I turn the shower on and jump in fast before Dom can tell me there's no time. Of course, he has to be a morning person. He has to have some fault and there it is - chipper morning person. Shoot me now.

My mind races along with my body as I try to hurry through my shower in case the five-minute warning is real. Showers are for thinking, and I need to wrap my mind around last night. It was intense and the most intimate I've ever felt with anyone. Not that I've had a gaggle of lovers, but I've had a few, and none of them have ever treated me with the care and tenderness Dominic did last night. I feel like he truly cares about me and that I'm someone important to him. Not to mention he didn't even look for anything in return. He put me first, and for that alone I'm finding myself struggling to cope with the feelings blooming in my chest. Is it possible he's the real deal and I might have finally found someone to trust?

Nobody has ever made me a priority, not even my family, for anything. Hope doesn't come easy to me, but I can feel it fighting to grow, like a tiny plant shoot in the darkest corner of the garden.

Shutting the water off, I hurry to dry off and dress. I do want to stop and feed Tux this morning. Roberta could do it, but he's my responsibility and I love him. I yank my hair into a ponytail and, after brushing my teeth, apply my usual lip gloss and a line of eyeliner. I blow myself a kiss in the mirror and I'm set.

I stuff all my things into my backpack and find Dominic in the kitchen, relaxing with coffee and not a care in the world, as he flicks through something on his iPad. He glances up when I enter and stands to greet me.

"Good morning." He reaches for a hug, and I allow myself to melt against him. The little plant sprout grows a teeny bit more.

"What's good about it?" I mumble into his chest and inhale his fresh smell. He smells domilicious. It's unique to him and I'm going with that. Maybe there's something good about the morning after all.

"For starters, it's a gorgeous day, and I got to wake up with you. Now you're in my kitchen. That's a pretty good morning to me."

Well, damn, he has a point. "Okay, you're right. It is nice to wake up with you, but you weren't in bed when I woke up."

He releases me and pours me a coffee, adding cream just how I like it and motions for me to sit at the kitchen island. "I wanted to be there when you woke up, but you sleep like the dead and Maggie needed to go out. I walk her around the neighborhood in the morning before breakfast, then she's had some activity before I come home at night. What would you like for breakfast?"

"I bet Maggie loves that." Sipping my coffee, I watch him rummage around cupboards. "I thought we only had five minutes?"

He smirks over his shoulder at me. "I lied."

"You woke me up when I didn't have to be up? What time is it, anyway?"

"7 A.M."

"Do you not like me?" I whine. "Why didn't you let me sleep until at least 7:30?" I drink more coffee and damn, it's good. I could get used to this coffee. Hell, I could get used to the whole damn thing. Maybe.

He stops his rummaging and walks back to me at the island. Palming the back of my neck, his voice is barely a whisper. "I like you very much and I wanted to have breakfast with you." His lips brush over mine. "Mmm, you taste like root beer again."

My heart jackhammers as I press my lips harder against his. "Then I suppose I can make the sacrifice of sleep if I get to share breakfast with you."

He snorts. "I'll take it. Your choice, omelet or pancakes?"

"Oh, omelet please! Mushroom?"

"Whatever your heart desires." He turns to gather his ingredients from the fridge, and it hits me. This, right here, right now. This is what my heart desires. But I can't tell him that, not yet anyway. What if this is just a one-night thing? My hope seedling flags a little in my chest.

I move beside him and help slice mushrooms. We work together like a well-oiled machine. When his knife stops moving, I hazard a quick check to see if something's wrong. His eyes are on me, and a silly grin is stuck on his face. I duck my head, feeling my cheeks flush. I want that grin every morning so badly. It's mine for the taking and I made the first step, but I need to keep a clear head. I need to protect myself here.

Dominic must sense my hesitance as he chatters about the day ahead and what he has planned. We eat our breakfast, which was delicious, and after a quick stop to see Tux, he's pulling into his spot at Wild Baloney, and for the first time in a long time, I'm going to be early for work.

"Do you want a coffee from The Bean to take with you?"

"I think I'll make it until lunch. I'm functioning now, so that's a good sign."

He runs his hand through his hair. "I, uh, had a great time last night. Do you think you... um, might want to come over again?"

Oh my God, just when I think he can't get any more adorable, he gets nervous and stammers to ask me over.

"I'd love to. I'll call you when I'm finished work if that's okay? Let's take that walk around the pond tonight, maybe?"

His face lights up with a giant, megawatt smile. "Can I surprise you?"

I narrow my eyes. "Am I gonna like it?"

"I guarantee you'll like it." He plants a kiss on my lips before we meet in front of his truck.

"You know, it's not really a surprise when you tell me you're going to surprise me, right?"

He chuckles. "Well, I didn't tell you what I was going to do, so it's still a surprise." He kisses me on the nose. "I'll see you tonight, Micha."

As I walk over to Fuzzy's, I'm not even sure my feet touch the ground. This is what it feels like to fall in love, I think. Real love, not something another person tells you how you should feel, but when you feel it yourself. But I can't be falling in love, can I? My hope seedling isn't even strong enough on its own yet. Maybe I'm just high on the hope it's love?

My hands are shaking as I unlock my door, and I run through my morning routine. Is it love or am I coming down with a flu? And where the hell is Travis when I need to talk to someone?

As if my thoughts summon him, his signature knock sounds at the shared door, and I rush to open it. I don't even wait for our usual jokes before I drop back into my office chair and wrap my arms around myself.

"Micha! You're white as a sheet. Are you okay? Should I get someone?" Travis kneels in front of me with a knitted brow.

"I think I'm okay."

"What happened? Is it Dominic?" His face clouds over. "Do I need to get a shovel?"

I laugh, but it's weak. "No, it's not like that Trav." He waits patiently for me to continue. "He's... I'm..."

"Mic, deep breath. I'll get you some water." He grabs a bottled water from my fridge and unscrews it for me. I take a small sip and when it no longer feels like I might throw up, I inhale to continue. "I think I'm falling for him, Trav. My hope is the biggest it's ever been."

He rubs my back with a sweet smile. "Are you going to tell me why you look like you might hurl, when that should be good news?"

"It's too soon."

He sighs. "No time limit on these things Micha, you feel what you want, when you want."

"I'm not right for him."

"He obviously doesn't think so. He picked you. I think he knows what he likes."

"He's a morning person."

"Oh, well, why didn't you start with that excuse because that's a deal breaker right there." He deadpans.

"It's too good, he's too good. It won't end well. Why does he want me?"

Travis scares the shit out of me when he smacks a hand so hard on the reception desk my pen cup crashes over. The pink sparkly one rolls onto the floor and I jump, sloshing water on my shirt, as I stare in shock at my normally jovial friend's outburst.

"Listen to me, Micha. Really fucking listen because I'm tired of you thinking you aren't good enough for someone. You. Are. Amazing. People love you. There's nothing about you that people don't like. Dominic is no exception. Stop fucking hiding. Take this and run with it. Have fun with someone. If it still ends after you tried, I'll eat a pint of ice cream with you while we watch The Fox and the Hound for the zillionth time, and I'll cry with you." He sucks in a breath.

"But I can't stand here any longer and try to support you if you can't even see how wonderful you are."

"Wow, uh okay. I'm not really sure how to take that last part. Are you still my friend?"

Travis barrels into me, his giant hug squishing the air out of my lungs with an oomph. "Of course I'm still our friend, you nincompoop. But I'm not listening to you talk bad about yourself anymore." He eases his grip. "Just follow your heart, Mic. He's a good one." He stabs me in the chest with his finger. "Let the hope win, just for once, okay?"

"That's the problem Trav. I don't trust my heart. It never steers me right."

He sighs, slumping his shoulders in defeat. "It's going to get it right some day. Either way, I'll be here. No matter what I say." He picks up the spilled pens. "You deserve it just as much as anyone else, Micha. Love yourself like everyone else loves you."

"Thanks Trav. For everything." I hug him quick again before he leaves.

Travis returns to the clinic, and I throw myself into my work, trying to calm my mind and all its racing thoughts. When I break for lunch, I grab my pack and head to the pond. It's always a great place to clear my head. The changing colours of the leaves is one of the prettiest sights this time of year.

I had shoved a granola bar into my pack when I left the house yesterday, intending to have a snack while I took a walk. It's what I used to do all the time to get Maggie out of the kennel runs. Melancholy settles over me as I come to terms with the fact I'll be walking on my own from now on. When I reach into my pack, my hand finds a paper lunch bag that I most definitely didn't put there.

I take it out with confusion and look inside. A tiny note sits on top of the contents.

Micha,

I didn't know if you had lunch plans today, but I wanted to make sure you had lunch just in case your day got away from you. Can't wait to see you again.

Dom

xo

My throat constricts as I inspect the items in the bag and wonder how the heck he snuck this in here without me knowing. But it gets better. The thoughtful bastard put notes on everything in the bag. As I read them, tears prick my eyes because this is the most thoughtful thing anyone has ever done and also the funniest.

A boloney sandwich - I'm sorry I didn't have ham, but my mom used to say I'm full of boloney, so I suppose that's true after all.

An apple - An apple a day keeps the doctor away. Unless I'm your doctor, in which case don't eat it then.

A fruit cup of pineapple chunks - I heard eating this makes you taste better, although I'm not sure how you can taste any better. You're already perfect the way you are.

A cherry chip cupcake - It may not be frosted but anything cherry makes me think of you.

I almost don't have the heart to eat of any it, but I tuck all the notes safely away. Even if things don't work out, I'll cherish those notes as long as I live. I eat the baloney sandwich and enjoy the fall sunshine, and I try really hard not to think about how I feel about Dominic.

That pesky seed of hope just had another growth spurt.

TWENTY-THREE

Dominic

THIS DAY CAN'T MOVE fast enough. I can't stop thinking about Micha. Everything from his impish smile, his hate for mornings, to the taste of his lips and the feel of him in my arms. All of it is on a constant loop today.

He thinks I was only up early because I'm a morning person. The truth is, I couldn't sleep, because all I wanted to do was kiss and touch and pull all those sexy sounds from him, over and over. I watched him sleep for so long I had to get up to do something. While it would've been great to wake up with sexy times, we both needed to work, and I didn't want to keep pushing him.

I know he took a giant step coming over last night. He's scared and I can't blame him. He's been through more than I have at a much younger age. But I know I'm ready to love someone again. Fiercely and with no reservations. I miss having that in my life and aside from Jenny, I've never felt this way before. While I never imagined being with anyone else but Jenny, Micha just fits. I thought part of my sleeplessness this morning was due to having someone else in my bed after all this time, but that wasn't it at all.

After I took my walk, it was clear. I wanted this man in my life. I wasn't feeling guilt for being with someone else. The world didn't implode and nothing bad happened after we spent the night together. It didn't even matter that I discovered I liked men at the age of thirty-two. I want to be happy, and Micha makes me happy on all planes. I don't need anything else.

I came up with the idea to make him a lunch while I was out walking Maggie at stupid o'clock. While I am a morning person, it's not usually so early I beat the sun out of bed. I made him a lunch, packed him cute notes and I'm dying to hear what he thinks when he finds it. I've never been overly romantic. Sure, I brought Jenny flowers a few times a year, or made her favourite breakfast some weekends, but Micha is different. I feel like he's never had anybody do anything nice for him just because they wanted to. That's a damn shame because he's beautiful inside and out.

"Hey Dom, someone's here to ask you about an urgent matter for catering? Can you talk?" Jade bursts into the back, knocking me from my thoughts.

Resting my cleaver on the cutting island, I remove my butcher garb. "Of course. Just tell them I'll be out in a few minutes."

When I'm presentable, I exit the back to find Jacob chatting with Jade like old friends.

"Jacob, hi. What can I do for you?"

His smile is warm and genuine. "I hope you can help is what. Do you have some time to talk? The shelter fundraiser hit a snag."

I frown and motion to the small table and chairs I have out front. He removes a very colour coded binder from his bag and flips open to the green tab. "Our caterer had to back out yesterday. We need food at the event since we've already sold tickets and based it on the cost with food. We floated an idea at our meeting to run it by you and see if it's something you might be able to help with."

"Isn't the event this weekend?"

He grimaces. "Yes, it's really short notice."

"What's the idea? Tell me more and I'll see if it's something we can do or not."

He inhales. "We're wondering if it's possible for you to do a mini charcuterie box of some sort? Small and portable. They could eat as they walk or take home. We need two hundred."

He slides a proposal to me. "This is our budget for the food portion of the night. Is it possible for you to crunch numbers and let me know if you can do something even close to this?"

"I'll work on it right now, and Jade will help. I'll see if we can come up with an answer before the day is out."

Relief washes over his face. "Thank you so much, Dominic. I know you're not committing, but even an answer today would be super helpful." He stands to leave. "Can you sit and help me out while you're here?"

He lowers himself back down. "Of course. Not sure with what, but I'll always help if I can."

"I want to surprise Micha tonight. What kind of food does he like best?"

Jacob beams. "Forgive me for being forward, but I think you're the perfect match for him. This makes me happy to hear."

My neck heats. "Um, thanks, I guess. He... makes me very happy. I know he was dealt a bad card with... the shark guy." I trail off, not knowing how much Jacob knows. "But I'm not like him. I'd never do that."

His eyebrows shoot up. "He told you already? Wow." He whispers. "Did he make you watch a shark show, too?"

"Uh, yes."

He's silent for a moment. "Dom, I'm going to tell you everything I know, and you're going to figure out how to use it to keep him. Because there's one thing about Micha, he doesn't believe in himself. For some reason, he thinks he's never worth the effort. He's going to fight you every step of the way."

"I get that impression. He said he has a hard time accepting when good things happen to him."

"Just don't give up. I think you can be the one to make him believe in himself."

Jacob spends fifteen minutes telling me about Micha and I soak it all up like a sponge. As much as I would love to learn all this information from Micha himself in my own time, I need some of it now.

After Jacob leaves, I give Jade instructions to pull up prices on items for Jacob's request, and I go next door for my lunch date with Owen. I need to bring him up to speed with my world.

OWEN SETS LUNCH DOWN for me, the same lunch I have three days a week with my best friend, and I'll never tire of it.

"You look like you're bursting to tell me something, Dom."

I spread a dollop of mayo across my sandwich before I take a bite and consider how to start this conversation. Ease my way into it or just put it all out there? I go with the second option. "Do you want the fifty bucks now or later?" I say with a grin.

"Shut up! You did it? You made a move?"

I nod as I chew. "You could say that, yes."

He laughs. "You don't need to tell me any details, Dom. I don't need to know any specifics, but I'm damn proud of you. How do you feel about it?"

"So fucking alive. Owen, I think I found someone to be with again. Is it weird it came out of nowhere and so fast?" I stare into my soup. "I went to visit Bonnie and Jack."

He lowers his voice. "What did they say?"

"Jack was out, but Bonnie was there." I pause to collect my thoughts as the feeling of being in the living room with Bonnie, surrounded by memories of Jenny floods back. "She was really happy to know I was moving on. She genuinely meant it."

"Do you feel better knowing that? That Bonnie's okay with it, I mean?"

"I didn't think I needed it, but when Bonnie urged me to be happy, an invisible weight lifted. I also wanted to make sure they knew. I didn't want them to be caught off guard to know Micha isn't a woman." I shrug. "It seemed like decent courtesy to tell them that."

Whether it was subconsciously my last step to moving on or not, I don't know. But I know I never want to go back to feeling how I used to. Drowning in a pool of silent loneliness was not my cup of tea.

I must have lapsed into silence, because Owen is waving his hand in front of my face. "I'm sorry, what?"

He smirks. "You've got it bad, my friend. And I couldn't be happier."

"I don't know if I have it bad, but I'm determined to win him over. I haven't dated anyone since I was seventeen. What should I do?"

Owen leans back in his chair, thoughtfully sipping his coffee. "What makes you think I'm such an expert? I'm still single, remember?"

"Then you have lots of practice dating."

He sighs. "Dom, I don't *date*. I fuck around. I have fun. I don't romance anyone because it's not my thing." He shrugs and stares out the window. My heart pangs for him. He's false bravado. He's just as lonely as I was until Micha found me. Owen will never admit it, but I know he's searching for someone.

I want to lighten the mood, but his attention has shifted to someone outside and I follow his gaze. Parker is friendly with a rough-looking biker type dude and if I didn't know better, he's trying to get Owen's attention. Parker paws at the man's chest right outside the front windows of The Bean, and I hear Owen growl. That's my cue to leave.

"Thanks for lunch, O. As always, it's amazing, but you obviously have things to take care of." I stand to clear my tray.

"What? No. Stay, Dom, there's nothing going on."

I raise my eyebrow. "I didn't say there was, but it's interesting you deny it, anyway."

"It's not what you think. I've been trying to tell Parker that guy is no good, but he won't listen. Now he's parading him outside like a prize pony."

I squeeze his shoulder as I walk by. "Uh, huh. When you want to talk about it, you know where to find me."

I deposit my tray at the bussing station and leave, nodding a hello to Parker as I walk by. I don't know what's going on, but Owen will tell me eventually. I may be waiting a long time, but he'll tell me. Until then, I have a surprise to plan.

TWENTY-FOUR

Micha

I LOCK THE DOOR behind my last client of the day and look at the clock. It's 4 P.M. and Dominic sent a message to meet him at 4:30 P.M. at the trailhead to the boardwalk around Dogwood Pond. It's only a walk, but it feels like a monumental event. Like something in our young dynamic is about to change. I don't know if I'm excited or scared out of my mind. I've been on pins and needles since I had my lunch filled with what I call love notes, and I'm lurching back and forth about how I want to proceed with this.

I could be very happy with Dominic. I know this and my heart knows this, but my blockhead can't seem to get on board with the plan. Travis is at his wit's end with me, that much I know. As great as Dominic has been, I'm waiting for the other shoe to drop. When does he do something that's cruel or decides he prefers women and goes back? I wouldn't be able to handle it if I grew accustomed to him and actually loved him, only to be pushed aside for a woman.

Despite my reservations, I'm excited to find out what he has planned for us tonight. I rush through my end of day tasks, feeling on edge the entire time. It's a funny thing when the anticipation of meeting and the urge to run in the other direction meet each other. As much as I don't want to be on the end of another *It's not you it's me* conversation, I want to be with him even more. Is it stupid? Maybe, but I'm going to take a tiny step and say it's hope taking root that for once, I'm going to have a happy ending.

Finishing the cleanup, I check myself in the mirror. Okay, this is it.

You've got this.

Gathering my pack, I lock up and begin the short walk to the trailhead. My stomach flip-flops as I walk down the trail path. The familiar scents of wet leaves and lake water hit my nostrils. When I arrive at the place Dom said to meet him, he's nowhere to be seen and my heart sinks. He doesn't like to be late. Has he changed his mind already? I'm about to start the walk home when I hear a familiar, deep voice.

"Okay, girl, you can do this for Micha. Be a good girl."

There's a rustling noise and I scan around, trying to find out where they are. It's not dark yet, there's still plenty of light, but I can't find them.

More rustling and Maggie pops over the grassy embankment followed closely by Dom. But Maggie has my full attention. She's carrying something in her mouth and proud as punch to do so. She stops in front of me, wagging furiously and plops the drool covered bag at my feet.

"Thank you, Maggie. Is this for me?" I scratch her ears hard just how she likes it and gingerly pick up the soggy paper bag. "You're a good girl. Thank you."

"I wasn't sure if she'd do it or not. She learns fast." He leans down and places a kiss at the corner of my mouth. His brown eyes sparkle. "I'm sorry it's soggy. She drools a lot, but what's inside should be okay."

I unfold the flap of the bag and peer inside. When I see what it is, I squeal and reach in, almost ripping out the bottom of the bag. "How did you know this is one of my favourite things, Dom?" It's a package of gummy bears, but not just any gummy bears. These come in unique tropical flavours, not the usual kind and are one of my guilty addictions. You can only get them at the specialty candy store in town, Your Sweetness.

Dom shrugs with a playful smile. "I'm not telling."

"Is this my surprise? My favourite gummy bears?"

Dom's sexy chuckle sends a shiver through me. "It's part of your surprise. A snack for our walk around the lake before dinner." He pauses and takes my hand. "If you'll have dinner with me, that is."

My mind has conveniently forgotten all the arguments I had earlier about being careful, and I blurt out the first thing. "Yes, I'd love to have dinner with you."

A slow smile fills his face. "Let's walk and talk first. You can eat your gummy bears."

Maggie leads us down the boardwalk, sniffing every bench or tree, smiling a hello to everyone walking by. I munch my bears like a toddler, happy with having dessert before supper. When I'm finished, I throw the bag in the next trashcan and Dominic immediately reaches for a hand and laces our fingers together as we walk. The seedling of hope hitches up a little farther.

"Did you take a lunch break today?"

"I did, yes. Turns out a thoughtful person packed me one without my knowing."

"Wow, that was really nice of them. They must really care. Did you like it?"

I recall the little Post-Its that marked each item in the bag and how he used a tiny piece of tape to secure them all to the right items, since the notes rarely stick too much. His squished, blocky printing to get all the words on the Post-It. He went through a lot of effort to do that. While I want to tease him about it, I can tell he's nervous about what I thought. I also loved it so hard, I don't want to make it a joke.

I stop walking and tug on his hand. "I loved it, Dom. Really. It was cute and very thoughtful." I stretch up on my toes to kiss his cheek. "Thank you for thinking of me like that."

His voice is gruff. "It was my pleasure. Truly."

We only do half the loop since darkness comes so early now that fall is here. I shiver with the loss of the sun and the sudden temperature dip.

"Are you cold, Micha? Do you have a sweater?"

In my haste to get here tonight, I left my jacket at work. "I'll be okay. We won't be out much longer."

Dominic has Maggie sit and shrugs out of his jean jacket. "Wear my coat until we get back home. I have long sleeves on. I'll be okay until we get to the truck."

"Dom, no. I'm not going to take your coat."

"Micha, take it. How does it look for me to be walking next to you shivering? I should take care of who I'm with." He takes no argument and forces his coat onto my shoulders while I limply accept.

"Thank you."

"Can I ask you something?"

"As long as it's not something personal, like wanting to know my weight. That's just rude." I snicker.

"No, you dork, it's not anything like that." He hesitates and we walk silently. I'm thinking he might have changed his mind about the question when he finally asks. "Does it bother you I used to be with a woman? Like, I've always been straight until now. Is that a problem for you?"

Well, he's full of surprises tonight and not just the gummy kind. How could he know that? Just from our conversation yesterday over the man who broke my heart? He certainly doesn't believe in beating around the bush.

"I'd be lying if I said it didn't bother me at all, Dom. It does. But bother isn't the right word. It's more like it makes me nervous."

We reach his truck and load Maggie, before buckling in ourselves. "Why does it make you nervous, though?"

I sigh. "You know that saying, fool me once shame on you, fool me twice shame on me? It's like that. I can excuse myself for one misstep, but I'm hesitant to make another." I pause when I notice him bite his lip. "You obviously have something planned. Let's focus on that, okay?"

With a nod, it's over and we begin the drive to his house. He's gone to great lengths to plan a surprise. I don't want to spoil it by having me get all weird and explaining why I can't just be happy for myself for once.

He parks in his driveway and turns to me. "Please don't get out yet. Stay here. I'll be right back."

Without waiting for my response, he enters the backyard and leaves me and Maggie waiting in the truck.

"Do you know what he's got up his sleeve, girl? I sure don't. I apologize if I adopted you to a weirdo. I swear, I thought he was the right one for you. Maybe even for both of us, really." Maggie wags and butts her head into my hand while I wonder what Dominic is up to.

Roughly five minutes pass before Dom exits from the front of the house. His face splits with a wide grin and he bounces down the front walk. When we first met, he was carrying an enormous burden I knew nothing about. He didn't smile, and he sure didn't bounce. Now his handsome smile comes easy and the sadness that was in his eyes has vanished. When he turns that look to me, well, it makes me feel like I'm on top of the world.

He stops at the truck and opens my door. "Thanks for waiting."

"Well, it's not like I had any other choice, is it?"

"Nope. All part of my plan." He winks, and that's all it takes for me to laugh along and allow my hope to grow.

After entering the front of the house, he leads me into the kitchen, and we sit at the island while he feeds Maggie.

"I don't know if you like to drink at all, but I have wine, beer and I'm a fan of rye and ginger ale myself. I can get you something if you'd like."

"I'm not a big drinker, but I'll have whatever you have tonight. So you don't drink alone and all that."

He laughs and my heart swells. "Fair enough." He mixes us each a drink and sits at the island with me.

"I thought you were feeding me tonight. Liquor before food might not be in either of our best interests. I have a low tolerance."

"I'm feeding you, don't worry." The wicked gleam in his eyes has me licking my lips, hoping dinner will consist of him. Or dessert. I'm not picky, but I suddenly have a very strong urge to taste him, all of him. I shift on my stool and, of course, he notices. "Something making you uncomfortable over there?"

He sips his drink while eyeing me over the top of his glass. "You're rather cocky tonight, aren't you?"

"Cocky. I like that word. What's it mean though, really?"

I snort. "You like the word cock?" I let it roll off my tongue, pausing at the end to make the k sound linger.

He licks his lips again and shifts on his stool. I smile, knowing he's enjoying this as much as I am. "Dom."

"Yeah?" His rough voice goes straight to my dick and I'm suddenly wondering if we'll even make it to dinner.

"Are you thinking about cocks right now?" I swirl the drink in my glass as I watch his eyes zero in on my lips. I lick the rim of the glass and he mimics my actions.

"What if I am?" His ice clinks as he sips his drink.

"I'd say it's a good thing as long as you're thinking of ours. Together." I know I am, but I don't think I have to say that out loud.

"Come here."

He spreads his legs and motions for me to walk over. I straddle one thigh, placing my hands on his shoulders. His hand slides up my leg while his lips find my throat.

"You make me lose control." He whispers in my ear.

"You make me want to give it to you." I breathe.

Dominic sucks down my neck while chilled fingers inch under the edge of my T-shirt, making me jump.

He chuckles. "Sorry. It's the ice in the glass."

Feeling bold, I take the closest drink and finish it while sucking an ice cube into my mouth. With the cube in my mouth, I press my lips to the base of his throat, next to that sexy dip I can't get enough of. I alternate swirling the cube, then my tongue across his skin, letting the melting water drip down his shirt. When my cube has melted, I lick up any water I can find on his skin.

His breathing is ragged, and his fingers grip my hips so tight, I'm sure there'll be marks. But I love it. He's losing control, but he's giving it to me instead of the other way around, and I'm drunk on it. Seeing his flushed face and the red marks on his skin from the ice is beyond sexy. My dick could break concrete right now. I want to taste all of him and be on my knees for this man. I brush my hand over the bulge in his jeans.

"Micha, this isn't what I had planned for tonight." His hand cups my face. "I mean, I'm not against it, but I have a surprise for you, and I don't want you to miss it."

I puff out a long, slow breath to settle my body. He planned a special evening. I can wait for this. When I open my eyes, he's staring back at me with an adoration I've never experienced. My heart both reaches towards for it and flies away from it.

Ding Dong

He taps my leg. "Stand up baby, that's the next surprise. Let me get it."

I stay in the kitchen and watch with amazement as he manages to walk with a massive erection to answer the door with no shame in the world. In record time, he returns to the kitchen with a take-out bag.

"Under trusted authority, I was told you have two favourite meals at the diner." He holds up the bag. "I got the one you eat when you're happy."

I can't contain my grin. "You got me chicken fingers and fries? Chef House's special fingers?"

"I sure did. Are you hungry?"

"I should probably eat. I had that drink pretty fast."

Dominic unpacks our dinner. He's eating chicken fingers and fries too. I don't know what it is about this meal, but chicken fingers always make me happy. Maybe it's because chickens don't have fingers. It's probably because Chef House makes the best batter for them. Either way, I can't help but smile when I eat them.

We have animated conversation and laughter while we eat. The previous sexual tension has dulled to a simmer, but it's ready to kick up again at a moment's notice. I've smiled more tonight than I have in a long time and our evening isn't even done.

"I'm so full. Thank you. That was the perfect dinner, Dom."

"I'm glad you liked it. But my actual surprise for you is out in the yard." He looks me up and down. "Are you comfortable wearing that for a while or would you rather change? You can wear a pair of my lounge pants if you want."

"Um, I wear this all day and it's fine. Unless you plan on having me in an awkward position?"

He wiggles his eyebrows. "I do, but not until later."

"Oh, that's promising. I should be okay like this for now."

He hands me an oversized sweatshirt. "It's chilly outside. You're going to need it."

I put his sweatshirt on, and it hangs to my knees, but it's snuggly, and I can smell his woodsy cologne. If we were ever apart, I'd wear this hoodie all day because it feels and smells like a hug from Dom.

"Ready?" He holds his hand out to me and I take it.

"As I'll ever be. Let's see the surprise."

He opens the patio door, and we step out into the cool fall air. It's dark enough now I need a moment to let my eyes adjust. Dom starts a propane fire bowl, flooding the area with light and warmth as I scan the yard to take it all in.

The giant hammock has been moved to the middle of the yard, and it looks like a large movie screen is set up in the distance. I look at Dom and find him watching me closely.

"Is this... is this an outdoor movie?"

He rubs his hand over his neck. "Do you like it?"

"How did you know I've always wanted to watch a movie under the stars?" I'm amazed he's gone through all this effort for me. I don't know what to say.

"I had a good source of information."

"Are we going to watch..." There's no way he has my movie. It's impossible.

His lips twitch. "We're going to watch what you always watch when you're happy. Or at least most of it, anyway."

"Monty Python and the Holy Grail? You actually got it to play tonight? Outside?"

"I did."

I'm ready to lose all the feelings on him because even though it wasn't his own idea, he asked my friends what I like and what I've always wanted in order to do this for me. Sure, he would have found out eventually the more time we spend together, but he wanted to pull out all the stops right away and I'm stunned.

How do you push away someone that's gone to such great lengths in a few short hours to make your day amazing? You don't, is the only answer and my hope seedling just flowered.

TWENTY-FIVE

Dominic

I WATCH MICHA'S EYES light up as he realizes what's about to happen. Yes, I asked Jacob, and even Travis, a few things about Micha's likes and dislikes, but I wanted to do something big for him right away. I'm only just getting to know him, but I want him to know I'm serious. We've already been intimate. It's not even me trying to get him into bed. I just want to show him I care and would do anything to make him happy. I think I may have succeeded.

"When did you even have time to do all this?"

"This afternoon. I left work and made it all happen."

His eyebrows raise. "You left work early to plan this? For me?"

I wrap my arms around his waist and bring him closer. "This is me, Micha. I do things for people to make them happy. More so for people I really care about." I drop a kiss on his forehead. "Don't be so shocked. I hope you'll get used to it."

"You're setting the bar high for me."

"Not at all. It doesn't take much to make me happy. If my partner is happy, I'm happy. The only thing you need to do is accept it. That's all I need."

He swallows hard and hugs me closer. I know this is new to him. He hasn't had people in his life like I have, and I wish I could have helped him sooner. Although if I met him earlier, we might not have ended up like this. I believe things happen for a reason. Maggie not being adopted, Micha being her caregiver, even Parker working with Owen to suggest I get a dog. It's all part of the master plan for my life, written in the stars long before I even entered the world.

I was fortunate to be raised in a loving family. All I ever knew was love and acceptance. It's hard for me to understand some things Micha has been through, but it's not hard to understand why he doesn't value his own existence. He's been made to feel lesser his whole life and I don't even want to think about what that asshole Robert did to him. If I have to work for years proving to him he's as fabulous as the personality he projects, I'll do it and smile the whole time.

He lifts his head from my chest, his doe eyes send my heart leaping. "You know I didn't miss how you called me partner. Yesterday you called me boyfriend too."

"I'm sorry. I may have overstepped. But when I want something, I just go for it."

His lips twitch. "I can see that. You've arranged for something I've always dreamed of in a few short hours. Go big or go home, right?"

I chuckle. "Something like that."

"Let's get this show started, then. I assume you want me in the hammock?"

"I want us both in the hammock."

"Is that your ploy to have me close? Such a schemer you are." He playfully smacks my chest.

"It was actually my plan to keep you warm. But if you don't want to snuggle up to me, I'll try not to be offended."

I make sure I have the remote for the projector and I settle myself in the hammock first. I motion Micha to step closer. "It's not going to tip. Don't be scared." He shuffles closer and, after much giggling, he settles next to me. I cover us with a fuzzy blanket I brought out and he burrows into me as I hit play and the opening sequence begins on the screen.

We stay like that for the entire movie. Laughing out loud together and Micha quoting most of it. I do admit; I watched him more than the movie itself. The way his face was in a constant state of smiling happiness. His animated expressions at his favourite parts of the movie and how he absently ran his hand over my chest as he watched. That was my favourite part. How comfortable he was laying here with me that he could touch me with no second thoughts. I don't want second thoughts. We should snap together without hesitation, like magnets. I want that all the time.

When the movie ends, we lay there under the stars, snuggled together and I find myself wondering when the last time I felt so complete and happy was? When Jenny was still healthy would be my guess. Which means no less than four years have passed since I felt this sense of peace. That's a long time to be at war with yourself and not enjoy the little things in life.

"Dom?"

"Yeah?"

Micha draws little circles on my chest under the blanket. "What are you thinking about? The movie's over."

I squeeze him tighter to me. My arm is going numb from being in this position for the whole movie, but I don't want to let him go. I love the feel of him tucked against me. "I was just looking up at the stars. It's such a clear night. Have you ever looked up into the night sky and wondered about it all?"

"About what, exactly? Like, are we the only life out there type thoughts, or why is it called the milky way thoughts?"

He giggles and moves up to rest his head on my chest. "About our purpose and why we're even on the earth to begin with. When I was a kid, I'd always look up at the stars and wonder if I was on earth as a human for a reason. Why wasn't I a human thousands of years ago when we didn't even know how to speak the language we do today? Why wasn't I a human during biblical times even? Why was I, this random kid in a small town, here at this time? Deep thoughts for a ten-year-old, probably because I watched too many documentaries growing up, but I still always wonder about these things when I look into the sky."

"Wow, that's rather deep. I wonder about a lot of things, but not that."

"What do you wonder about?"

He sighs, and his hand that was drawing on my chest stills. I miss it immediately. "Sometimes I wonder why I was even born at all." His voice is barely a whisper and my heart breaks. "I wonder why me. Why did I get given the life I have? Why am I made different? Why did I end up having to start over when I was only nineteen?"

"Those are deep thoughts, too. Can I say something, honestly?"

"I think we've reached the point where we can be honest with each other."

I'd been thinking of this a lot, and while we've spent time out here tonight, it came back to my mind again and I couldn't get it out of my head. Maybe if I voiced these thoughts, Micha would truly see how I feel about it all.

"I think you were put here so we could meet each other at the time we needed it the most. I don't believe in a god like the traditional religious way. I believe in karma, I suppose. At a time in my life when I needed someone to make me laugh and teach me to live again, I met you. While I have no doubt we would be friends if I met you at a different time, we're more than friends. You entered my life at the perfect time, when I needed you. The time when I wanted to love someone again, and I needed to be shown the way, you were there." I lift my head to kiss the top of his while he rests on my chest. "I think I'm here to show you why you're here now with me. To make you see you're not different, but special."

We lay in silence for several minutes. While I rub his back, I realize with great clarity I'm falling in love with Micha. Hard and fast. Something I didn't think was possible, but I can't deny the connection or my desire to deepen it. All the guilt I had been carrying about being with someone after Jenny has washed away, because I've realized sometimes people get multiple chances to love. I'm the lucky one. The universe has gifted me with another person to feed my soul and fill my life. It's not something I should feel guilt over, but something I should celebrate. It doesn't lessen my love for Jenny at all. It means I have more to give.

How lucky am I to experience this twice in a lifetime?

TWENTY-SIX

Micha

OUR LIGHT AND ANIMATED evening date has taken a serious turn as we gaze up at stars and turn to deeper thoughts. I can hear what Dom's saying, and it scares the crap out of me to understand it. I had every intention of keeping him at arms length and not letting him in, but that fell apart when I let him kiss me, and it exploded spectacularly when I let him put my dick in his mouth.

All day I'd been fighting that seed of hope. The hope that he'll be different, and I may have finally found the one to love me for who I am. It's a terrifying thought, to think I've been put on this earth specifically to help Dominic navigate his way to a second love. But I have to admit, nobody has made me want to give up the fight like he has. He says I make him lose control, but it's really me losing control. I've been managing my loneliness perfectly fine until he swept into my life like a handsome tornado, ripping out all my excuses and defenses with an ease I've never experienced.

Travis says I need to live and take a chance, and as scary as it is, he's right. I'd be a fool to not let Dominic in. Everything he's done for me the last few days has never been about him looking for something in return. It's been about him wanting to make me happy. All of it. He hasn't asked for a single thing and by doing so, he's succeeded in his mission to make me feel special.

I try to shift in the hammock without spilling us over. "These things are just as tricky to get out of as they are to get in."

"You want to get out now?"

"I'd like to be out of this and closer to you somewhere more solid, please."

He wiggles his legs out and plants his feet on the ground. "That can be arranged. Swing your legs over and stand up."

When we're both standing on firm ground and out from under the blanket, the chill hits me instantly. I take Dom by his hand and lead him into his own house, before turning and plastering myself to him.

He chuckles and pulls me closer. "I'm not complaining, but if you're cold, I could get you another blanket. Or make you hot chocolate or something." His hands glide up my back, strong, reassuring and comforting.

"I'd rather get naked and warm up that way." I rasp.

Dominic's eyes almost pop out of his head. "My intention tonight wasn't to get you naked." His lips brush over mine. "I wanted to make you happy and do something all for you."

"You did. No one has ever done anything like this for me before." I sneak my fingers under his shirt. "But I'd be extra happy if you'd get naked with me."

He snorts. "Extra happy? Is that what you meant before when you said you were extra with a capital E?"

"Hmm, maybe. But right now, it's with a capital D because that's what I want."

I fumble with the button on his jeans and kiss the sexy dip at the base of his throat before planting my lips on his. Our tongues dance as my hands roam everywhere.

"I want to taste you. I've been wanting you in my mouth since before dinner. Please don't say no."

I drop to my knees before he can protest and yank his pants to his thighs. Pressing my lips over his cotton covered cock, my mouth floods with saliva. God, I've never wanted something as bad as I want this. I raise my eyes to gauge how Dom is feeling and the face staring down at me draws a gasp from my lips. His hooded eyes project his desire and his wet lips part in anticipation. His expression oozes want and lust. I want to do it all right now, right here. No longer cold, I rip off my sweater and shirt. I'm on fire from head to toe for this kind and gentle man.

A man that gazes at stars and questions the universe, but still reasons the bad things we've experienced in our lives had a purpose. A single purpose for us to meet here and now, and to bring us together. I've never believed in fate because it was never good to me. But right now, I want to kiss that bitch and apologize to her. If fate is delivering me Dominic, she just moved to the top of my Christmas card list.

With shaking hands, I push his boxers down. His thick cock springs out and I dart my tongue out for a quick taste before taking him into my mouth. His bittersweet flavour floods my taste buds. Saliva pools in my mouth, making me choke while I try to swallow it along with Dominic's length.

His fingers work their way into my hair. "Micha... " Dominic's voice drips with pleasure, his head falls back with a moan. I swallow him deeper and feel my erection grow impossibly harder. I struggle to free it from my pants until Dom's deep voice has me still.

"Micha, stop." He pants and tugs on my hair until I release him with a pop.

"What is it? You don't like it?"

"Stand up, baby." He holds out his hands and I reluctantly stand.

"Let's take this to the bedroom. I love your spontaneity, but I'm not a boy scout today. There are things I want to do with you and it's all in the bedroom."

I snort. "You don't keep condoms and lube all over the house, then? That's just the kitchen? We can do it in the kitchen if you want."

"I'm not going to fuck you in the kitchen, Micha. At least not today, anyway."

My breath hitches. "You want to fuck me?"

His eyes soften as he holds my face in his hands. "That might have sounded too crass. I want to be inside you and make you come undone. To watch your face when you let go and moan my name. I don't want to come down your throat, at least not right now. I'm always up for that another time."

His eyes plead for me to agree and, like everything else he'll ask of me, I give it. We shuffle to his bedroom and collapse on the bed, still half dressed. Now that I've had the taste of him I so desperately wanted, we slow it back down and I'm glad he took control back.

We help each other out of our pants. Dom removes his shirt, and we finally find ourselves skin to skin, like I wanted to be out in the hammock. Much like he did to me the first night we were together, I want to explore every inch of this man and tell him with my hands and mouth how I feel.

Dominic has other plans though and hauls me on top of him. I grind my hips over his, pulling a moan from him, and his strong hands grip my ass to press me harder against him. He slides a finger through my crease, and I press back against it, welcoming his silent question.

"I'm not gonna hurt you, right?" He murmurs across my lips while pressing lightly against my hole.

"I'll tell you if you hurt me, but it'll be okay. I... use things." Good grief, I'm laying naked on the man, and I can't bring myself to say the word dildo.

He chuckles and presses harder, drawing a wanton moan from my lips. "Are you telling me you have sex toys? Something you use on yourself back here?" He presses harder and I whimper into his mouth. "That's a pretty hot image in my head, Micha. Would you show me sometime? Let me watch?" He bites into my neck, and I hear the lube cap pop before the cold fluid flows down my crack. I squirm around, searching desperately for the pressure at my entrance to return.

"If you want to watch I'd give you a show." I pant. "Maybe even ask for audience participation."

"Is that right? I may have to get a front row ticket for that, then."

His words are enough to distract me, and I feel two fingers breach the tight ring of muscle. "Oh, God." I thrust back onto his fingers.

"More Dom, so much more. Please." I moan into his ear.

"You're so fucking beautiful, Micha. I could do this all night. Do you even know how hot you are right now?"

I moan again as he gives me more. My body is on fire for this man. All of him. Not just for his cock to be inside me, but for his thoughtfulness, his love he has to give, his goddamn smile that breaks me every time it's flashed my way.

I sit up to gaze in his eyes. Those soulful brown eyes. "Dom... I haven't been with anyone for over two years. I get tested every year and I'm clear." My voice is ragged and gravelly.

His soft lips brush mine. "I've only ever been with one person in my life. I trust you."

"I want to ride you. Bare." A shudder passes through his body.

"Fuck, yes." He rasps and smashes his mouth on mine.

I reach for the lube bottle and slick his cock, taking the time to jerk him slow and watch his eyes roll back. "Why does it always feel better when someone else does it?"

I chuckle. "If you think that's good, wait until you're buried inside me. Balls deep, Dom. You can watch me ride you and know I do this by myself sometimes." I lower myself onto his cock that feels impossibly larger now that it's not in my hand. He's big, but I can take him. Even if I couldn't, I'd make it work because I can't tear my eyes away from his face right now.

His face is flushed, and a sheen of sweat covers his chest. Hickeys are already popping along his neck and the sight of them compels me to take more of him, to claim him even more than hickeys do. An external marking outside has nothing on what's about to go down on the inside. I lower myself bit by bit, until he's buried, just like I promised.

I lean down to kiss him. "You, okay?"

His fingers bite into my hips as he kisses me back. Breathless, passionate, and wanting. "I've never been better."

I rock slowly, relishing the feel of him filling me. I shift and increase my speed. "Fuck, Micha. I won't last long if you go that fast." He bites out a curse as he looks between us.

"It's okay, Dom. I don't want you to hold back. Give me all of you."

I find the right angle for him to hit the sweet spot and I progress from low strung, to taut wire, to snap in an instant. "Oh, shit." I pant. "I'm gonna come, Dom."

And I do. It's the most epic orgasm, even tops our cupcake sex. Cum spurts all the way up his neck. "Dom... " I collapse against him, utterly spent while he thrusts into me.

"Fuck, Micha." Dom empties into me with a shout so loud it might reach the neighbours. I take his face in my hands, kissing him over and over as he shudders and shakes until he finally stills.

Our ragged breathing is the only sound as I ease his softening cock out and lay myself next to him. What a turn of events this night has been. I started today thinking I'd need to politely decline his invitation and take a step back to preserve my heart. Now I'm laying next to him covered in sweat and cum, trying to catch my breath after we just had mind blowing, bareback sex.

I think I've just sealed my fate because I can't resist this man any longer. Why did I even want to in the first place?

Sometimes I can be as thick as a brick wall. No good can come out of denying what we have building. Here goes nothing. I'm jumping off the end of the dock and I'm not even going to hold my nose.

Dom opens his eyes to find me propped up watching him. "Are you okay? Did I hurt you?" His hand caresses my cheek.

"I couldn't be better." I place a kiss on his nose. "You didn't hurt me. I would've said something."

"I had no idea you'd be such a filthy talker. Where did you pick that up?"

I laugh, running a finger through a rope of cum drying on his chest. "You must bring it out of me." I paint his lip with my spunk, and he draws my finger into his mouth, sucking the rest off before licking his lips.

"I'll never get enough of your taste."

Dominic rolls and pins me underneath him, pressing all the stickiness against me. "Will you stay again tonight? I promise I won't get up so early and have you wake up without me." He sucks my earlobe, sending a jolt through my body. "Hmm, is that a good spot, baby? Did I just find out another thing you like?"

"If you keep doing that, you'll find out." I can already feel my cock coming back to life. "Do you have what it takes to keep up with me, old man?"

"Who are you calling old? I only have eight years on you." He grinds his hips and I'm pleased to discover I'm not the only one looking to go for another round.

"Dom?"

He rests his forehead on mine. "Micha?"

I swallow hard. "I'd love to spend the night with you." Truth be told, I don't think I can ever leave now.

And I do spend the night, but I don't sleep much. We wake each other up over and over, finding something new and different to drive each other wild. I can't get enough of him.

When I fall asleep finally, wrapped in his arms, I know it's where I need to be. All the walls have been torn down and hope has taken root alongside something new.

I'm falling in love.

TWENTY-SEVEN

Dominic

WAKING UP WITH MICHA this morning is what I was missing in my life. It feels like I've come full circle and out of my grief, I've found a reason to want to keep going every day. A bright, effervescent, sexy as hell reason. With his playful gleam in his eyes and root beer tasting lips, I'm gone. Totally, completely gone.

I can't even wrap my mind around the sex. Mind blowing, hot as hell sex, and we've only just begun down that road of discovery. I let him sleep late this morning, since I know he's not a morning person now. I didn't leave the bed until he was awake and knew I was there.

He's curled up against me, like a tiny teddy bear, arm flung across my chest and a leg over mine. I have to move him to get my day started, and I really don't want to. Kissing his temple, I peel his arm away. "Baby, I need to get up. I'll wake you a little later."

"What time is it?" He mumbles, reaching for my hand blindly.

"It's still early, but I need to let Maggie out and get ready. Sleep, I'll wake you when it's time."

He squeezes my hand with a muffled "Okay." He's back to sleep instantly.

I throw on a pair of sweatpants and a t-shirt and Maggie trots after me down the hall. I clip on her leash, grab a jacket, and we start our now morning ritual of walking around the neighbourhood. My breath clouds in the cool air as Maggie smiles and wags as we walk to the end of our street and stop at the dead end to admire the view. It's while I'm there I watch the trucks delivering the tent for the shelter's Fall Fling fundraiser happening in a few days time.

I created a charcuterie box within Jacob's budget, so he was thrilled. Well, it was slightly more than what he had proposed but I didn't tell him that. It's my honour to help and I consider it part of the donation. Jade will help me assemble them with the assistance of a few other volunteers and we'll get them delivered in time for the event. An event I'm looking forward to attending with Micha. He tells me the few he's helped with since coming here have been a lot of fun. Since it's part of who he is and it's a big thing for the community, I'm all in to attend now that I have someone to enjoy it with.

Maggie does her business and I clean up after her. Thankfully, there's a garbage can where she likes to stop. I thought there was nothing worse than having to clean up warm dog crap. I was wrong. Worse is carrying said crap several blocks because there's nowhere to put it. I learned my lesson early, changed the route and now we're golden.

We cross over a short walking path behind some houses and pop out a few streets over. As we walk down that street, there's a lot more traffic than usual for this hour. All the cars are turning into the same house and as I get closer, I see why. It's the Larkman residence, one of the largest homes on the hill with a coveted property that leads to the water. All the vehicles must be Austin and Logan arriving for the festival with their friends. As we approach the driveway, voices carry in the morning air and I can't contain my chuckle.

"Oz, the cats are fine. It's only a weekend and we've barely left. Jordan doesn't need you to send another video message for them to watch."

"I know, baby, but what if they forget who I am while I'm gone? I'd be crushed."

"You're unforgettable for both man and beast alike, trust me."

I laugh, perhaps too loudly, and they both turn to see me passing by.

"Sorry, I wasn't eavesdropping. It's just really quiet and your voices carry. I heard you before I even got here." I wave and keep walking. "Enjoy your morning fellas."

"Wait!" Austin stalks forward, clad in his New York Mafia sweatpants and jacket. He stops at Maggie and crouches down. "Is this Maggie?"

My eyebrows shoot up. "Uh, yeah. Why?"

He grins. "Did you adopt her?"

"I hope so or I'm going to be in trouble having a dog that's not mine." I stick out my hand. "Dominic Morenzo, nice to meet you."

Logan joins our party, sliding an arm around Austin's waist and offering his hand as well. "I'm Logan Larkman. This is my husband, Austin Maloney. You're the guy that owns Wild Baloney then, aren't you?"

I shouldn't be surprised these two know all about me. With Austin's brother Jacob running the shelters, I'm sure he keeps them in the loop frequently. "That would be me."

Austin continues to pet Maggie, a kid in a candy store look on his face as he lavishes attention on her, and she laps it up. The dog is an attention whore. "We have two cats, but I love dogs."

Logan sighs. "We can't have a dog. You know that, babe."

"I know." He pouts and stands up.

"I should let you guys get on with your visit and I'll see you at the festival. Nice to meet you." I wave and turn to leave, but Austin stops me again.

"Dominic?" I turn to face him. "Be careful with Micha. He loves this dog, and we love him like one of our own." He sticks his hands in his pants pockets with a blank look on his face.

I can only imagine what he's been told about me so far to even know I'm with Micha. His message is clear though, hurt Micha, and he hurts me. Got it.

"He's safe with me. Enjoy your day fellas." With another nod, I get back to our morning route.

"That was a bit awkward wasn't it, Mags? I wonder how many other people will threaten me to not hurt Micha?" Maggie doesn't answer, just smiles and wags while she trots beside me, happy as a clam to be out walking. Now I'm talking to dogs like Micha. Speaking of, it's time to get back and finish the morning so we aren't late for work.

MUCH TO MY SURPRISE, when Maggie and I arrive back at the house, Micha is already awake and making coffee. Maggie runs up to him before sloshing her water dish all over and I stand in the doorway, dumbstruck he's even out of bed, let alone showered and making coffee.

"Did I do something wrong? Why are you looking like that?" Micha pauses at the coffee machine and worry creases his brow.

"I wasn't expecting you to be awake. Just a little off guard, I guess."

I walk over and plant a kiss on his lips. "Can't say I don't like it."

He smirks. "Well, the problem with me staying last night was I didn't bring any extra clothes. I found a pair of your lounge pants." He hitches up the waist with a grin. "We'll have to swing by my place this morning though, so I can get clean ones."

He's both adorable and comical. He already showered and has his hair pulled back, but he's wearing a pair of my pants, which are far too big. The legs are rolled up several times, so he doesn't trip and he's folded the waistband over twice as well. Like a child playing dress up with their parent's clothing, it's cute as hell.

He's not wearing a shirt and now in the daylight, I notice how rough we were and the bruises from my mouth over his upper body. I trace a finger over one spot on his shoulder, which is clearly a bite. I remember doing it because he egged me on that round when he was on his hands and knees. It was raw and animalistic. "Did I hurt you? They could identify my body with this dental impression." I place a tender kiss on the spot and gather him into my arms.

"No, Dom, I wanted it and I liked it. I'd let you know." He pushes away and gestures to the counter where he has breakfast items ready. "Now go do your routine and I'll make breakfast. It's the least I can do since you did it for me last time."

With a peck on my cheek, he shoos me out of the kitchen, and I go off to do exactly what he asked me to with a smile on my face. When's the last time I've been this happy just to wake up and go to work? Fuck, when's the last time I've ever felt this light and happy about anything?

I take a shower and root out clean clothes. If Micha needs to stop at home first, we have to leave soon. I know Jade will open on time for me. I can afford to be a little late if needed. Micha will need to get to his shop on time, so his day doesn't go sideways right off the bat. I don't want him having a bad day if I can help it.

Padding up the hallway, I pull up short outside the kitchen when I hear Micha once again having a discussion with a dog. A smile forms on my face before I hear the full conversation and I pause.

"I think I made your dad forget to feed you when he came in, didn't I?" Maggie stomps and pants, her sign of agreement she's lacking in the food department.

"Okay, miss thang. Let me get it for you." I hear him rustling in the food bag and the kibble plinking in the bowl as Maggie amps up her excitement. "I'm sorry you had to wait so long for your breakfast. You must be starving." The thunk of the bowl hits the floor, followed by Maggie's hearty crunching. "Next time I'll make sure you get fed first, okay? I won't let his shameless sexiness distract me every time I'm here. What kind of co-dad would I be if I did that, huh?" More crunching and smacking from Maggie.

I round the corner and find Micha has made semi burnt toast and questionable scrambled eggs. "You made breakfast."

"As you can tell, I'm no cook, but I know we're short on time. Hope you need some charcoal in your diet."

I snort laugh and sit with my plate at the island. "Did my shameless sexiness distract you from cooking, too?"

He mock gasps. "You were eavesdropping on me again. Rude."

"Sorry, I'm not used to you always having conversations with animals yet." I lean over and kiss his cheek. "I will always appreciate whatever you make for me." I slather the toast with peanut butter. "Even if it's blackened so much I wonder if you were trying to make an offering to the gods."

He sniffs. "Are you mocking my breakfast effort now?" He takes a bite of his toast and grimaces. "Fuck, never mind, it's horrible. Don't eat it. Can I buy you a muffin at The Screaming Bean instead?"

I push away from the island. "Deal. I'll clean up and you go get your things. We'll drop by your place first."

I scrape his attempt at breakfast into the compost bin with a smile on my face. If it means he spends more nights here, I don't mind a little wasted breakfast.

TWENTY-EIGHT

Micha

Dominic trails behind as I rush into my apartment. "I'll change and see if Tux needs anything before we go. I'll be fast."

I bounce down the stairs, and Dom follows. Tux meows and runs after me. "Oh handsome, I'm so sorry I haven't been here for you. I'll get you a special treat tonight." I kiss Tux on the head and sit him in front of his dish which I heap full of wet cat food. Guilt feeding has begun.

"I'm so horrible. I didn't even think of him last night."

"Hey, don't feel bad about it. He's okay." Dominic hugs me, but I feel like I've betrayed my trusty companion.

I rush into my room and empty my backpack, adding more laundry to the growing pile. I really need to get that done soon. As I yank open my dresser drawers, it's going to need to be today, because I'm down to my last pair of clean boxers.

I'm not one of those guys that does the whole commando thing. I need to have my jewels snugged away, thank you. Zippers are dick vampires and I'm not willing to take that chance. I'll have to take a break and stay home to do the laundry tonight. Which works because I can ease my guilt by staying with Tux at the same time. Talk about a win-win decision.

I throw on a pair of jeans and a clean t-shirt, my usual attire, and check my reflection in the mirror. I apply black eyeliner today instead of the purple, and when I'm satisfied, I step back into my living room and find Dominic... not there. Frowning, I listen and follow the voices upstairs where it sounds like he's talking to Roberta. I grab my things to join them as Tux races up ahead of me.

"There's my boys!" Roberta smiles and sweeps up Tux. Dominic stands from the table where he and Roberta were sitting.

"Are you ready to go?"

"What were you two chatting about so early in the morning?" I wag my finger between them.

"Dom was just asking how I was and if I needed any help around the yard. If I minded him bringing you home this early in the morning."

I snort. "You're up at the crack of dawn, woman. Me coming home after 7 A.M. will not disturb you in the slightest."

"You're right, but it's still a nice gesture to ask me that." She sets Tux down and takes her coffee cup to the living room.

"Have a good day, my boy. We'll catch up soon." She winks and disappears around the corner.

"I'm ready to go. Even have time to buy you breakfast."

"Ah yes, you promised me a muffin. Let's get going so you have time to eat it before you're elbow deep in dog fuzz." He pecks me on the lips and together we leave the house for The Screaming Bean.

Dominic reaches over to take my hand while he drives us the short distance to his shop. "Do you have any plans for lunch today?"

"I don't. Unless someone snuck a secret lunch into my bag again, I have no plans."

He aims a goofy grin my way and strokes my knuckles. "Would you like to have lunch with me and Owen at The Screaming Bean today? I'd love for you to spend some time with him. He's my best friend."

Full speed to meet the best friend. Okay, I can handle this. I've already decided I'm going to do anything Dominic ever asks me to, and he may not know it yet, but I handed him my heart on a platter. What's a lunch date with his best friend?

"I'd love to. I can be done by 1 P.M. Does that work for you?"

"It's perfect." He brings my hand to his lips. "Just like you."

My cheeks flush and I drop my head. He could charm the habit off a nun this guy.

He pulls into his parking spot in the shared lot between his and Owen's building. Together we enter The Bean, and the cute blonde server from the first time we were here together greets Dominic.

"Hi Dom! The usual this morning?"

"Hi Paige, almost. The usual coffee and one of the giant banana muffins, please." He pulls me forward. "And whatever this beautiful one wants."

My cheeks burn for the second time this morning. I wasn't expecting him to be so open with affection. I'm not complaining, but it's a pleasant surprise. Another sign, if I needed anymore, that it's right to allow the hope to bloom with this one.

"Uh, I'll have the same please, Paige."

I pull my wallet from my backpack to pay and Dominic steps aside, but not before he whispers in my ear. "Do you mind if I kiss you in public?"

My shaking hands barely control the debit card to pay as I feel his hands on my hips from behind. I turn my head to meet his gaze. "Not even a little."

With his hands on my hips, I tilt my head back and let him kiss me. At the front counter of the busy coffee shop. Is this my life?

A throat clears and Paige has our order ready. "Here you go, fellas. Have a great day."

"Can you let Owen know Micha will join us for lunch today?"

She assures Dom she will, and we leave, each of us with a muffin bag and a coffee in our hands.

"I'll meet you here for lunch, then. If I'm late or anything goes off schedule, I'll send you a text."

With another kiss, this one a little more X-rated. I leave Dom at his shop and walk to my own just down the next street.

When I open the door to Fuzzy's, I curse. As soon as I enter, I remember I have plans to help set up for the Fall Fling this afternoon. I only have a half day booked and then I'm setting up displays at the animal shelter and preparing for Friday's special meet and greet for VIP ticket holders. I can't believe I forgot.

I pull out my phone and swipe to Dominic's contact and call.

"Miss me already, Micha?" His soft laugh warms my heart.

"I do, but I have bad news." I inhale. "I completely forgot I'm helping set up the animal shelter for the fundraiser today. I only have a half day booked and I'm heading straight there after. I'm so sorry, I can't do lunch today."

"Don't be sorry. I'll miss you, but it's okay. Call me tonight?"

"I will, I'm so sorry, Dom. I was looking forward to properly meeting Owen."

"Lots of time for that, baby. Have a good day."

M Y MORNING FLIES BY and I'm rushing to get over to the shelter for first, the lunch Jacob promised me, and second, to get started on the work that needs doing. When I enter the animal shelter, the aroma of fresh baked pizza hits my nose and my stomach growls. All the other shelter volunteers are here, and we hope to make quick work of the open house set up. I ditch my pack under the reception desk and immediately wolf a slice of pizza.

"Did you stop to chew, even?"

"I'm so hungry. No time to chew, Jake."

He smirks. "You're not usually a big lunch eater. Did you work up an appetite or something? You know, lots of activity happening?" He wiggles his eyebrows suggestively and motions with his head to follow him to the back. I snag a root beer from the table and follow him. He leads me into the laundry room and closes the door behind us.

"Spill it."

I eye Jacob. "About what?" I know damn well what he's fishing for, but I want him to say it.

"Seriously Mic? You come in here starving for lunch, practically glowing, and you're not going to fill me in?"

"Oh please, says Mr.- I'm- fucking- a -hockey- player, but won't breathe a word of it to anybody."

He exhales and knows I have him. "If that's the way you want to be. I get it."

We stare at each other until I crack. It's Jake, after all, and the closest thing I have to a brother. If he's keeping a secret, he has a reason to, and I'll respect that. "Was it you who told him about my favourite movie?"

"No way! He did it? Did you watch it outside?" He sighs, like a love-struck teenager mooning over a movie star crush.

"We did." I swallow a lump as I think of how special last night was. "It was the most heartfelt thing anyone has ever done for me. It was perfect."

Jake hugs me and I clutch onto him, not letting go. Much like I did the first night we met, and he helped me settle in here. "I'm happy for you, Micha. Are you okay?"

"I'm scared shitless." I laugh and release him, swiping at my eyes. "It's been fast, but he knows what he wants. He's made that clear."

"What does he want?"

"Me. All of me." I shake my head, still in disbelief. Jake's kind eyes watch me. "I'm falling for him, Jake. It's really hard not to want to be with him."

He smiles. "So be with him. Problem solved."

"I'm going to try. Trav already told me he'll pick me up if it ends in flames, but Carl was right." Jake furrows his eyebrows. "You know the dog that told me to just go for the Poodle?"

"Oh, for fuck's sake, Micha, you and your bloody dog conversations." He turns to open the door and we head back to organize the volunteers as I laugh at Jake's response.

This afternoon's job is to clean the animal shelter as spotless as possible, set up information on adoptions and have a table with spay and neuter information. There also needs to be a table accepting donations and filling in ballots.

Everyone that passes through and makes a donation gets a ballot for signed memorabilia from Austin and Logan. All those items need to be displayed. We also need to make goodie bags for the kids and packages with pet items for anyone with pets. This part of the Fall Fling is time consuming because it lasts for two days instead of just one. Everyone wants to see all the kittens too, so there needs to be traffic control and a tour schedule in place. It's a lot of work, but one I'm more than happy to help with.

Jake and I split everyone into groups, and we divide and conquer. I'm in the lobby rearranging our picture wall and dusting everything from top to bottom before I set up our donation table and display. The knock on the door has me squeak in surprise. I place my cleaning supplies on the table and find a woman outside the door.

"I'm sorry we're closed today to prepare for the weekend's open house. Did you have an emergency?"

"Oh, I'm so sorry. I just wanted to know if you still had the black lab for adoption."

"No, I'm sorry she finally found a home." I start to close the door, but her next words rock my entire world.

"That's wonderful news! My boyfriend was supposed to come and look at her. I've been out of town. He must have adopted her as a surprise."

I paste a fake smile on my face and ignore the rapid churning in my gut. "What's your boyfriend's name?"

"Dominic, he loves dogs. You probably can't tell me if he adopted the dog, I get that." She squeals. "I can't wait to see her. I'm going to track him down and find out."

I slam the door harder than necessary and throw the lock back into place. This can't be happening. What are the odds she has a different boyfriend named Dominic? Pretty low since I know every person who's come through to try to adopt Maggie. Exactly one of them was named Dominic.

How could he do this? Did he not think I'd find out? I trusted him and I fell for every filthy lie out of his handsome face. I almost told him I loved him! This is why I should never let myself have hope.

I stumble to the chair behind the reception desk and collapse.

"Hey Mic, are you - " Jacob rushes over to me.

"Micha, what happened? Are you hurt?"

"I feel like I'm going to be sick."

"Oh, shit." He kicks a garbage can next to me. "I'll grab my keys and take you home. You okay for a bit while I do that?"

I nod and listen to his footsteps retreat as my heart breaks into a million tiny pieces.

TWENTY-NINE

Dominic

IT'S GETTING LATE, AND I still haven't heard from Micha. I spin my phone on the arm of my sofa and wonder if I should call him. I don't want to monopolize his time. He did say he wanted to spend time with Tux and feels guilty for not being home. I don't want to intrude on his alone time. That could be all this is.

Part of me feels itchy, like I should check on him. It's hard to explain, but after our connection the other night, it feels extremely odd he wouldn't call. I'm probably just overreacting, and he's caught up in the shelter preparations. He likes to throw himself into his tasks and shelter work is no exception. That's all this is.

Maggie stretches with a groan across the floor and I absently pet her with my socked foot. I have a baseball game playing on the TV, but I'm not even paying attention to it. My mind has been stuck on Micha all day, like it has been since I met him. I don't like sitting here at night without him, nor do I like the prospect of not waking up with him. Maggie sure helps when I come home every day to her happy, wagging tail. I love our nightly walks together, too. She's only a part of my puzzle, though. Micha is my last missing piece.

I wander into the kitchen and finish cleaning up the mess from my dinner. Last night, I almost told him I loved him. I know he's skittish about trusting people, but he was fine this morning. If that made him uncomfortable, he would have said something already. I'm sure of it. Jesus, the man told me he fucked himself with toys for crying out loud. I'm pretty sure he'd tell me if I was being too overbearing. Wouldn't he?

I tap my leg and call Maggie. "Let's get to bed, girl. Doesn't look like we have company tonight."

I flip off the TV and Maggie trots to the bedroom with me, curling up on her bed with a groan. I slip under the covers and lay on my side, staring at the spot Micha was in only this morning. The sheets still smell like him, and it makes me feel less lonely tonight.

I pull his pillow over and hug it to me. Tomorrow night he'll be here. I can wait until then.

IT'S FRIDAY BEFORE THE Fall Fling and I arrive at work as I normally do. Although a little less rested, since I couldn't sleep well. Jade has already started building the tiny boxes we need to fill for tomorrow's event. Today I have a lot of slicing to do so we can finish it.

I still haven't heard from Micha. I'm waiting until I know he's on his way to work before I check in. I settle into the shop and set up for the day, but before I start my work, I pull out my phone to call Micha. It rings and goes straight to voice mail. Frowning, I send him a text before placing it in my pocket and get to work. I'll try him again in a few hours.

My day gets busier than I expected, and lunchtime arrives before I know it. I keep my lunch date with Owen and make my way to The Bean, intending to keep it short and run over to the shelter to check on Micha and the volunteers. I know he had today off as well, and they were working on getting the youth shelter, Auslo's Loft, ready for the VIP signing event later this evening.

I wave at Owen, and he seems shocked to see me as I slide into our usual table.

"Dom, I didn't think you'd be here today."

I frown. "Why wouldn't I be?"

Owen's expression is blank. "Uh, no reason?" He drops his eyes and my pulse spikes. What the fuck is going on?

"Well, if I wasn't coming, I would've told you. But it's fine. I'll take something to go and then drop by the shelter."

"Do you think that's a good idea?"

I narrow my eyes. "Why wouldn't it be? What the hell is going on?"

He stands. "Follow me." He walks to the back, and I follow him into his office. He closes the door behind us and continues to stare at me.

"Jesus, Owen, tell me what the hell is going on. I'm freaking out that something happened to Micha and you're not telling me."

He sighs. "Micha was upset yesterday. Parker said Jacob took him home and he wouldn't talk to anyone. He barely helped get anything done."

"What!? Has anyone checked on him? Is he alone? He didn't answer his phone this morning when I called." I run my hands through my hair and move to leave, frantic to find out if Micha is okay. Owen blocks the door and places a hand on my chest.

"Dom. He doesn't want to see you."

His look of sadness for me makes me want to scream. I don't need anymore looks of sadness. I want Micha and I want to know what the hell happened.

"How do you know this? I didn't do anything. What the hell is he saying this for?"

"I'm just relaying what Parker told me this morning. He said Travis was with him last night, too. He's not alone."

A feeling I thought I was finally over comes roaring back. Grief and the pain of having lost yet another person I cared about. Not just cared. I loved him. That's the only reason I feel this way. I went and fell in love with him and now he's leaving because of a reason I'm not even aware. I swipe at my eyes. Was I going to cry? I don't need to cry anymore fucking tears. I've shed enough over people that have died. I don't need to cry for someone alive who wants nothing to do with me.

But that's my problem. I want desperately for him to have something to do with me. How do I find out what the hell happened in the span of less than twenty-four hours?

I need to get the fuck out of here.

Owen grabs my arm as I try to muscle around him. "Dom, take a bit to calm down. Don't fly off the handle."

I aim a withering look his way. "I don't need to calm down." I bite out. "I need to know why a man I care about very much suddenly walked away without a fucking word."

I rip the door open and fume out of The Bean and get in my truck. I don't know where I'm going yet, but I need to get some air. I need to calm down, but I also need to wrap my mind around what I just heard.

I END UP DRIVING to the town limits and aimlessly driving dirt roads until I pull over and scream until my throat is hoarse and throbbing. The anger has dissipated enough I can manage it, but I'm crushed. Utterly crushed. I fell in love, something I didn't think I would ever do again. I had hope. My life was about to take a great turn for the better and now... well, now it seems like it's been ripped away. Again.

And now I have to get back to the shop and finish the meat prep for a fundraiser Micha is supposed to help with. This is shaping up to be a fantastic weekend all around.

When I arrive back at the shop, Jade rips into me for not calling. "Dominic, where the hell have you been? Mrs. Morgansen was here for her order, but you hadn't cut the steaks yet. Jacob has called to confirm details twice and I need to take a piss!" She stomps her foot and whirls around to the back, where I'm assuming she's going to pee.

When Jade returns, she apologizes. "Sorry, Dom, I didn't know where you were, and I was by myself with people bitching at me. I shouldn't have taken it out on you."

"No, it's my fault. I should've called. I'm sorry Jade. Thanks for manning the fort."

"You okay, boss?" She cocks her head, no doubt noticing everything I'm trying to hide.

I sigh. "No, not really. But I will be. I'll get those steaks done right away for Susan and get back to cutting for the fundraiser."

I should've come back here instead of driving aimlessly. Slamming a hunk of meat with a very sharp knife is oddly satisfying when you're angry. I fill the steak order and let Jade know before returning to slicing for the charcuterie boxes. Donning my chain-mail gloves and setting my slice thickness, I cut slice, after endless slice, of prosciutto, Genoa salami and sopressata. The repetition of slicing and making piles of sliced meat is calming.

I'm so lost in my task, I don't hear Jade behind me. I jump and almost drop the salami on the floor.

"Jesus, Jade. You scared the shit out of me."

"I called your name twice, Dom."

"Oh, sorry. Guess I'm just focused on the task."

Jade shuffles her feet. "Dom, it's getting late. Do you want me to stay and help you longer?"

Checking the time, I startle. I've been back here for four hours and didn't even notice it. I survey what I have left to do. It's only a few hours more and the volunteers are helping assemble tomorrow.

"No, I can finish up, Jade. Thanks though. You should get home, enjoy the weekend."

She grabs her jacket and purse from the staff area and readies to leave. "Jade?"

"Yeah, Dom?"

"I'm sorry again for being an asshole today. I should've called."

She shrugs. "We all have bad days, Dom. It's okay. But if you need anything... call me."

After Jade leaves, I quickly clean up and decide I'll finish in the morning instead of staying late. Maggie needs to be let out, too.

At least I know she's not going anywhere.

THIRTY

Micha

J ACOB BRINGS ME HOME, but I don't say a word about what happened. He assumes I'm feeling sick from a flu, not from anything else. He helps me into bed and even leaves me a can of ginger ale by my bed with a bucket.

"Micha, I'll let Roberta know you're not well before I leave. But call me if you need to, okay? I'll be here."

He rubs my back and I curl into a ball under my blankets, wishing like hell today was a different day. Jacob lets himself out and once he's gone, I feel guilty lying to him about what happened. After I admitted to him earlier today I was falling for Dom, I felt too stupid telling Jacob what the woman at the door said.

It's going to come out eventually, but I don't want it to be today.

After curling under blankets for several hours and ignoring the entire world, I call Travis to come over. I hate needing to ask anyone for anything, but Travis will be here. When he arrives, he finds me in the same place Jacob left me.

"Hey, Mic. You okay?" His soft voice, full of love and concern, is all I need to tip me over the edge and make the tears flow. Hot tears of sadness and pain flow freely as I roll over to face my best friend.

"Oh, Micha. What happened?" I sit up to take the offered hug and try to breathe.

"We were wrong, Trav. It was a lie."

His hands smooth over my back. "Back up, Micha. You need to start at the beginning. What happened?"

I gulp in some air and wipe at my face. "Dominic. He lied. I knew I shouldn't have trusted him."

"About what, though?"

I sigh and reach for a dirty shirt on my bed to blow my nose into. I'm classy like that.

"I was in the lobby cleaning for the open house at the animal shelter. She knocked on the door and told me she was Dominic's girlfriend."

"Who?"

"I don't know!" I wail, throwing my hands in the air. "She asked if the black lab was adopted, and when I said yes, she said her boyfriend Dominic must have done it to surprise her." I sniffle again and fresh tears flow. I crawl back under the blankets and curl up as tiny as I can get. Travis pushes me over and crawls right in next to me, cuddling against my back.

"Micha, there has to be an explanation. You know I'm always on your side, but is there anyway you made a mistake? Maybe it's a misunderstanding?"

"She said she was his girlfriend and had been out of town, Trav. Pretty clear."

"Have you talked to him?"

"I can't yet. It's too hard." I clasp his hand and pull it around me, desperate for human comfort. "If it's really true, I can't fall apart in front of him. Trav... I'm in love with him." I whisper, swallowing hard. "I let my guard down. Now I have to pay the price."

Silence blankets us as I fold in on myself and fall asleep. It might not be the arms I want to hold me when I sleep, but I'll take the comfort while I can.

When I wake up, it's late evening and Travis has left. He left me a note saying to text him again if I need him. I'm not surprised he's gone. I left the shelter when they need all the hands they can get. Travis is probably doing double time to make up for me not being there. Propping myself up against the headboard, I stare at my phone. There's a missed call from Dominic and a text I missed.

My heart thumps. He sent this early morning, after I had the bomb drop on me. My thumb hovers over it as I battle with myself over reading or deleting it. Self preservation wins and I delete it without opening the message. I stare at the contact longer and make my final decision. I block Dominic in my phone and delete him.

With a heavy sigh, I drag myself out of bed and start a load of laundry. Since I'm home, I might as well be productive. Dragging my hamper down the hall, I sort everything out into the proper piles. I make a pass around my room, gathering up stray items, and I spy my backpack. I remove clothes from it I forgot about and add them to the pile.

After stuffing a load of darks in, I flop on the couch with my pack. Now is as good a time as any to clean it out. I should wash it. It's full of fur from the shop and Lord knows what else. As I empty the pockets and compartments, my hand closes around a stack of paper sticky notes. My breath hitches and I carefully pull out the notes in Dominic's scratchy block lettering.

I flip through them carefully and remember how I felt reading them for the first time. How special it made me feel he went through all this trouble to surprise me. How he cared enough to make sure I even had lunch. My fingers brush over the words as I recall our conversation that day. It meant so much to him to make me happy with a simple gesture. God, it was only two days ago. How did this go so bad so quickly?

I can't bear to throw them away. I at least have some power left in my brain to recognize the sweet memory for what it is. A memory. Maybe it was an empty gesture, but deep down, I know it wasn't. Why would he lie to me? That's what makes all this so much more confusing. Now that I've had the time to calm down, I can acknowledge it was a time in my life when someone made me feel good about me, like I was cared for. I'll try to hang on to the feeling and forget the rest. I place the notes in my bedside table and shut them away.

Meow

Tux has arrived for his dinner. I scoop him up and flop on the bed. He purrs and kneads my chest. A picture of happiness and carefree attitude only cats seem to possess. "Looks like I'll be home for a while, handsome. Just me and you against the world."

I scoop him food and sit on my couch, staring off at the wall, because I still don't know how to proceed. Tonight is the VIP event at Auslo's Loft, and I already begged forgiveness and ditched helping. Tomorrow is a much bigger event. Dominic will be there since he's the caterer. Unless I don't go at all, I won't be able to avoid him. I can't do that to Jacob and the others. I also don't want to. People get broken all the time and they don't wallow in their rooms forever.

I'll lick my wounds tonight, but tomorrow I'll put on my fabulous Micha face and get back to my life. I hope.

THIRTY-ONE

Dominic

WHEN I ARRIVE HOME, there's a car I don't recognize in my driveway. It's Travis. We exit our vehicles together and meet in the driveway. When the motion light turns on, I see his clenched jaw and flexing fists and I'm immediately on the defensive.

I nod. "Travis, what can I do for you this evening?"

He marches right up to me, toe to toe, and stares me down. A sneer curls his lips. "I trusted you." He spits out through a clenched jaw. His expression is one reserved for shit on the bottom of your favourite shoe. "Do you have any idea what you've done to my best friend? A man so kind, he hates killing spiders, for fuck's sake."

I bristle. "Actually, Travis, I don't know what I've done, because he won't answer my fucking calls." I puff out my chest so we actually touch, and the bastard doesn't even flinch. "You've got a lot of damn nerve sitting here on my property waiting to ambush me."

Travis steps back. "You hurt someone I care for deeply. I'm the one picking up the pieces because of you."

"And I'm not hurt, Travis? That's rich. I don't even know what the hell happened! Everyone has Micha guarded up in his ivory tower and I can't even find out what I did that was so damn bad he's no longer talking to me." I clench my fists. "He's not the only one with pieces to pick up here."

He scoffs. "As if you don't know what you did."

"I don't fucking know!" I roar and he flinches away. "I didn't hear from him last night and I couldn't reach him today. I found out there was a problem because somehow Owen knew about it, and he told me Micha didn't want to see me." My voice has raised high enough I'm going to draw the neighbours out but I'm spitting fire right now at the gall Travis has to come here and lay into me when I don't know the issue. I can't even defend myself against his accusations, which only ramps my anger higher.

He chews his lip, surveying me. He opens his mouth to say something but stops when another car pulls into the driveway.

"Jesus Christ, do people not warn you when they come over anymore?" I mutter. I groan even louder when Tara gets out of the car. I don't have the patience to deal with her right now.

"Dom!" She singsongs. "I'm so glad I finally caught up with you. I've been out of town and out of the loop." She pauses and acknowledges Travis.

"Hi. I'm Tara. Are you a friend of Dom's?"

"You could say that." He gestures to the bag she's carrying. "Are you spending the night?"

She doesn't even flinch at the implication in his tone. "Well, I always come prepared to spend the night." She winks and Travis blanches at her innuendo before staring at me with new fury in his eyes.

"Back up a minute, Tara." Travis turns to leave, but I grab him by the arm. "Wait. We aren't finished here."

"Is this your boy toy I heard about, Dom?" She peers at Travis with a renewed interest. I see her scheming look and it hits me. She has something to do with Micha's silence. "I mean, he's cute, but I thought it was just a rumor." She pats Travis on the arm. "It's okay. You can go. He made a mistake."

"What the hell is your game, Tara?"

"My game?" She titters an annoying laugh and pats her perfectly styled hair. "Baby, I was giving you space, but enough is enough. I heard you were holding hands with some guy and got a dog and all kinds of weird things. I came back as fast as I could." She moves to walk up to the house. "You obviously need me to step in. When Bonnie mentioned you adopted a dog, I rushed down there to see if you had already done it, but I was too late. You don't need a dirty dog in your house, you need a woman."

Travis has leaned back on his car with a new look on his face. Curiosity and, if I'm being hopeful, a smidge of understanding.

"You're not setting foot in my house, Tara."

"Dom, I know you're upset, but I'm doing what's best for you. It's what Jenny wanted."

Why did I never see this side of Tara before? Her perfect manicure and perfect hair and perfect outfit. Single and looking for the perfect man and house to park her perfect fucking Lexus at. Now she's using my dead wife's name to guilt me into... what I'm not quite sure, but I don't like the sounds of it.

"First, don't you dare talk to me about Jenny. Second, she's my dog, and she's not some kind of filthy, untrained animal. She brings me great happiness and I don't regret adopting her." I narrow my eyes. "Did you just say you were at the animal shelter?"

"Yes, I went first thing yesterday afternoon hoping it wasn't a done deal, but some blonde man with horrendous eye liner told me she was gone." She clucks her tongue. "Someone really needs to give him an application lesson."

The hair on the back of my neck stands up. "What did you say to him?" I seethe.

She waves her hand in the air, like it doesn't matter. "Gosh, I don't remember. Something like my friend Dominic adopted her. I don't remember, Dom. Now let's go inside."

She pats the bag she's carrying. "I brought you a casserole. Thought we could have dinner."

"Are you out of your fucking mind? Get in the car and drive far away from me." I grab her by the elbow and lead her to her car.

"Dom, what's gotten into you? This is just you grieving. You don't really want a man." She slides a manicured finger down my chest, and I barely resist the urge to gag. "Let me help you."

I'm shocked I've remained as calm as I have. But I place her casserole on the floor in the back and she finally gets into the car.

"Tara, you're not in touch with reality. Don't come back here. I let you help because you were Jenny's friend. Yes, I do want a man. If your little stunt has ruined everything with said man, I will never, ever forgive you." I inhale a steadying breath. "If you ever come back here, I don't think I'll remain this polite. You crossed too many lines."

Finally, her cool façade crumbles, and what I sensed lurking underneath emerges. Her lip curls in a snarl. "I won't be back, Dominic. Don't worry about that. If you want to suck dick for the rest of your life, be my guest. You're not worth the effort. I don't know what Jenny ever saw in you."

She slams her car door with another sneer and peels out of my driveway. I sag against my truck in disbelief. I knew something was off with her, but I didn't think it was anything as bad as sabotaging my life and being homophobic. Fuck, how am I going to repair this? Micha must think I have a secret girlfriend.

I curse. That's the one thing he was afraid of. This is what happened to him with Robert. He mentioned he was afraid of me changing my mind and wanting to go back to women. Now that's what he thinks has happened and he won't even talk to me. Jesus, if this was my run in with Tara, what did she say to him?

A throat clears, making me jump. I forgot Travis was here watching the whole thing.

"Uh, I'm sorry I doubted you, Dominic. She's something else."

I laugh, but it's hollow. "She's something all right."

I turn to walk up the pathway inside. I need to let Maggie out still, and I feel like my guts have spilled outside my body. Tara was a hidden crackerjack. Micha thinks I was playing him, and Travis saw the whole thing.

"Are you going to call Micha? Tell him what happened?"

Am I? He believed the worst in me without even giving me the benefit of the doubt. I didn't get a chance to explain anything. He just shut me out, and I suspect blocked my number since my calls go straight to voicemail with no option to actually leave a message. How many times might that happen as we go along in a relationship?

I run a hand down my face. "Travis, he won't take my calls, and I don't know. It's a lot to process here." I swallow hard and turn to face him. "If you're going to go back and tell him what you've witnessed, I can't stop you. Just make sure you add in how I'm disappointed in his lack of belief that I would never hurt him."

I enter the house and poor Maggie has been waiting at the door this whole time. I grab her leash, click it on, and head back out the front door for a long walk to clear my head. Travis is backing out of the driveway and I wave, but keep on walking.

Maggie knows the route and leads me along, rather than the other way around. As I trail behind her, the man holding the leash, my mind tries to reconcile the events of the day.

Night has definitely arrived and when Maggie pauses for a long sniff around, I stare up into the clear night sky filled with stars. Which brings me back to my thoughts of what's my purpose here? I thought it was to be here for Micha and he for me. Not just a thought, I believed it. With all my heart, I believed we were meeting each other at a time we both needed it most. We fit together. I've never been happier than with him.

Yes, it fucking hurts. He doubted me and ran as soon as happened to make him scared, but I can also understand why he did. I had a loving relationship with my high school sweetheart, and she died for reasons beyond my control. It ended with death. There was no deceit or questions about sexuality. It was a relationship that saw no major disruptions other than a fight about what colour to paint the spare room and whose family was hosting Christmas.

Micha doesn't know how genuine relationships work yet. He was manipulated and deceived from day one. He's only known betrayal. Not just by a lover, but his family too. Our paths couldn't be anymore different. Shouldn't I try to show him how good it can be? To share with him the joy of a partnership where one supports the other?

Maggie tugs me down our path and as we return home. I feed her and change her water dish before sitting in the darkened living room. I remember how great it felt having Micha snuggle into me and watch shark shows. How amazing it was to wake up with him and how cute it was when he tried to make breakfast and even burned the toast.

He tried to do something out of his comfort zone then. He needs to try again now.

THIRTY-TWO

Micha

I HAD THE SHITTIEST sleep of my life. Well, almost. The shittiest sleep was when I did actually sleep in a park on the ground. At least now I have a bed of my own and a roof over my head. No need to fight the alarm today. I've been awake since 4 A.M., staring at the ceiling and wondering if I stared hard enough at it, could it give me the answers to a happy life.

I've wallowed for a full day, but today is the day of the Fall Fling. Not only have I committed my time to it, but it means a great deal to me to give back to the place where I found a new life. I need to face the world, but most importantly, I have to face Dominic. He lives here. He's involved in his community and our paths will cross. He also adopted Maggie, and that's a whole other issue I need to cope with. My limit is one major crisis at a time, though.

Dominic is catering this event, and he's going to be there. Time to pull up my big boy pants and deal with it. I'd rather give cats flea baths all day than face my issues, though. Why don't they warn you about the traps of adulting?

With a deep sigh, I drag myself to the shower. I smell coffee upstairs and once I'm dressed I follow my nose. I don't need to be anywhere early today, looks like today is the day to enjoy coffee with Roberta.

"Hey momma Berta! Today is your lucky day. I'm up and moving and I can sit for that morning coffee."

She shuffles out of the living room, beaming a smile, but when she sees me, her smile vanishes. It's such a night and day shift in expressions that I look behind me to see if, I don't know, the ghost of Christmas past made an appearance or something. When it's clear there's no ghost behind me, I return my attention to Roberta and her face hasn't changed.

"Micha, what's wrong?" She passes a thumb under my eye, where there's dark circles no amount of makeup can hide. "You're not sleeping and there's no sparkle. Sit."

I take a seat at the kitchen table with my coffee and fail to meet her eyes. "I haven't been feeling well. I'm sure I'll be okay later."

"You don't have to lie to me. You can tell me anything you know."

I sigh and raise my eyes to meet hers. And that's when I see it. She's worried, and she loves me. I shouldn't lie to her.

She's never done me wrong. It's not fair for her to be kept in the dark.

"I got some bad news yesterday. Dominic lied to me. He has a girlfriend."

Her eyebrows almost touch the ceiling. "Are you sure, Micha? I've known Dominic his entire life. I changed his diapers. He's been nothing but honest and upstanding. There has to be a mistake."

"I thought so too, but I met her myself. Even told me Dominic was her boyfriend." I shake my head. "It's just another case of trusting the wrong person. This is why I prefer being around animals. They don't say or do stuff to break your heart."

Roberta drums her fingers on the table. "Did she tell you her name?"

"Nope, I didn't give her a chance to, actually."

"Hmm, and what did Dominic have to say for himself?" She sips her coffee and peers over the cup at me.

"Uh, I haven't spoken to him."

"Micha, you didn't even get his side of it? You owe him that much, you know." I bristle. "I don't owe him shit. He did exactly what I was afraid he would do. He lied, and I was just an experiment."

"Micha Jones."

Shit, she said my full name. My eyes widen as I snap my attention to her. "Roberta Handy." I joke, but she's not having any of our usual playful banter.

"Your puppy dog eyes and cheeky attitude aren't going to help you with me. You're an adult and you solve problems like an adult. You don't run and hide when stuff gets hard. Have I taught you nothing?" I want to respond, but she shushes me. "I've taught you plenty. I've taught you to give everyone a fair chance, have I not?"

"Yes."

"I've taught you to see the good before the bad, yes?"

"Yes." I hang my head.

"I've taught you, most importantly, to listen to your heart, Micha. Honestly, what is your heart saying?"

I stare into my coffee. She has a point, and I don't want to admit it, because it's way easier to live in my bubble and wallow. To cut all the ties now before shit gets too deep. Deep down, in the part of me where the hope was growing strong, it's bleeding a message I've been ignoring. I've been ignoring it because it's easier that way.

"My heart says to let him explain and that it can't possibly be true." I whisper and clutch my cup closer. "He's a great guy."

"Micha, why are you being such a blockhead right now? You were happy. Why would you not give him a chance to explain? If it's true, then go ahead and shut yourself in your room and watch The Fox and the Hound, while you cry yourself to sleep. But don't duck and run without an explanation. Last I checked, you're not a coward."

I tilt my chin up. "I'm not a coward. And leave The Fox and The Hound out of this. It's one of my favourite movies."

Why didn't I talk to Roberta first yesterday? Why didn't I listen to Travis? They both told me the same thing, to ask for an explanation, and I tucked my tail and hid. Even if I wanted to talk to Dom now, he's most likely written me off. He has to have figured out by now I blocked his number. He's not going to explain away everything and be all forgiving when I mistreated him, even if he deserved it. The bottom line is I sabotaged myself. I'd rather not know if I was wrong, and he has a valid explanation at this point.

"Listen, honey, you're gonna do what you want to. I can see it on your face. I'm not trying to sway you in either direction. I'm going to state the facts as I know them." She pauses to make sure she has my attention. "The Dominic Morenzo I know would never be that cold. It's not his nature. Never has been and never will be. I've never seen you as happy as you've been the past week. I can see you have your heart on a string." She stands up. "My advice to you is to make sure you want to cut it."

She pats my hand and goes back to the living room where she has the Saturday morning news and weather station on. I stare blankly at the screen and notice they're calling for an evening thunderstorm and some woman in the town over grew a thirteen-pound potato. Must be a slow news day.

I rinse my coffee cup and place it in the dishwasher before going back downstairs. I pull clean clothes from my fresh laundry stack and out of habit, have a change in my backpack even though I don't work at Fuzzy's today. I'm not due to help with anything for another hour, and I was on the list to be at Wild Baloney to help with the food. I want to get to Auslo's Loft and convince Jacob to switch me with someone. Dominic and I can't be in the same room right now. If I need to build my courage to ask him what happened, it's going to take me some time to get to that point. I can't build up my courage when he's staring me in the face.

THIRTY-THREE

Dominic

I WOKE UP EARLY because I could barely sleep. I couldn't stop thinking of my plan to get close to Micha and tell him I understand why he didn't believe me and I'm still here. I'm desperately hoping Travis has already told him what happened and Micha might call me first, but that's all it is. Hope he will call. I need to show him I'm here for him and I hope what I've come up with will be enough for him to trust me.

Since I'm not sleeping, Maggie and I had an earlier than usual walk. I'm counting on her to make my plan come together. Operation show Micha it's okay and I'm in love with him, needs to include my sidekick.

Owen was livid to hear what happened with Tara yesterday and has agreed to help me out with more enthusiasm than I expected. He roped Parker into helping him and the two of them will take the place serving at the Fling for me. It's not a wise business decision. I should represent my company, but I can't be tied up for that long if I have any hope of getting Micha to listen to me.

First things first, though. I need to get to the shop and finish what I didn't do yesterday. Jade will help me assemble, and Owen will take over from there. Now that I have that organized, I need to track down an accomplice, because I don't even know if Micha is going to the event at all now. He could be completely hiding from me and stay home. For my plan to work, I need him to be at the event. With the help of Parker, of all people, he gets me Travis's contact and I call him.

"Hello, Travis speaking."

"Uh, hey Travis. It's Dom. From Wild Baloney."

"Oh... hey."

"Listen, this is probably a weird request, and you can say no, but can you help me with Micha? I mean, you were there yesterday and if he doesn't want to talk to me after I have my say, I'd really appreciate you backing me up."

"You're going to talk to him?"

"Yeah, I have a plan to get him alone but I'm gonna need -"

"Yes! Whatever you need me for, I'll do it."

"You don't even know what I want yet." I can't deny his enthusiasm has eased the churning of my guts. Travis was my first step, and he's on board. As Micha's best friend, my hope that this plan will work is buoyed with his backing.

"I don't need to know anything except you're going after Micha. I'm in full support. He needs you."

"Um, thanks Travis. It makes me feel better knowing you support this."

"Dom, I didn't say anything to Micha yesterday. He knows nothing. I didn't want to interfere unless he was going to do something stupid. I was hoping you'd come around and see he's worth the fight."

A grin splits my face. "Oh, he's worth it. It took me awhile to understand where he was coming from, but I'm not going anywhere just yet."

"Good. What do you need from me?"

So I lay out my plans for Travis and what I need from him. He's like an eager beaver, agreeing to everything and squealing with delight. By the time I end the call, I'm feeling more confident this will work. But I've got a long day ahead of me.

I'VE WATCHED THE FESTIVITIES from the outside. I'm saddened the evening didn't play out like it was supposed to. Micha and I were going to man the food table, and I was going to promote the business with him next to me. I could introduce him to my regulars. Maybe I saw it as a celebration of us being a couple. Perhaps next year that can happen if my plan works.

I've been waiting at the shop for Owen and Parker to return crates and signage and give me an update if anything has changed on Micha. Pacing around the front of the shop, I swallow my anxiety. I know I've decided to go after him and now that I'm feeling a lessened sting; the nerves are kicking in. What if he already decided he doesn't want this? He might not be ready for it.

I release a long, slow breath. All I can do is say my piece and hope he's on board. If not, well, I don't know what I'll do if not. I'm not even going to think that way.

There's a knock on the door and Owen waves for me to let him in, while Parker rushes over to The Bean.

"How're you holding up? You look nervous." Owen drops his armful on the corner before facing me.

"I am nervous. I've never been in this position before."

"Dom, don't stress, okay?" He places his hands on my shoulders. "What will be, will be. But I'm confident Micha is going to come around. From what I've heard from Parker, he's had a tough life. This is going to help him see there are good things out there."

"I hope you're right. How did the food part go? Any complaints? Did people like it?"

His grin splits his face. "Everyone loved it! Huge hit! Don't be surprised if you have a crap load of orders for Thanksgiving and Christmas. All your info sheets were gone.

You done good, buddy." He slaps me on the shoulder before gazing out the window. We both watch as Parker shows up with my special request.

"Hey, Dom. I had to put the finishing touches on this, but I think it'll do the trick for you." He proudly places the box on the counter, and I don't miss the look shared between him and Owen.

The three of us leave the shop together. Owen and Parker leave me for the coffee shop, and I slide the white bakery box on the floor of the truck. It's time to go pick up Maggie and set the plan in motion.

Thirty-Four

Micha

IT WOULD DEFINITELY BE more exciting to be under the tent at the Fling, but I've stayed busy here at the animal shelter. I pack away our displays as the evening winds down. We've had steady traffic all day, but now with the party ramping up under the tent, it's time for me to shut this side of things down. Our donation bin is stuffed, and I'm thrilled the generous people of this community have opened their wallets yet again to help.

I haul the donation jar back to the safe and I secure all the autographed items in the back room and lock the door as well. I'm about to lock up the shelter and begin turning off lights when two of my favourite people burst through the door.

"Micha! There you are! We missed you. Come and give me some sugar." Logan holds out his arms for a hug, and I'm more than happy to take it. He releases me and gives me a once over. "Are you sure you don't want to model? You have the best cheek bones. Fresh Faces would eat you right up."

I laugh. "I'm sure. I don't think I'd like the spotlight on me."

Austin snorts. "Logan doesn't have that problem. Right, babe?" He squeezes his arm around Logan's waist and draws him closer for a sizzling kiss. My cheeks heat as I witness their overt display of affection. God, I want what they have someday. Austin releases Logan with a satisfied smirk at his husband's glazed expression.

Logan sighs. "I just like your spotlight on me, Captain." He walks over to the photo wall and browses.

"Micha, you know we appreciate your efforts here, right? This wall is amazing." Austin looks over his shoulder and they comment on a few pics before Austin singles out the photo of me with Dominic and Maggie.

"How come you and Dom weren't at the tent tonight?" He taps the photo. "This is a great shot. Must have been hard for you to let Maggie go."

I swallow hard, remembering again how I'm not just losing Dominic, but Maggie, too. "It was, but I had to do what's best for her and Dominic was a good fit. She'll be great with him." I force a smile on my face and hope he'll let it drop, but as expected, he doesn't.

"And what about you?"

"What about me? I'm happy she found a home." I turn away and tidy up more things. Right now, I don't want to talk about

Dominic. I know Austin means well, but I just can't do it. I've been able to keep my mind off him all day until now.

A gentle hand lands on my arm, and I know I have to face the music. "We know something is up, Micha. You can talk to us you know."

I take a moment to compose myself before facing Austin. As soon as I see the concern on his face, I crumble. "It's not going to work out, okay? Can we just leave it at that?"

He folds me against him gently, and I sink into the safety of his arms. Logan rubs my back and murmurs comforting words as I break down in front of them. I feel like all I ever do is fuck up my life. It's one disaster after another. When will I ever learn?

We break apart when there's a knock on the door and a young girl around the age of ten enters with Maggie. I stride across the room and crouch in front of her. "Hey there, pretty lady." I stroke her ears and a quick once over reveals nothing wrong, allowing me to breathe a sigh of relief. She's wearing the pumpkin sweater I picked out for her and my heart pangs. My concern amps up though as I wonder who this girl is and why she's here with Dominic's dog.

She thrusts an envelope at me. "Are you Micha?" I nod. "I was told you'd know what to do and give you this."

She spins on her heel, but before she leaves, she notices Austin and Logan in the corner. "Oh my god! Mr. Maloney, you're my favourite player in the whole wide world. I play center, just like you. Can I have your autograph?" She's breathless and vibrating as Austin steps over to the desk and finds a scrap of paper and pen.

"You bet. I love giving fans autographs and thank you for being one. What's your name?"

"Callie."

"What's your number, Callie?"

"Thirteen. Just like you." She breathes as she watches Austin scribble a note on the paper. He hands it to her, and she squeals.

"Thank you so much! I'm framing this. Best day ever!"

Austin pulls his phone from his pocket. "Want to make it even better? Let's take a photo. I'll send it to Micha here. You come back with a parent next week and he'll make sure you get it."

He curls an arm around her, bends down to press their cheeks together and snaps a pic. He shows it to her, and Callie's smile could light up the night sky. She waves and gushes again before flying out the door.

I look down at the envelope in my hand. It has Dominic's blocky handwriting on the front with my name. Maggie smiles at my feet and watches me. She's so damn adorable in her sweater and I don't know how to process this. I didn't think I'd get to see Maggie again, and here she is with a note.

"Are you going to open it or stare at it all night?" Austin takes Maggie's leash and leads her to the back. "Let's find some treats, girl. I know they're back here somewhere."

My hands are shaking so badly it feels like eternity passes before I finally get it open and read a note in Dominic's same blocky writing.

Micha,

Maggie brought us together once. I hope she can do it again. You're worth all the fight I have in me to give.

If you want to talk and fix this, meet me at Maggie's favourite spot on the boardwalk.

All my love,

Dom

Logan stands by, waiting for me to say something until his patience finally caves. "Well, are you going to tell me what it says?"

I'm still letting it all sink in. He wants to talk. Roberta and Travis could be right. He has an explanation and I, in perfect Micha form, assumed the worst and ran. I read the note several more times before passing it to Logan.

He skims it and cocks an eyebrow. "What happened?"

"Ah, the other day a woman knocked on the door and said she was Dominic's girlfriend."

"Come again? Dominic doesn't have a girlfriend. I have it on good authority he doesn't."

"How would you know? You don't even live here."

He scoffs. "True. But my mom does, and she knows everything about everybody in this town. Dominic has been alone since Jenny died. Now word is, her best friend Tara was trying to make moves on him, but he never took the bait.

In fact, mom seems to think Tara was trying to break them up before Jenny got sick." He waves his hand in the air. "But that's a whole other story. Trust me. I also know if she's the one that said or did something to make you think this... she was playing you. She's not a nice person."

"I don't know her name, she didn't say. But she was done up like a supermodel with her hair, nails and outfit. She was pretty, but she had too much makeup on."

"Sounds like her. So, she showed up and what? Dropped that bomb on you and you ran away? Didn't ask him to explain or anything?"

I hang my head. "That's exactly what I did. I blocked his number too."

Logan pushes the note in front of my face. "He's not buying your bullshit, and I say that with love, Micha. Go listen to him and decide then. He obviously cares about you enough to do this, and you should allow him to defend himself. Make a choice after that."

"What if he doesn't forgive me?"

Logan taps the note. "It's right in front of you. He already has. Go find him."

Dare I believe he's right? Is this when life finally forgives me and stops kicking me at every corner?

"Okay, I need Maggie. Time to face the music and hope for the best."

We enter the doorway to the back part of the shelter and find Austin staring into the kitten room while Maggie lays at his feet. He sees us and rushes over to Logan, pulling him by the hand to the window.

"They have a litter of orange kittens, baby! Come see!"

"Oz, we can't take one home." Logan groans.

"We could make it work."

Logan sighs in defeat. "Micha, take Maggie and go. I can lock up here. Looks like we'll be staying for longer anyway now."

We both watch as Austin has already slipped into the kitten room and pulled one out of its cage to cuddle.

I chuckle. "Do you think you're going to win this battle?"

"I honestly don't know. When he gets it in his head to adopt an animal, it's hard to talk him out of it. I usually have to resort to creative methods of distraction."

"Um, I'm going to guess I don't want to know what that entails. So, if you two are okay, I'm going to leave."

"Good idea, because it means it involves sex." He laughs when my eyebrows raise. "Don't worry, nothing will happen here. Well, not inside anyway." He pushes me back down the hall. "Just go already. Side note, public sex on the boardwalk at night is frowned upon. Don't ask me how I know. So, make sure you take it home when you make up."

Maggie trots with me to the reception area as Logan pushes me out the door and locks it before racing back to Austin. I can only imagine what those two will get up to.

I puff a shaky breath. "Well girl, let's go find your dad."

MAGGIE AND I MAKE the short walk to the trailhead and my guts roll as I realize I have to listen to Dominic's explanation, as well as explain my own actions. Even if he has an explanation, and it seems like he does if I listen to everyone else, what if he doesn't want to deal with me after?

As I approach Maggie's favourite spot, she slows to begin her sniffing stretch and I search for Dominic. It's dark outside, but there are a few outdoor lights in this area casting a yellowish glow on the boardwalk. I shuffle around in a circle and freeze when a tall figure moves my way. Dominic.

When he's finally close enough to me, my knees tremble. How could I have believed this man would hurt me? His soft eyes cast only understanding my way and guilt surges through me again at having put him through all this.

He stops a few steps in front of me, jamming his hands in his pants pockets and rocking back on his heels. "Hi."

"Hi."

"I see Maggie found you, okay."

"With some help, she did."

He clears his throat. "I wasn't sure if you'd show up if I simply asked you. I knew you would if you had Maggie to care for. I had to pull out all the stops." He chews on his bottom lip.

The dull thump of music from the festival carries over the water, and waves gently lap the shore. We stand there staring at each other, and I don't know what to say. How do I start a conversation and admit I was an insecure dumbass? It's not easy to admit you made a huge mistake. Maggie groans and lays down with a thump, too bored waiting for us to figure out our shit.

"Micha, I know what happened. Well, not exactly, but I have a pretty good idea." He tilts his head back and looks at the sky. "There is no girlfriend." He croaks.

"I shouldn't have just believed her without asking you."

His shoulders sag, and he steps closer. "I'm won't lie and say it didn't hurt knowing you would believe the worst of me like that. Because it did, and I was angry for a while."

I swallow hard. "I'm sorry. It's just... you know where my issues come from. It's hard to shake sometimes."

Dominic nods and inches closer. "I do know. That's why I'm here. After having time to be angry and then cooling off, I got to thinking and seeing how different your life experiences were from mine. I looked at this from your point of view and I understand." He reaches a tentative hand towards me, and I allow him to caress my cheek. Oh, how I've missed his touch and how he makes me feel.

I squeeze my eyes shut. "Are you able to forgive me?" I whisper.

"Micha, I'd be a fool not to. You're my light. Don't you see what you bring to my life? When I told you I believed the stars led us to be together, I wasn't kidding. You're the sign I was looking for and I can't walk away from you." He brushes his lips over mine. "I forgive you because I know you struggle to forgive yourself."

"I don't deserve you."

"You deserve everything, Micha. Everything."

"I can't promise I won't jump to conclusions again."

"But can you promise me you'll not run away, and we can talk about things?"

"I can definitely try."

He makes the final step and engulfs me in his arms. My head swims as I breathe in everything Dominic. I almost fucked this up, but somehow karma gave me a man who not only gets me but has a heart big enough to forgive me. I've never had anyone give me the benefit of the doubt.

He kisses me on the top of my head, and I cling to him as I take the moment to appreciate how amazing Dominic is and how lucky I am he's forgiven me. It's peaceful and serene until a hacking cough behind us ruins the moment.

We turn to find Janice and Brandie, the ladies from the town offices, on a bench nearby. They're sharing a joint and Brandie seems to have inhaled a bit too much. Sounds like she might cough up a lung.

"Hey, Sausage King!" Janice yells and waves. "You two are just so dang cute together. Sorry we ruined the moment. I was hoping to see a kiss, but the rookie here doesn't know how to smoke."

"Put a sock in it, woman." Brandie wheezes. "I know how to suck and blow just fine."

They burst into laughter, and I turn to Dom. "Should we get out of here?" A drop of rain splats on my face.

Dominic wipes it off, grinning. "Yeah, let's get out of here. I don't want to get caught in the rain."

He takes my hand as we walk back to the path for the parking lot, and the rain falls harder.

"Woo-hoo, wet t-shirt time!" Is all we hear, followed by cackles of laughter from the two ladies on the boardwalk.

I burst out laughing and run to the truck. "Race you!"

Thirty-Five

Dominic

MICHA HAS A FEW steps on me before I register his call to a race, and I take off after him. He's faster than I thought he would be. Just as he makes it to the truck, Maggie and I catch him before he can open the door. The rain has picked up and tiny rivers are cascading down his cheeks as I turn him around to face me.

His cheeks are rosy from the exertion of running and his hair sticks to his neck. In the rain, his eyelashes appear to be a thousand times longer. His smile is blinding even in the middle of the downpour and he takes my breath away. How he can think he doesn't deserve good things in life, I don't know, but it's my new mission to make sure he knows he's deserving every day for the rest of his life.

I press my body into him, pinning him against the truck before I crush my lips to his and revel in the taste of Micha.

Root beer lip gloss and fresh rain flood my taste buds. The rain comes down harder, but I don't want to stop. This broken man is trying to be better for me, and I'm beyond grateful for the chance. I would've kept going, rain and public parking lot be damned, if Maggie hadn't whined.

I break away from Micha, and poor Maggie is drenched. Her ears are hanging, plastered to her head and her sweater is soaked as she begs to get out of the rain.

"I'm sorry, girl. Here, get in." I open the truck door and she jumps up. I don't miss the stink eye she aims my way before shaking her wet body as soon as I close the door. Some water dog she is.

Micha, with his wild and yet innocent beauty, still stands in the rain, waiting for me. His shirt is plastered to his skin and we're both standing in a puddle now, soaking our feet.

"Will you come home with me?"

"I thought you'd never ask." His devilish grin makes my heart pound harder in my chest. I plant another kiss on his rain-soaked lips and open the door for him, before rounding the front to take the driver's seat.

I crank the front defroster since Maggie's panting has already fogged the windows. Micha shivers and I feel terrible I have nothing dry to give him.

"I'm sorry you're cold. The heat will kick in shortly. I have nothing to dry off with in here."

"It's okay, that's not why I shivered." Again, with his trouble making grin. "I was thinking it's a shame to waste the foggy windows."

I chuckle. "Don't worry about that. I guarantee you we'll make our own steam soon enough."

He shivers again, releasing a whimper as I drive home far too quickly.

When I pull into the driveway, the rain has slowed to a light drizzle, and the first order of business, as much as I wish it wasn't, is to deal with a wet dog.

"Stay here with Maggie. I'll get some towels."

I slip off my shoes and soaking socks and leave them in the front foyer while I go to the spare bathroom and drag out a stack of towels. When I return, Micha already has her wet sweater removed, and it's creating a puddle on the floor. I hand him a towel and both of us rub her down as best we can. I take extra care with her muddy feet and squeeze out her tail.

When we've used four towels and there's black fur everywhere, she curls up on her dog bed in a tight little ball in the living room. I adjust the control for the gas fireplace, and it roars to life. In a few minutes, Maggie will have all the warmth she needs to be dry and comfortable. I turn back to the foyer and find Micha holding all the wet towels and her sweater in his arms.

"We should get these into the wash right away." I nod and he follows me to the laundry room. He shoves the wet fuzzy towels in and prepares it to start.

"We should also leave our wet dog fur covered clothes here, don't you think?" I lift the hem on his T-shirt as he raises his arms to remove it.

"Yeah, good idea." He rasps as I find the tab of his zipper and loosen his jeans. It's already difficult to take wet jeans off your own body. But to do it from someone else's body, a hot body that distracts you, that's a whole other kind of difficult. Especially when Micha likes to wear tight pants.

"If I can't get your pants off, I'm going to take you right here." I growl. Touching him and being this close to him has amped up my want to be with him. I thought a slow, sensual love romp was how we could spend the night, but the longer we fight with wet clothes, the more persistent my erection becomes.

He grins and his body sags like a wet noodle. "I wouldn't complain about that."

I back him into the wall hard enough for a gasp to escape and I smash my lips over his while struggling with my own pants. I can barely do one thing well at once, let alone two, but I don't want to stop touching Micha. My lips need to cover every inch of him. The cold, wet clothing is doing nothing to extinguish my burning desire. I growl again in frustration.

"That's sexy. You should growl more often." Micha breathes.

"I'm growling because I don't have the patience to get naked. I just want to feel your skin against mine." Curling my fingers around his neck, I yank him to me. "I want to know you inside and out. I want you to never leave here again, thinking I might hurt you. I want... " I trail off, squeezing my eyes shut. This is not how I wanted to spill my feelings to him. Half naked, smelling like a wet dog in my laundry room. It's supposed to be a special moment, romantic.

"Dom, look at me."

I open my eyes to find Micha's deep brown ones staring back. "I'm not good at patience either." He brushes his lips over mine. "But I want you to be impatient. Right now. I want you to know my... insides." His hands work at my wet jeans and together we get them yanked to my thighs with my boxers. When Micha licks his lips and eyes my cock like it's his next meal, I combust.

With greedy hands I wrangle his own pants down, panting with the effort and victorious when I get one leg free. He wraps the leg still wrapped in jeans around my waist and pulls me closer. I palm his ass, perhaps too rough, but I'm out of my mind with the want to be inside him. I grind our hard lengths together, making my eyes roll back with the pleasure of it all.

"Dom, holy shit." He bites and nips my neck, panting in my ear. His hand wiggles between us and he strokes us both together.

I mutter a string of curses and rock into his hand. "I'm gonna come and I want you to fuck me." His hot breath passes over my ear as I feel the warm, sticky fluid slide down my cock. Micha shudders against me and all I can do is watch as he lets go, covering his hand and my cock with his release. His eyes burn into mine as he tilts himself back, pushing all the cum he can into his hole and slicking my dick with the rest.

Holy shit.

Holy. Shit.

Mad with desire, I spin around and perch him on the table I fold laundry on, almost falling on top of him because I forgot my pants are still at my thighs. I rub my dick through the sticky mess he made and push against his entrance.

"Do it, Dom. It's not gonna hurt me." He wraps both legs around me, digging his heels in.

His head thuds on the table when I breach the tight ring of muscle and his hands scramble to find something to hang on to before finding purchase on my biceps as I bury myself in him. The table screams in protest, and I pray it doesn't break because I can't stop now even if I wanted to.

"Micha... oh my God." I breathe as my orgasm barrels into me, and I pull out to mark him with stream after stream of cum.

The washing machine sloshes away as we continue to pant and try to come back to earth. I'm afraid the table might collapse with Micha on it. I reach a sticky hand over and pull him up into me.

"This isn't what I had planned when I asked you to come back home with me." I chuckle and place a soft kiss on his lips.

"I've never been much for plans, you know. I like to be spontaneous." He laughs. "And this was definitely spontaneous."

"Are you sure you're okay? I've never done anything like this before." I run my hand down his side and notice the goose bumps chasing after it.

"I'm more than okay." He reaches up and kisses me. "In fact, I'm never going to look at a laundry room the same ever again."

I laugh against his lips. "That makes two of us." I pull us apart with a wince. "How about we actually get our clothes off this time and have a hot shower together?"

"That sounds like another place for us to get dirty and clean at the same time. Let's do it." He winks as he removes his pants and leaves them in a pile in front of the washer before strutting past me, bare assed to my bedroom.

I can't wipe the smile off my face as I strip and race off after him.

I T'S JUST AFTER MIDNIGHT; we fell asleep on the couch watching more animal documentaries. Thankfully, none involving sharks this time. My stomach grumbles and Micha laughs sleepily.

"You hungry, Dom? That was really loud in my ear." He smiles as he rests his head in my lap.

"I'm starving. Join me for a snack?"

He yawns and stretches up. "I thought I was your snack."

"You are. But I need real sustenance to keep up with you." I peck a kiss on his lips and head to the kitchen. He trails after me with a blanket wrapped around him. He's an adorable, fluffy walking burrito.

He plunks down at the island, and I open the fridge to see the white bakery box I forgot about. Seems like the perfect time to take it out.

"I picked something up earlier today, hoping you would come home with me and listen to me."

I place the box on the island, and he raises an eyebrow. "The last time you had a box like that, we got nasty in the kitchen, and I can't even smell cherries without getting hard now."

I chuckle. "While I appreciate that memory, it's not that. Well, not completely anyway."

"Micha, I'll never stop doing things to make you happy. I'll never stop giving you the benefit of the doubt. I'm always going to believe in you and you're enough." I take his hand in mine and stroke his knuckles. "I love you."

His mouth drops open with a silent gasp as he stares at me and says nothing. I open the box and spin it around so he can see. Parker made me a star-shaped cake with cherry frosting, but it's the words I want him to see.

"Oh my God. Dom..." His hand covers his mouth as he focuses on what's inside. "You did this for me." He whispers.

"I'd do anything for you."

He drops the blanket and crawls onto my lap. "I don't know what brought you to me, but I'm going to do my best to never let you go." He brings his lips to mine and leaves a tender kiss. "I love you too."

The cake is almost forgotten as we make out like teenagers on prom night in the back of dad's station wagon. But Micha being Micha, swipes some frosting and spreads it across my lips. "Fuck, cherries taste so much better on you."

And we forget about the snack and the cake.

What did the cake say, you ask?

Never dull your shine.

You're more than enough.

I love you.

Epilogue

Micha

JANUARY

I hate winter. I hate the snow.

Yet here I am, manning a hot chocolate station at the Winter Festival, freezing my ass off. Where's Dom? I asked him to bring me more of those little heater packs you can stuff in your mitts and boots. The only thing keeping me from being a complete miserable asshole is watching the guys playing hockey on Dogwood Pond.

We tried a new thing this year for Auslo's Loft and Austin's Animal House and arranged a day long 3-on-3 hockey tournament. This time, the funds raised won't be for the shelters, but for a young family struggling to start over after a tragic house fire. Austin could come last minute as he wasn't voted to the NHL all-star team, and he had five days open in his schedule. He brought two of his teammates with him as well. Logan, unfortunately, couldn't get out of a photoshoot, so he had to stay in New York.

I'm impressed watching Jacob skate and keep up with the other players. I didn't know he could skate. He never seemed like a hockey guy to me, regardless of who his brother is. I look on as he and one of Austin's teammates, Matts, fool around by themselves one on one. I don't know a lot about hockey, but since I've been with Dominic and he likes to watch, I've been learning. What I'm watching right now, well let's just say I don't think there's supposed to be that much body contact. If there's nothing going on with those two, I'll eat my hat. Well, not my tuque, I need that because it's cold, and you'd have to tear it from my frostbitten fingers.

"Hey beautiful. Sorry it took me so long."

Dominic has finally come back to rescue my icicle ass. "Did you get the goods?"

He snorts. "You make me sound like a drug dealer."

"Well, if I don't get warm soon I might die. It's not a stretch."

"I found something better." He removes a pair of mitts from inside his jacket.

"It's another pair of mitts, Dom. How is that going to help right now?" I whine. I know I'm whining, but I hate being cold.

"Not just any mitts." He takes one of my bundled hands and rips off my current mitten. I want to yell a string of expletives, but he places the new mitt on my exposed hand and it's... warm as toast.

"Oh my God, so warm." He repeats the process with the other hand and it's like I have my own little furnace on each hand. It's blissful really.

"They're battery powered mittens. You don't have to worry about those little package things. Just turn on the mitten and it'll stay warm for hours."

I throw my arms around his neck. "Have I told you I love you today? You found me battery operated mittens. Nothing says true love like keeping me from freezing to death."

"You have told me that today, but it never gets old hearing it." He brushes his lips over mine. This time I shiver with something other than cold.

"Hey guys. Feel free to leave. I'm here to take over."

Parker plunks a giant bin of cookies on the table with a grin. "I thought I was here for another hour yet?"

"It seems your boyfriend talked to my boss and made a deal to spring you earlier." Parker nudges me out of the way. "So go on and be all swoony and in love somewhere else now."

"Thanks Parker, I owe you one."

He pushes me farther away and waves me off, setting out hockey themed cookies he baked and iced himself.

"What kind of deal did you make with Owen to get Parker here early?" I loop my arm through Dom's, and we walk towards the path for the parking lot.

He chuckles. "Nothing you need to worry about. I knew you'd be cold, and I have a surprise for you. I didn't want to wait any longer."

"I love surprises. Especially yours." Which is true. Dominic is a romantic with all things he does for me. It could be warming a towel in the dryer for me while I shower or giving me his sweater when he knows I'm cold. He goes out of his way to make me feel special and cherished. It's like a personal mission of his to make me smile and cry happy tears every day. Can't say I hate it.

As we pass by the ice surfaces where several games are going on, my eyes find Jacob again and I nudge Dominic. "Dom, you know I'm just learning hockey, but you can't do that in a game, right?"

Dominic follows my gaze. Matts has both of his arms around Jacob, and he's locked him against his giant body by using both hands to hold him there with his stick. Matts has his head lowered next to Jacob's ear, and I'm one hundred percent sure it's not a talk about game strategy.

Austin's voice carries across the ice. "Hey Matts! Is my brother giving you a hard time? Don't let him fool you! He's got skills on the ice." Matts drops his hold, and they break apart quickly at the sound of Austin's voice. "Not at all Austin. I was just showing him a trick from behind." He smirks at Jake before skating to Austin where they start a conversation and Jacob takes a moment longer before joining them.

"Ah no, that's definitely not allowed. Hope Austin isn't a protective brother."

"Oh, he is." I've seen it firsthand. Nobody fucks around with Jacob if Austin can help it. "Thanks for clearing that up for me, Mr. Hockey." I pat his arm as he throws his head back, laughing.

"Micha, Mr. Hockey is Gordie Howe, not me."

"Oh, is he here? Should I have met him?"

"No baby, he's a hockey legend, and he passed away a few years ago. One day, I'll tell you all about him."

Suits me fine. He can tell me inside where it's warm then. I'll never understand sports and their nicknames. I'll stick to animals.

We make the short drive to Dom's, but before we enter the house, he pulls a blindfold out of his pocket.

I raise my eyebrow. "You know I'm up for anything, but it's too cold for me to be kinky on the front porch."

"It's what's inside I don't want you to see right away. Trust me?"

"Always."

I close my eyes and let him place the blindfold. He leads me into the house and makes me stop on the mat in the foyer. He removes all my winter layers and even takes off my boots while I stand there and let him. He places a kiss on my neck and pulls me forward until we stop in what I think is the middle of the living room.

"Before I take the blindfold off, I want you to remember when we went to PetSmart the very first time."

A grin fills my face. "I remember. That was fun."

He removes the blindfold and in front of me is the most gorgeous cat tree. It's right in front of the window, looking out into the garden. It would be heaven for Tux if he were here.

"Wow, that's awesome, Dom. Some lucky kitty is going to love this."

"I'm hoping one kitty, in particular will like it. Permanently."

His eyes roam my face as he takes my hands in his. "You told me that day it was your dream to have a giant cat tree for Tux in a window. Specifically on a main floor and hopefully of a house you own." He places a soft kiss on my lips. "Move in with me, Micha. I hate it when you're gone, and I want us all to be together. You, me, Maggie and Tux. It might not be a house you own, but you make it yours every time you come here."

I blink. "You want me to live with you? Like, move all my shit and sleep with you every night? Burn your toast every morning and have our pets together under one roof?"

"I suppose that sums it up. Although, you left out the part where you're the only person I want to see first thing in the morning, and the house always feels too empty when you're gone." He places a trail of kisses across my knuckles. "Don't leave me hanging, beautiful. Will you move here?"

Never, ever at any point in the last four years did I think I would arrive at a point in my life where I could say I had it all. I'm not rich with money or possessions, but I'm rich with a circle of friends that love me and a boyfriend worth his weight in gold. I'm in awe of this man every time he does these things that may seem so insignificant to some but mean the world to me. Sure, it's just a cat tree, but he remembered what I told him on a day almost six months ago and what it meant to me. You can't put a price on that.

"Of course, it's yes. How could I ever say no to you?"

Thank you for reading!
Owen and Parker are up next. Finding The Right Forever is their story!

Acknowledgments

Behind every book, there's a team of people to make it happen.

To you dear reader, the biggest thank you of all. Thank you for taking a chance on someone new. With so many great indie authors clamoring for attention, I'm grateful you chose me.

An immense thank you to Hayden and Lindsay for the early input. It was invaluable to me and I appreciate your time more than you know.

Janice and Brandie, I owe you a thanks for allowing me to use your names and present you in the funniest way I could. Your banter, some of which you force me to be a part of, has provided so many comical ideas. Please don't make me kill your characters off. I'd really like them to stick around.

Alex, thank you so much for proofreading for me when you already have so much on your plate. I appreciate it so, so much.

To all of you that have rallied around me, lifted me when I'm down and gave me the boost to believe in myself - Thank you!

About Author

I'm just a small town, Canadian girl writing fun and filth.

I'm a wife, mom, animal lover and a hopeless romantic.

I want my stories to make you smile, swoon and snort laugh, but not necessarily in that order.

I hope I can be the author you turn to when you need a story to make you laugh, or add light to an otherwise dark day.

Coffee always wins, you can't change my mind.

You can find me on facebook in Neill's Naughty List or visit my website rmneillauthor.com

Also By